when comes the Joy

ALSO BY CHARLENE CARR

A New Start Series
Where There Is Life
By What We Love
Forever In My Heart
Whispers of Hope

Behind Our Lives Trilogy
Behind Our Lives What We See
The Stories We Tell

Standalone
Beneath the Silence
Before I Knew You

When Comes The Joy

A New Start, Book 1

Charlene Carr

Published by Coastal Lines, 2019.

Library and Archives Canada

When Comes The Joy
Book One of the A New Start Series
ISBN: 978-1-988232-15-7

This novel is a work of fiction. Names, characters, places, and
incidents either are the product of the author's imagination or are
used fictitiously. Any resemblance to actual events, locales,
organizations, or persons living or dead is entirely coincidental and
beyond the intent of the author.

Typography by Coastal Lines
Cover Design by Coastal Lines

Second Edition, July 2019

This book was originally published in 2014 as *Skinny Me*
ISBN: 978-1501067396

This work is also available in electronic format:
When Comes The Joy
ISBN: 978-0-9939238-3-8

I dedicate this book to every woman who has ever looked in the mirror and not liked what she's seen, to every woman who thinks her worth is somehow connected to a number on the scale, and to every woman who strives to overcome the societal expectation to fit into a certain mold.

Love yourself.

Seek health and fitness in the hope that you can continue loving yourself for many years to come.

I wish you happiness..

CHAPTER ONE

The woman in front of me steps up to the teller. She is tall, at least five foot nine. Her brown hair flows down her back in graceful waves. Her waist is slim, and her hips are round. She can't weigh more than one hundred and twenty-five pounds. She smiles at the man who steps out of her way, and it looks to be an easy gesture. She is gorgeous. She is everything I want to be. It's bad enough that the bank machines are down and I have to stand in line where all these eyes can look at me—see the way my shirt clings to my bulbous form, how the waist on my pants digs into my flesh, letting the fat hang over. I can almost hear their thoughts—*she should just eat less. Why doesn't she exercise more?* To have that woman here, a stark contrast to my sweaty self, makes it so much worse.

Another teller waves me over, so I reach for my wallet and shuffle forward. His eyes look vacant. "How can I help you today?" There's no intonation in his voice.

"I'd like to take out some cash," I say. He doesn't look at me, his gaze somewhere over my shoulder as he takes my card. I'm just another client. He's a glorified ATM. I glance to the woman at the teller beside me. Her teller smiles at her. He laughs. I try to focus my mind back to the task at hand.

"How much?"

"Uh, one hundred and fifty," I say. Now I'm the one who's not looking at him. Instead, I envision the skinny girl inside of me. I know when I leave here and squeeze myself into a seat on the bus, suffering the annoyance of whoever's seat I'm spilling over into, I'll close my eyes and work out a whole scenario for this girl, for the me I'm supposed to be. The me who walks into the bank lobby without shame. The me I only dream of. She is skinny, yes, but not only that, her skin is smooth, her bottom is firm and round, her breasts are perky. She is kind and sweet and can tell a joke like nobody's business. She isn't bitter. She never gets angry at simple, unimportant things.

"Do you want a receipt?"

"Yes, please."

She barely cries. If she does it's because of something beautiful, like a child's first step or a reunited couple at the airport. She shares in other's joys. She doesn't begrudge them. She doesn't need to. Like the brunette at the other teller, she's everything I'm not.

My teller has to ask me twice, "Is that all?"

"Yes, yes, thank you." I gather my card, the cash, the receipt, and work on stuffing it all into my wallet as I step into the sunlight. I wish I'd worn something lighter. It's 18 degrees, warm for spring in Halifax, and with the sun glaring, sweat runs down my back. I stand at the crosswalk, surrounded by people, just waiting for the light to change. I pull at the collar of my shirt, trying to let the breeze. My wallet falls. I cuss under my breath and bend to get it. A horrible rip sounds as the fabric of my pants spread. My world stops. My throat tightens. My breath ceases. I close my eyes, frozen, willing this to be a dream, begging whatever power is out there in the universe to let me sink into the ground.

"Check it out," says a male voice behind me. I glance back and see a flash of pimpled skin under the shadow of a sideways hat. "She actually split her pants." Glee dances in his voice. I fling my hand to my backside and feel the hole that spreads beyond the reach of my fingers. I whip up and drop my wallet in my bag, then hold it behind me as the light changes and we enter the intersection like cattle.

Heat works its way up my neck and into my cheeks. I know my face is red. Tears squeeze from my clenched eyelids as I try to tune out the muffled laughter. I glance around. Most people have averted their gaze, pretending it hasn't happened, pretending they didn't notice, but that muffled laughter reminds me it's real. These are my fattest pair of fat pants—were my fattest pair of fat pants.

Rather than wait at the bus stop, where the teenage boys are heading, I continue along the street. It's further from my destination but away from them. I keep my bag behind my bottom, hoping it covers the bright blue underwear that is now exposed. When I make it to the next stop, out of breath and damp with sweat, I'm thankful the bench is empty and sit down, panting. The tears have stopped, I've willed them to, but the heat is still in my face. I imagine I'm blotchy and grotesque.

When I get home, I pull the pants off like they're on fire then throw myself on the bed. I moan into the pillow and clutch my hands onto it, hard. I want to eat this feeling away, to indulge in cookies and ice cream and chips, but I don't. That's what got me here.

I was five and my cousins Daniel and Autumn were over. We spent the afternoon running through the yard, jumping up and down as the ice-cold water shot out of the sprinkler. After, we lay in the sun, laughing at whatever two five-year-olds and an eight-year-old laugh at. We came inside, asking for snacks. Ice cream sandwiches. My mom hesitated before giving them to us. She handed Daniel and Autumn an ice cream sandwich each and told me I'd already had a snack this morning, but I could have some carrots if I wanted. She'd just cut up some fresh ones. She said that like I should get excited, 'I've just cut up some fresh ones.' I remember being confused. I remember looking at my cousins eating their sandwiches, the milky white cream dribbling down their fingers, and not understanding why I didn't get one. Then I saw Daniel's knobby knees and Autumn's slim belly. I looked down at the rolls that stuck out of my bathing suit and wasn't confused anymore.

I've often wondered what would have happened if I'd reacted differently that day. I don't know what that different reaction would have been—taking the carrots, chewing on them happily? Maybe my whole life would have taken a different course. Maybe I wouldn't have grown up as the fat girl. Maybe I wouldn't be lying here now, humiliated, dejected, and obese.

I didn't take the carrots. I grabbed Daniel's sandwich and ran into the bathroom. I locked myself in and ate that sandwich with more joy, more delight than I'd ever eaten anything before. My mother banged on the door. 'Jennifer,' she called. 'Jennifer!' She was using my full name, so I knew she was angry, but it didn't matter. Nothing mattered except how good that sandwich made me feel—the chocolate cookie coating and the sweet and creamy ice cream sliding over my tongue. I was happy. I was safe. In the white tiled walls of that small room nothing and no one judged me.

A LITTLE OVER twenty-two years after that pivotal ice cream sandwich, I wake up to the sound of my alarm clock and realize I must have fallen asleep during my cry fest. I'm on top of the covers and still wearing the shirt I came home in. With a grunt, I roll over and turn the buzzer off. My fat jiggles, pulling me over further than I intend to go. It's a feeling I'll never get used to. I glance at the clock, though I know what time it is—10:45 on a Wednesday morning because I've decided to sleep past eleven signifies that you've given up on life.

For some reason it hits me this morning. I'm twenty-seven. I'm twenty-seven, have been for a few weeks now, and I'm unemployed. I'm an unemployed fat loser who has just grown out of her fattest pair of fat pants. I don't want to admit to myself that I'm a failure, but it seems pretty evident.

My phone rings in the other room and I almost trip as I hurtle myself out of bed to reach it in time. I pick it up, my voice still groggy with sleep, though I'm panting with the sudden dash. "Hello."

"Hi. Jennifer, are you all right?"

"Yeah, yeah, I'm fine."

"You don't sound—"

"I ran to the phone."

"Oh."

"What is it, Autumn?" I lean on the arm of the couch.

"My mom wanted to invite you over for dinner Friday night. It's Daniel's birthday. We're doing a family thing before he heads out with his friends."

I hesitate. "I don't know. I—"

"Just come."

"I'm busy."

"No, you're not."

"Hey!"

"You're not, are you? I mean," she pauses. "I didn't even tell you what time."

"I was an after thought."

"Jennifer."

"It's Wednesday. You're just planning this now?"

"No. Mom was nervous, embarrassed. She wasn't sure you'd come."

"Well."

"I told her you're family."

"Yeah, well,"

"Be there for 6:15. Okay? I met this new guy. He seems like he may be a keeper. I'll tell you all—"

I cut Autumn off, not wanting to hear about yet another

new guy who, if history's any indication, will definitely not be a keeper. "Okay. I'll be there."

"It'll be fun. You'll see."

"Sure." There's a long silence.

"So, how are things going, anyway? Is the job search—"

"I'm actually kinda busy right now, Autumn. I'll talk to you later. On Friday."

"Okay." Her voice wavers. "See you Friday."

"Yep."

"And, Jenn?"

"Yeah?"

"I'm thinking of you."

Her words cut like a knife. I take a deep breath. I don't want her to be thinking of me, pitying me. "Thanks." I say. "Bye."

"Bye."

I let Autumn hang up the phone and stare at it. I don't want to go. I really don't want to go. It will be a good and well-balanced meal, the one plus. But I don't want to go. I return to my room and stare at the clock. I look to my bed, shake my head, then walk to the scale for the first time in months. I step on and squeeze my eyes shut, but I have to open them. I open just one—like a child, like that will make a difference. Twelve more pounds. I step off and breathe deeply. That explains the pant episode last night. I battle to keep back the tears.

I head to my desk and flip open my laptop. It's been almost four months since I quit my job at the Boys and Girls Club and I've almost run out of money. That's why I went to the bank; I figured if I operate with cash, I won't risk the embarrassment of having my card declined. There's no point dwelling on my dwindling funds though, what I need to focus on is getting a job. And, for probably the fiftieth time, I wish I had just held my tongue. At first, I enjoyed working at the Boys and Girls Club, but I'd forgotten how cruel kids can be. Their taunts still filter through my mind. It was like grade school all over again. Fatso, Lard-Ass, Waste of Space, and that wasn't even the worst of it. As the weeks passed, it seemed a game to them—who could come up with the most heinous insult. And I took it, every time, sometimes pretending I didn't hear, sometimes laughing their words off or joining in, acknowledging the most recent dig as witty or challenging them to up their game. If you can't beat 'em, join 'em, right?

One day I told a group of loitering grade eight boys they needed to leave the hall. They had to either join the other students or go home for the day—centre policy. They swore at me, taking the insults to the next level, spouting nasty, obscene things about my weight, my supposed hygiene issues, my imagined sexual preferences—bestiality was mentioned.

I couldn't take it anymore. I snapped. I went crazy. 'Your mothers are a bunch of skinny sick bitches who didn't have the sense to take a morning-after pill,' I hissed. My body shook with rage. The four boys stood there, looking at me like I'd just spontaneously combusted and all they could do was stand in amazement.

'You can't—' said Richard, the smallest one, but I cut him off.

'I'm going,' I said. 'You'll never have to see my fat ass again.'

I walked away with such shame I could feel it, like a hand around my throat. They were kids, just kids. I was supposed to be the level-headed adult. It didn't matter that I felt awful. It didn't even matter whether they ratted me out or not. I couldn't work there anymore, not if that's who it turned me into. I walked into the manager's office and resigned.

When I passed the boys on my way back out, they were laughing—not at me, just laughing, the moment forgotten. Jonathan, the instigator of all the taunting, had made some joke.

Not knowing what I'd do next, I went home. I cried. I ate a bag of Old Dutch Rippled Sour Cream and Onion chips—my favourite—and washed it back with a chocolate milkshake made with skim milk. I tried not to cry again. I grabbed a paper, flipped it to the job listings, realized I wasn't looking for a job fifteen years ago, and went to my computer. As I scanned the ads online, wiping the tears from my eyes, I tried to think of where my skills best fit. There were dozens of jobs I felt basically qualified for and I applied to dozens of them. And then I applied to dozens more and dozens more, for weeks.

I SIT AT MY COMPUTER, contemplating my options. I have some decent qualifications. I'm University educated. I have a double major in Science and English. I'm not stupid. I can work hard and have a good head on my shoulders, but that hasn't seemed to make a difference. I've actually had four on-site job interviews. Not bad, I'm told. But I've had zero call backs and although I'd like to think better of the world, I know why. I open the email from the one job I've been offered. It only required a phone interview and doesn't require me to leave my apartment. I haven't replied because I don't want to become one of those fat people who gives up on life. It starts slowly. First, they get their family members to take care of small things—picking up the groceries perhaps. They go out less and less because they're tired, they're busy, their favourite sitcom is on, and then one day they wake up and that show *600-Pound-Life* is at their door. I never want to be on that show. Never.

I let my mouse hover over the reply icon. I think of those pants, those twelve pounds, my mom, my dwindling bank account. If I take the job, I'll be working twenty-five hours a week and it will pay more than my forty hour a week job that had almost two hours on transit travelling back and forth from Halifax to Dartmouth every day. I stand and walk to the mirror above my dresser, hating what I see. I return to the desk, hit reply, and write my letter of acceptance.

This job will fix one problem in my life, but it's not even the biggest problem. I can't keep being the woman who walks into a bank lobby ashamed because she knows she's the biggest person there. I can't keep bursting out of my clothes. I make a decision. In the extra hours this job provides I will transform myself. I won't just succumb to being a stay-at-home. I'll transform myself into the skinny woman I've always dreamed of. I press send and feel a jolt of empowerment. This won't be a yo-yo diet. Mom and I had done those before, and they don't work—Juicing for hours a day gets old quick. No, this will be a life change. This will be different. I will wake up exactly one year from today and I will be the person I've always wanted to be. The person I was born to be.

My first reaction is to call my Mom and tell her I have a job, tell her I'm going to change my life. But I can't. Mom won't be here to help me. She also won't be here to sabotage me with bags full of McDonald's burgers or our favourite, the Harvey's Poutine. I stop as I think this, trying to resist the sorrow that threatens to flood through me. It stressed Mom, me quitting my job like that, but I tell myself there's no correlation to the heart attack that took her two weeks after. If there is a correlation, Billy's accident could have been to blame as well. He was always reckless on that motorcycle. Mom hated it. But her doctor didn't mention stress. He kept talking about her health, her weight, how her heart was clogged with plaque. He was explaining what happened, how it had happened, and he gave me this look, like he wanted to make sure I was taking in every word.

I consider calling my best friend, Tammy, instead. But I doubt she'd join me. She might not even be happy for me.

Amazingly, annoyingly, she's one of those fat girls who seems fine with her weight. She's active, and her doctor says although she does need to lose weight, she's healthier than some of his skinny patients.

There's not really anyone else to call. Tammy and Mom, before she died, made up the base of my social circle. It's not even a circle anymore. It's just Tammy. There is my cousin, Autumn—5'3, 134 lbs, a personal trainer with muscles that glisten as she leads her boot camps in the park and, lucky bastard, still curves. But I don't want to be a project for her. Last time she tried to help me get fit we came close to disowning each other. It doesn't matter. I don't need to call anyone. I can do this. I'm motivated. It's not just the whole miserable life thing—no boyfriend, no job, almost no friends, and the fear of becoming a recluse who lives entirely in the confines of a none too spacious one-bedroom apartment. There's more than that. If I don't do this, I'll die—probably sooner than later—just like Mom. And at least Mom had a life. At least Mom had me and Billy and a husband who loved her at one point in time. When Dad met Mom, she was slender. After me she became voluptuous, slowly creeping up into the two-hundred-pound club. After Billy, it seemed like a race to tip the three hundred mark.

By that time, I was racing along with her. I saw the numbers on the scale creep up to 203 on the same day I got my first visit from good ol' Aunt Flo. I was crying when I asked Mom for a pad. She looked at me. She smiled. 'You're a woman now,' she'd said. 'Be happy.' She didn't know the real reason for my tears. By that time the yo-yo diets had pretty much stopped. She'd accepted her fate. I guess she accepted mine too.

"I'm going to do this," I speak to the walls. "I have to do this." In the past few months I've hardly cried for Mom. I've hardly cried for my lack of a job. I don't even let myself think about Billy—I won't cry for him. He's dead to the world in that hospital room, and dead to me too. I cry today though—for Mom, for my dwindling bank account, for the split of my fattest pair of fat pants. It's all too much. I close my eyes and press my hands against them, trying to push out the images that won't go away. I've been trying not to think about Mom. When I do, it's always the same image that pops into my mind. I'd erase it if I could. If there were one memory in my whole life I could eradicate, that would be the one. It would trump every obscene comment that's come my way; it would beat the day my father left us. All of that is berries and cream in comparison. But this memory won't go away. It unrolls before me like a surround sound, IMAX theatre presentation, complete with sensory overload. I'm living it all over again....

CHAPTER TWO

I turn the key in the lock and push open the warped door of my mother's mudroom. The scent of chocolate and vanilla floats in the air. I pull my foot back, just missing a pool of what must have been a milkshake. Shards of glass stick in the thick liquid. Another smell hits me— urine—and my chest tightens. 'Mom!' I call out. She didn't show up to our dessert date at the Middle Spoon, a fancy dessert bar downtown, and didn't answer the phone when I called.

I waited at the restaurant for almost an hour. On the bus ride over I'd oscillated between worry and outrage. I step over the milkshake and tiptoe my way through the kitchen. 'Mom?' I whisper. Turning into the hall I see a foot, one of her favourite purple pumps lays just beside it. I stop. My breath catches. I debate fleeing but step forward instead. My mother lies across the living room carpet, one hand under her chest, the other hand reached out. The phone lies on the floor, just inches out of her grasp. I am frozen. Literally frozen. My mind tells me a million things. It screams— check for a pulse, roll her over, call 9-1-1, check for a pulse, move, move, move! And my body just won't listen.

When the paralysis finally leaves me, I catapult forward, trip, and land on her so hard it knocks the wind out of me. I lie there for a moment, gasping for breath, and when it comes, I repeat, 'I'm sorry, I'm sorry,' then stop. I get on my knees and put my fingers across her throat. There's no movement. She seems colder than she should be, but I tell myself I'm just being paranoid.

I push her over as far as I can and she ends up stuck against the couch, half on her side. The tears are flowing hard at this point, and I choke and gulp like a blubbering child as I pull and yank her away from the couch so I can get her on her back. Her body jiggles as I do this and revulsion flows through me—which morphs into disgust at myself. All I should be thinking about is how to save her. I clench my teeth and put my face up close to hers, listening for breath, hoping to hear or feel something. I do a quick mental checklist of the CPR formula as I hover over her. 'Idiot!' I scream and grab the phone, then dial 9-1-1. 'My mom. She. I don't know. A heart attack? She's on the floor. No. I. I don't think so. I'm not sure. Just get here, okay? Just get here—30 Springvale Ave. Yeah. A house. Are you coming?'

I hang up the phone and start compressions. After two rounds the sweat pours off me and I have to stop. I forget to breathe—into her I mean because I'm trying so hard to catch my own breath. I need to push deep to even have a chance of reaching her heart and it's hard. It's really hard, and I can't stop crying and I want to call Mom, get her encouragement, ask her what else I can do, but of course I can't and the thought makes me more desperate, so I start again with the compressions, my arms burning. I'm strong but not strong enough, and I'm crying so hard my nose starts to run. A plop lands on my mother's neck, and I frantically wipe it off, saying, 'sorry, sorry, I'm sorry.' The paramedics knock, then burst through the door Mom must have left unlocked.

They usher me out of the way and ask all these questions. I try to get the words out but can't think, can hardly speak. Nothing makes sense. One man cuts open my mother's shirt as the other opens a box. The guy with the scissors cuts through my mother's bra. I gasp and start to say something—it's one of the new ones she'd ordered online, it actually gave her support and was seventy-five dollars plus shipping—I stop myself before the words are formed.

They place the paddles on her and set up an automated breathing device. They're working with slow focus. After what doesn't seem like nearly enough time, they stop. One of them, the younger one with wavy black hair and ocean blue eyes, looks at me. 'I'm sorry,' he says. 'There's nothing more we can do.' I don't respond. For a moment, we're all silent.

The other guy stands. 'We need to get the body ready for transport.'

'She's my mom,' I say quietly.

Blue eyes puts a hand on my shoulder. He looks at me, into my eyes, like I matter. I start crying all over again. 'We need to get your mom ready for transport, okay?'

I nod. The other guy averts his gaze. I sit back as they struggle and manoeuvre and ultimately fail. I don't offer to help, but I do go over and pull the blanket blue eyes laid over her chest up higher. It slipped as they tried to move her. She shouldn't be exposed like that. He tells me they've called for some more help and I'm embarrassed, horribly embarrassed, and make a silent promise to Mom that I won't let anyone know about this.

Remembering my manners, I ask if they'd like something to eat or drink while they're waiting. The older guy makes a noise that could almost be called a scoff and his expression seems to say—isn't food what got us into this? Blue eyes says, 'No, thank you,' and sits on the couch. I sit across from him and wish I hadn't told Mom to back off and mind her own business when she was lecturing me a couple of weeks earlier.

When I told her about quitting my job, she was mad. She took the boys' side. I didn't tell her what they said to me, what they'd been saying to me for months. Maybe if I had she would have understood. But I couldn't repeat those words. I just wanted her to tell me things would be okay, tell me they were little jerks, and I'd find another job, a better job. She was upset about Billy, so maybe that was part of it. Now that you've made your bed, you'd better sleep in it, she'd said…whatever that means. I snapped back, if I wanted her advice, I'd ask for it. That was the last time I saw her.

Today's dessert date was me making up. I'd even put on some makeup for it, did my hair, added a little wave. During the argument she'd also told me I needed to spend more time on my appearance, like Tammy, like herself, though she didn't say that part out loud. Mom wasn't like me in that department. She wasn't Tammy either, but she was always presentable and never left the house without at least some light foundation, lip stick, and mascara.

Blue eyes gives me the littlest of smiles as the additional paramedics enter the house. They manage to lift Mom and I'm glad this happened after she'd gotten ready. It was bad enough all these men seeing her so exposed. If they'd seen her face naked too, it would have been too much.

I LOOK INTO THE mirror again and shake myself free of this memory. It's left my throat tight and my hands shaky. It will haunt me again I'm sure, but I won't allow it to eat up anymore of today. Today I have a mission, though I don't know where to start. I think to the episode of *The Last Ten Pounds* I saw yesterday—I don't know why I watch that show, maybe to comfort myself with the fact that even skinny girls feel fat, it's just a matter of perspective—A new mom lost fourteen pounds in a month. At the start of the episode the host filled up a whole garbage can of junk food from the mom's cupboards and fridge. That's where I'll start. I pull out a fresh garbage bag and fling open the cupboards. I pause. I'm technically still unemployed and I'm running low on money. Would it be ludicrous to throw out all this good food? It'd be a slap in the face to the starving children of Africa.

That last thought tells me I'm being ridiculous. This is garbage food, despite how good it tastes. I say it out loud to make myself believe it. "This is garbage food." It's not what I would give those children. If that's where the fifty cents a day Alyssa Milano asks us for goes—to buy this junk—people would be outraged. So, I start throwing things in the bag and it kills me. I consider starting slowly, eating what I have and adding healthy food little by little, but I've tried that before. It doesn't work.

My resolve breaks through and I end up with a garbage bag that's half full. I look at all the things I love piled in there together. There are Fudgee-Os—so good for a quick pick me up. Semi-sweet chocolate chips. Milk chocolate chips. My beautiful, plump, newly bought bag of sugar. There's Taquitos—delectable. Three boxes of frozen pizza, which were multigrain thin crust and prompted a debate within me since that sounds somewhat healthy. A half-empty bag of Ripple Chips. Onion and garlic dip. Pepperoni sticks, individually wrapped—the ideal nibbler. Full fat whipping cream—divine. I turn toward the cupboard and my favourite cookie tin stares back at me. I just baked the batch of peanut butter fudge oatmeal bars yesterday. I take it out of the cupboard and tilt open the lid. More than half are left. I pull the lid off and hold it over the garbage bag, and hold it, and hold it. The sweet scent makes me salivate. I close the lid and push them to the back corner of the cupboard. I won't forget they're there but still, they don't need to be so obvious. I don't know as much as I should about healthy food but I know oatmeal and peanut butter are healthy so the bars can't be all bad. Besides, I need something around for the occasional treat. Everyone deserves a little indulgence.

I turn back toward the bag, tie it up, take it into the elevator, down to the parking garage, and toss it in one of the dumpsters. This is resolve. I'll do a lot to get my snack on, but I will not climb into a dumpster. I go back upstairs, proud, terrified, and ferociously hungry. My cupboards and fridge aren't empty, but they look pitiful. Oatmeal, milk, mini carrot sticks that are getting those white chalky lines in them, sliced roast beef, eggs, honey, some lettuce leaves that have seen better days. Nothing I can make a meal out of. I regret tossing my bread. It was white, and white bread is supposed to be death, but I could have made egg in a basket. That would have been something. My stomach growls. This isn't mental hunger, but I got rid of all my food, so now what? I could go to the grocery store, but I don't know what to get and I know you're definitely not supposed to do grocery shopping when you're hungry—I heard that somewhere. Shop the perimeter, I think. I heard that somewhere too. So, that's what I'll do. Go to the grocery store, shop the perimeter, and figure out how to make the food into healthy meals after. But I'm too hungry. I can't do that. I need food now. The cookie tin calls to me.

Fifteen minutes later the tin is empty and I'm sitting on my couch with chocolate smeared on my fingers and tears running down my cheeks once again. I'm a failure. A failure who really wants her Mom. I need her to tell me beauty comes from within, not that I've ever believed it, but I need her to say it and I'm pissed at her because she isn't here to and that's because she was a failure as well.

CHAPTER THREE

I t's 11:45am and it feels like the whole day is over—it's a waste, which translates to me being a waste, which makes me disgusted at myself for how weak and pathetic I am. I'm guessing only pathetic people think of themselves as a waste. It's all a vicious cycle. I step over to the window and place my hands against the glass. The warmth reminds me that the day is not done. It's just starting, and my moment of indulgence was just that, a moment. It doesn't mean I'm a waste; it just means I'm not perfect. But I will be. I close my eyes and see myself the way I've always dreamed, as this happy, wonderful, fit person who isn't a slave to her desires, who isn't weak in body or in soul, and I tell myself—you'll meet her soon. "So, first things first," I say aloud. I need to figure out what to eat. I grab my laptop, head back to the couch, and type in 'Healthy Eating Plan.'

Before I hit enter, I scan the other possibilities Google brings up for me: healthy eating plan for women, for men, for weight loss, for beginners, and a healthy eating planner. I let my cursor hover over the weight loss option then click down—healthy eating plan for beginners.

The first two results show sponsored sites, Herbal Magic—been there done that—and some kids' foundation thing. I scan on: A Beginner's Guide by Nerd Fitness, a fancy nutrition plan, Dr. Oz's plan. I contemplate clicking the Doctor's page but am sceptical about that guy.

Everything he pushes seems to be the solution for weight loss, flat abs, or overcoming cancer. It can't all be so amazing. I continue to skim down the page and the choices seem overwhelming, but I only have a couple hours to make some decisions or I'll end up ravenous again and that's not a position I want to be in at the grocery store. I decide to see what the old Doctor has to say. The article is all about meal planning. I can relate to some of it. When you don't know what to cook or have the food in the house to cook it, of course it's easier to fall back on frozen pizza or a bag of potato chips. But the article doesn't give any real tips about how to go about planning or what to plan. My resolve starts to wane. I've tried before and failed. What makes me think this time will be any different?

You don't want to end up on 600-pound-life, my mind whispers. *Or on your living room floor. Who would even walk in to see what was wrong?* I scroll to the bottom of the page and look at the linked articles. They're all full of promises. The link titled, 'Three Ways to Get Your Fat to Eat Itself' is the most appealing of the seeming lies, albeit a little creepy. I shrug. Cannibalism is interesting if nothing else. The article talks about eating only the good, healthy fats—avocado, olives, olive oil, nuts, nut butter, dark chocolate chips—but in portions that seem barely worth it. Two tablespoons of nuts? How about two cups! Still, it's better than nothing. I grab a piece of paper and write: nuts, dark chocolate chips, peanut butter…then remember peanuts aren't actually a nut so the author must mean something else. The next type of fat seems even less appetizing—fish, seaweed, pine nuts. I don't even know what a pine nut is. Finally, the article talks about some fibre I can't pronounce and doubt I'd even be able to find.

All this thinking about food makes me want to munch. I click back to the original Google search and open a link that promises a grocery list of healthy foods. I add a bunch to my own list and experience tingles of fear. I have no idea how all these foods will magically combine to make good and filling meals. My mind drifts back to Autumn. She'd know what to do with all of this information, but she'd probably use it to take over my life.

I don't want Autumn's help. The list in my hand is something. It's a start. It's better than just eating what I want and counting calories. Calorie counting is death. Instead I'll eat these healthy foods and focus on portion control. I walk to the bathroom and turn from the mirror as I strip down. I'm just about to step over the tub when I stop and turn back with my eyes closed. I can't even guess how long it's been since I've looked at myself naked in the mirror—most likely years. Heck, it's probably been years upon years upon years. I've seen glimpses here and there, of course, but I haven't looked. I open my eyes and grit my teeth. This is me. I stare a moment longer. The reflection cuts off slightly past my navel, so I grab a stool, pull it over, then step up so there's more of my figure in the glass. This is me. I close my eyes then open them again. This is me. These rolls, this dimpled skin, this disproportioned body, all the stretch marks is…No. I take a deep breath. This isn't me. This is the fat that surrounds me. I say it out loud. "This is the fat that surrounds me." This is not me. I am going to find me. For good measure I stare at my reflection a little longer, soaking it in, trying to see the woman who's hiding somewhere inside. I can't see her though. All I see is the mammoth that stares back at me. A person should like her own reflection. I should be able to look at the woman staring back at me and not have this kind of loathing. The tears start all over again. It has to be a record, three times in one morning. Like a roller coaster on steroids I ride through fear, hope, disgust, resolve, disappointment and, finally, determination. That's the emotion I decide to hold on to. I turn away, step into the shower, and begin a cleansing process. Old me, goodbye. New me, I'll see you soon.

≈

WHEN I ENTER THE grocery store it seems bigger than I remember. I'm not sure how to navigate it. Despite nobody here knowing my mission, I feel exposed. All they see is a somewhat unkempt fat girl—her clothes too tight, her hair lying lifeless against her scalp, her face in need of some foundation. I'm not obscenely fat. Not so fat children will either point and stare or hide behind their mother's pant legs, but I'm fat enough that some will snicker.

The sweatpants I'm wearing make me feel even more conspicuous. They're not even the tight, spandex kind that have become so popular. They're cotton, and baggy, and everyone who sees me in them will probably assume I've given up on life. But I didn't shave and my fattest pair of fat pants, the only pair that still fits, has a huge hole in the butt so I didn't exactly have a choice. At least the dinner at Aunt Lucille's is a special one. I can wear a cotton dress—so forgiving.

I grab a cart and pull out my list. The perimeter isn't completely foreign of course—bread is on the perimeter, and milk and eggs. But I generally just make a beeline for those places.

I enter the produce section, also not foreign, but not a place I spend a lot of time in. I do like apples—smothered in peanut butter or Cadbury's chocolate creme. I pick up about twice as many apples as I usually would and scan the other options. I read somewhere that the more colourful the fruit and vegetables the more nutrients they have. I also read that bananas are pretty much sugar sticks. I pick up a container of strawberries and one of blueberries. They're bright for sure. They're also pricey. I cringe. Apparently getting healthy is not very cost effective. I grab some oranges and decide I don't want to go overboard so I move on to the veggies. Baby green spinach—also pricey. I grab the bag instead of the carton, which is the same price for more ounces. Carrots. Peppers. I opt for green because they're cheaper. I look at the squash—what would I do with that?—and head to the bread aisle. No white bread for me. Not anymore. But there's whole wheat, 100% whole wheat, brown bread, Ancient Grains, Oatmeal, and Quinoa. I don't even know what Quinoa is. This is ridiculous. Bread should be bread.

A woman with beautiful black curly hair and skin as smooth and rich as milk chocolate stands beside me. She's trim and looks fit. After reading the ingredients list of a bag of Ancient Grains bread, she glances over at me. "I'm checking to make sure it's got the germ," she says. "That's how you know it's really whole grain."

I smile back. "Yeah. Of course." She tosses the bag in her cart and I wait until she's a few steps away before picking up the same one. Maybe that's what I'll do, find trim, healthy looking people and stalk them through the grocery aisles to make sure my cart replicates theirs. I spy the curly-haired woman up ahead buying chicken breasts—seems like a good option. After glancing at my list, I grab some fish too—haddock and salmon. In the dairy section, I scan row upon row of yogurt. I pick up a fat free strawberry yogurt and quickly move on. Almost an hour later my cart is loaded and I'm staring at the price on the screen trying to wipe the deer-in-a-headlights-with-its-mouth-wide-open look off my face.

"Ma'am?" A teenage cashier with dyed pink hair and nose, lip, and ear rings questions. "Ma'am?"

"Mastercard," I say. I didn't take out enough cash for this. Two hundred and twenty-eight dollars. Insane. I'm used to having a full cart of food but it's rare that it ever goes over one hundred. The first thing I need to do when I go home is make sure that job is secure. Heck, I may even see if I can get some extra assignments if this is what it costs to eat healthy. I stare at the bags of food in my cart. What am I going to do with it all? I may have been overzealous. Packaged food doesn't have the expiry dates this stuff probably does, and I didn't think to look. Maybe when you're buying healthy food you just can't buy so much all at once. Either way, I'm about to find out.

I GET HOME, PUT everything away, and feel as if I still don't have anything to eat. I'm hungry though, so I go for what seems easiest—yogurt. I open up my computer browser and before I know it, the container is empty. This is not the best start, but at least it was fat free. I need some more guidance. I open a new tab on my browser and type: quick, easy, healthy recipes. I print off a few featuring ingredients that now line my fridge and cupboard shelves and a sense of success floats over me. Moments later, an overwhelming desire for Fudgee-Os takes its place. It's just food—why must I want it so bad even after I've made all these resolutions? Of course, it's probably partly because I'm lying on the couch about to watch my favourite show, a show I often watched with Mom. The cravings are worse when I'm missing her, which is just about always.

I wasn't a popular teen. Before Tammy came along in grade eleven, I was pretty much on my own, so Mom filled the role of best friend. We would cuddle up together on a Friday night with chocolate covered almonds, popcorn, and sour cream and onion chips, watching our favourite lineup of shows. We'd laugh. I'd tell her about my day. Sometimes I'd tell the truth, like how Billy started calling me Elephant at school, and how the whole school seemed to pounce on the nickname. He became Elephant Jr. for awhile, which wasn't fair, but poetic justice. He was hardly pudgy, but the name stuck because of me. He cried and cried about that one. He said he was barely even my brother. Barely. I never knew what he meant by that. Of course he was my brother. Fully. He yelled at me, 'you don't have to be fat,' like it was something I could change with a snap of my fingers.

Other nights I'd pretend and tell Mom things were wonderful. I turned Janie McCarthy getting first in an art competition to me getting first. When she asked to see the winning painting I said, 'there'd be a problem with that, it got ruined when I slipped on the way home and dropped it in a puddle.' It hadn't rained in a week, but she nodded her head and said, 'that's too bad.'

As we watched Cory, Shawn, and Topanga, we'd lick the seasonings off the chips or come up with new ways to dunk our Fudgee-Os in milk; I made us a Fudgee-O/popcorn sandwich one night. It wasn't good, but it was fun.

The phone breaks me out of my reverie and I reach over to answer it.

"Jennifer?"

"Dad. Hi."

"How are you?"

"Does it really matter?"

"Jennifer." His voice has an all too familiar edge to it—disappointment and frustration masked by a veneer of patience and concern.

"What?"

"I just thought I'd call. See how you were doing?"

"Your preferred family isn't interesting enough for you?" My disdain for my father would be more suited on a fourteen-year-old. It's juvenile, but old habits die hard.

"Jenny, stop that. I care about you, I worry."

"It's Jenn now. I told you that."

He sighs. "Do you need money? Have you found work?"

At last I have the right answer. "I got a job today actually, just accepted an offer."

His tone lightens. "That's wonderful. What is it?"

"Writer. It's something I can do from home."

"Oh. Excellent. Very excellent." He pauses. "It's a

legitimate position? Not one of these make twenty thousand dollars a month from the comfort of your own home scams?"

"Thanks."

"I just—"

"It's a real job, Dad."

"That's good. I'm proud of you, honey." There's silence and I wonder if he'll say he has to go. "How's Tammy?" He's grasping by asking about my friend, but at least he knows her name.

"She's good. Obsessed with Colin, her boyfriend. I don't see her as much."

"Hmm. Meet any new people, lately?"

"Nope."

"Oh, well," he pauses again, "maybe you could come over for dinner. Sometime next week? It'd be really nice if you—"

"It's a nice thought, Dad, but I'm pretty busy."

"Well, okay then." He sighs again, this time I'm pretty sure it's of relief rather than frustration. "I'd like to see you though. I know you're probably busy with your new job, but how about coffee next week? Starbucks at Spring Garden and Dresden?"

"Steve O' Reno's." I counter.

"Sure. Great. That's great. I'll look forward to seeing you then."

"Okay." I end the call and realize I didn't say bye. He hates that. I hate that he made plans with me without actually making plans. Real plans require a set date. I toss the phone on the couch and all of a sudden, my apartment feels far too small. I want out of it but have no where to go. I put on my shoes anyway, grab a jacket, and head for the door. I walk to the end of the block then turn and walk another block. By the time I reach the third block I've started to pant but I don't slow my pace.

I'm steps away from my apartment when I decide to do

the same thing in the opposite direction. These blocks are much bigger, and it takes me forty-five minutes to get back home. At the end of it, I walk up the five flights of stairs instead of taking the elevator. Tired doesn't even begin to explain how I feel, but I'm breathing. I'm breathing and I doubt I could be more proud if I'd just finished a ten-kilometre run. I feel fresh, invigorated, alive. I puke in the toilet and feel less of all those things. I need to refuel. On my walk I decided that's what I'll call eating from now on. Fuel. Food is fuel. I heard that on an episode of *My 600-Pound-Life*. Food is not life. Food is not love. Food can be pleasurable, should be pleasurable as long as it's serving its purpose—to fuel me. I pick up one of those newly printed recipes, head to the kitchen, and prepare a meal to fuel me. I smile. A journey has begun.

CHAPTER FOUR

On Friday I'm standing in front of the closet trying to decide what to wear to Aunt Lucille's. I've lost three pounds, and it's only been two-and-a-half days. I'm not sure if that's even possible—for it to be actual fat loss. I read some stuff online about water weight and sugar detox or some such thing. What did people even do before the internet? I've also taken to reading blogs of other fat people. It's discouraging and encouraging and depressing and uplifting and makes me feel less alone. I haven't heard from Tammy all week and I haven't heard from Dad about next week. I won't contact him though. I don't need to see him.

Most of my dresses from last summer don't fit and I finally decide on a plain purple one Tammy calls my muumuu. I consider calling her to ask if I can borrow something, but then I'd have to admit my clothes don't fit. I pull the muumuu on, put a little product in my hair and apply the mascara I picked up at the grocery store last night. Maybe my old ideas weren't altogether sound. If I feel better, if I feel somewhat worth it just as I am, I may start treating my body like I am better—something a blog inspired in me. I'm drawn to the bitter, caustic chicks—they justify me, but I also like the more motivational ones, the ones who talk about worth. I'd like to feel that way. I'd like to feel I'm worth the effort. I reach for my tub of Vaseline and smooth a smidgen of it across my lips. The woman staring back at me in the mirror is slightly better than the me I'm used to. I don't look repulsive. I look kind of nice. I can only see my head and shoulders in this mirror. I try not to think about the fact that to see myself from head to toe may create an entirely different picture.

∾

WHEN I ARRIVE AT Aunt Lucille's the lights are on, silhouetting the figures moving back and forth through the curtained windows. I hesitate in the driveway, trepidation flooding me. The last time I was here was for my mother's wake. My mother was nice to everyone. She was kind and sweet and eternally optimistic. She loved showing love through food. Cookies, pies, squares, casseroles, she made it all. When Aunt Lucille's husband took ill—prostate cancer—my Mom fed their family through his months of chemo and recovery. Every night. For months.

I stand in front of the house and debate turning around. I could do it. I could call on my way home, say 'I'm sorry it's so last minute, I was really hoping to come but I just couldn't, I'm far too sick.' I could. But just as I'm about to turn and leave the scent of honey and French vanilla wafts over me.

Autumn's hand lands my shoulder. "Hey there, what are you waiting for?"

"Nothing, I was just—"

"Let's go in. It's chilly." She looks as she always does. Peppy. Smiling. Long waves of hair flow through the back of her high ponytail. It's practical and pretty—Perfect. Just like her. Even her scent is perfect. It always arrives just a moment before she does. Not overpowering, but lovely. I follow her into the house and am greeted by a new myriad of smells—onions, garlic, fresh baked bread—all tantalizing. A festive mood floats in the air. Aunt Lucille hugs Autumn casually, more of a pat than a squeeze. She holds onto me a moment or two longer, then steps back with her hands still on my shoulders and smiles that pinched smile people have when smiling is the last thing they really want to do.

"How are you, Jenny?" I cringe at the name as Aunt Lucille tilts her head to the left, her signature indication of concern.

"I'm all right."

"That's good." Her smile looks a little more natural this time, her hands still on my shoulders. "You're looking nice," she says. I'm sure I hear surprise in her voice.

"You too."

"Well, come in. Come in." She releases me.

I follow her into the living room where Uncle Leo sits on the couch. When I was little, he made me think of Luigi from Mario World. The thick black hair, the bushy moustache. He even had a green cap. I pass by without a word and make my way to the kitchen.

I turn to Aunt Lucille. "Is there anything I can help with?"

She puts her hands on her waist and looks around. "I don't think so." She rubs her index finger and thumb along her chin. The motion makes me yearn for my mother. Genetics or simple observation, it's hard to tell, but it doesn't matter. Sadness gurgles within me and I fight to shut it down. There will be no tears. This whole lack of sugar and comfort food thing, it's making me an emotional wreck. "You know," she says. "You could set the table for me. That'd be a help." I nod with rapid movements and shuffle over to the cupboard.

"For five?" I ask.

"No, eight," she says. "Two of Daniel's friends and Autumn's new beau are joining us."

I nod again and push down the anger that erupts. Just being here makes me angry, and Autumn said nothing about additional guests. She said this was family. I grab the plates and head to the dining room. I ask Aunt Lucille where the extra flap for the table is, and she calls to Uncle Leo. He comes into the room, a mix of bravado and tempered embarrassment. I'll never see him as Uncle Luigi again—I used to call him that sometimes, and it always gave him a laugh.

I avoid eye contact, trying to suck myself in to not brush against him or even breathe the same air. Part of me thinks I'm being ridiculous, the other part thinks—Screw him. Just as I think he's about to leave me to finish setting the table he hesitates, his shoulders slightly hunched.

"Jennifer?" His usual booming voice is a murmur. I look up. I look into him. "How've you been doing since…" His voice trails off.

"Splendid," I chirp falsely, and immediately feel like a bitch.

"Cynthia, she was a good woman." he rubs a hand along his opposite arm. "A really good woman."

I nod, then feel my mom deserves more than this. "She was great," I add, the tears fighting to escape. He's already said sorry. He said it that afternoon and I know he won't say it again. I want him to though. He's passing me an olive branch, but I deserve more than an olive branch. Mom deserves more than an olive branch. He should hand over a full tree, all ripe and plump. I've acknowledged what he's offering though. That's something. I can't do more. "She was better than most," I continue, a bite to my voice.

Uncle Leo nods and steps backwards out of the room. I watch him go before bringing my attention back to the table. Is it fair to blame someone for something they did when so obviously tipsy, when their faculties were out of whack? Maybe not, but I blame him anyway. Alcohol induced mishaps and slips of the tongue just reveal the core of a person—who they really are without their inhibitions trying to hold back their true self. If that's who he really is, if he thought so little of my mother, my mother who did so much for him and his family, then I reiterate (in my head, of course)—Screw him.

I finish setting the table as the front door opens. Male laughter travels down the hall. It's Daniel's thirtieth today. His buddies are sure to have some big things planned after this dinner. There may have already been some big things before it. He needs a good night after what he's been through. He caught his fiancée sleeping with her best friend—a girl—a month and a half before their scheduled nuptials. Awful as it was, it's at least nice to know I'm not the only one who has problems.

Daniel's handsome, tall, a brilliantly successful chartered accountant, and he doesn't have a satisfying love life either…at least not anymore. Tammy, with a sympathetic shake of her head, had said that's what you get when you go for looks over substance. Daniel's fiancée was gorgeous, sickeningly so. She'd even done some modelling, but her beauty was definitely skin deep. The few times we met her she treated Tammy and me like we were a disease. She'd probably insure her looks if she could and walks around as if 'fat' is something she's in danger of catching. I never saw her eat anything but fish and vegetables.

I hope the guys Daniel invited tonight are nice like him. Not all of them have been. I think back to a Halloween party he'd invited me to a few years ago. I went as a ghost. I figured it'd be an easy enough costume that would mostly hide who I was. One of his friends dubbed me the Pillsbury Dough Boy and went around the whole evening cracking up as he tried to get people to poke my belly and see if I'd giggle. I wanted to leave, but the party was away from bus lines and about a seventy dollar taxi back into the city, so I ended up spending most of the evening holed up in the bathroom while people banged on the door, trying to get in.

On the drive home Daniel had sighed. 'He didn't mean anything by it Jenny, he was just having a laugh. You were all dressed in white.'

'And round and roly-poly?' I questioned.

'Come on,' Daniel had said, 'you know he didn't mean any harm. It was an honest mix up.'

I stared in front of me, furious at Daniel for defending him. It was probably only the third time in my life I'd felt angry with him. Sure, it was an honest mistake the guy held onto even after I repeatedly told him I was a ghost, and would he please stop poking me? The jerk had just gotten a kick out of it—'Hey guys,' he'd said to some of his other buddies, 'I was wrong—it's the GHOST of the Pillsbury Dough Boy. Will it giggle or say boo or both!' So very clever.

We go through introductions and no one giggles or smirks or even raises an eyebrow. None of them pay me much attention, but why would they? This is Daniel's night. I'm just a relative on the fringes. Autumn's new beau, as Aunt Lucille calls him, must be a trainer as well. His muscles show through his fitted dress shirt—tight, lean, athletic muscles. Muscles that could come from hours at the gym, or from actively engaging in manly sports or—my mind slips into fantasy—from labouring in the woods as a lumberjack under the hot sun. I like this lumberjack scenario and envision him in a white muscle tank with a red plaid shirt that's left unbuttoned, blowing slightly in the breeze. He lifts a dirty, sweaty forearm and pushes it across his forehead as he wipes away the sweat and moves his just-past-eyebrow-length nutmeg brown hair out of his eyes. Beads of sweat pour down his chest and moisten his tank so it clings, revealing the rippled abs beneath the now sheer fabric.

"Jennifer? The broccoli?"

I snap back from my reverie. Rajeev, one of Daniel's friends, must have said my name a few times because everyone's looking my way. Rajeev's gaze fixes on me, a patient looking smile upon his face. My cheeks heat and I hope they're not as red as I imagine. I pass the broccoli. Still pleased by my reverie, I let it take over, pushing embarrassment to the side. One of the best things about the lumberjack scenario is that it would justify Matt's beautifully tanned skin. I don't like the idea of him going to a tanning salon. It's barely spring and, unless he works outdoors, or recently went down south, tanning is probably the only other explanation.

I'm cautious with my meal, taking small portions and ensuring there is still white space on my plate. I laugh as the group kind-heartedly makes 'age' jokes at Daniel's expense. It feels good. I haven't laughed in a while. My favourite sitcom hasn't even been doing it for me, rarely prompting more than a restrained chuckle. I find Rajeev especially amusing. His voice is soft and deep, has a British twinge to it, and he speaks slower than most, as if he's tasting and assessing every word. He looks at the people around the room in a similar way, as if he's looking into, not just at them. It makes me feel exposed and I can't decide if I like it or not.

Autumn is especially animated tonight. Her hair bounces from shoulder to shoulder as she darts her head back and forth, telling the story of how she and Matt met at a trainer's convention. "He used to be this crazy soccer pro," she says, a hand resting gently on Matt's shoulder. "Was going to go national until an injury stopped his game. After a slump, he decided to start coaching and—"

"Don't you think you should let the man tell his own story?" says Uncle Leo, a grin on his face.

"Sure, Dad." Autumn laughs.

"Oh, she was doing a good job." Matt looks so comfortable, so at ease among us. I'd be a sweaty mess around all these new people. "I got certified as a trainer. I wanted to help other athletes get over their injuries, just like people had helped me. It was a way to get purpose back in my life. Focus."

It's not a lumberjack, but I approve. He's more than just a straight set of teeth and a tight body. Certainly better than most of the self-absorbed nitwits usually hanging on Autumn's arm. It's about time too. As hard of a time as I give Autumn sometimes, she's not the vapid exercise Barbie you might expect at first glance. She's got substance. She's smart and, more than that, she's kind and loyal to a fault.

She almost got beat up for that loyalty once. We'd been swimming at a local rec centre. We were thirteen. It was the summer Autumn developed her breasts and curves. The summer I developed from fat to obese. Some jerks hid my shorts, and I came out of the man-made beach with nothing to cover my massive jiggling thighs. The pool was gritty with sand from dozens of dirty feet; it clung to our skin. I had to walk home short-less, with a towel not big enough to tie into a full skirt. My inner thighs started to sting. I later learned they were bleeding with the friction from the granules of sand being smooshed between my huge legs. It's one of those burdens of fat girls that skinny ones don't even know about—the way our own skin can cause us such pain. Miserable doesn't even begin to describe it. Two boys started walking behind us, mocking me. One walked with legs spread, arms out, saying stupid things like 'oompaloompa, look, I'm the big oompaloompa.' The other just taunted and threw M&Ms at me. I walked silently. What could I say? They were right. I was monstrous.

Autumn walked beside me, getting madder by the moment. Her fists clenched. Her teeth gritted. The boys were big. In tenth or eleventh grade and Autumn was barely five foot two back then, probably less than a hundred pounds soaking wet. That didn't matter. She ran over to the oompaloompa one, shouted that he was a stupid moron and his face looked like an oompaloompa. The other one, the bigger one, came over and told her she better watch her mouth. She picked up a rock and threw it right at his nose. He grabbed her by the shoulders and lifted her in the air.

Just then, one of the fathers who'd been volunteering at the rec centre came over. He yelled at the boys, making them scatter, then walked Autumn and me back to Aunt Lucille's house. I never loved her more than at that moment. I should remember it more often. She's loyal. Loyal to me.

I've zoned out again, but I draw my focus back to the group as Matt finishes answering a few more questions. He looks over at me. "You've kept pretty quiet all night," his smile makes my stomach flip-flop. "I'm sure everybody else knows, but what do you do?"

Autumn tries to shush him, "She's just, uh, in between—"

"I'm working for an international curriculum organization," I interrupt. "I write short stories, articles, and plays that are designed to help English learners improve their comprehension of the language while familiarizing themselves with the customs, traditions, and current colloquialisms of North America. The learners are primarily in the big three—Japan, Korea, and China—but there are quite a few throughout South East Asia. A couple sectors throughout Africa as well." I'd prepared this answer, wanting to show my family I wasn't a failure. Not anymore.

They all look at me, a little shell-shocked. "When did—" says Aunt Lucille.

"They offered me the position a few weeks ago, but I just accepted a little earlier this week." Autumn and Daniel congratulate me sincerely, Uncle Leo nods.

"That's great, really, great," he says.

Rajeev leans forward. "That sounds awesome. So, do you get to do any travelling with it?"

"No," I say. "Not yet. But it's possible I may get to do some one day." This is almost assuredly a lie.

"Cool, cool." He nods. "So, is there an office here or do you work from home, or?"

"It's an at home job."

"I've always wanted to work from home, to write," he

says, and sits back, like he's about to enter his own little daydream. I've never seen a guy, a decently good-looking guy especially, look at me with such interest, almost admiration. It's unnerving. "How'd you get into it?"

"Well," I say, feeling nervous at the sudden attention. "I've always really liked writing. English was part of my double major and when I …left my last job I applied to this one, did some sample write ups. They liked my work. It's really nothing too glamorous."

"Is it enough to, um," Aunt Lucille hesitates, "pay the bills?"

"Yeah, it's pretty decent." I say. "It should work out to a few thousand more a year than my last job. Could be more if I get faster at it or decide to take on more than the required assignments, which right now is only taking up about twenty-five hours a week."

"That's amazing," says Rajeev again, nodding with approval. "More pay and less work."

"Yeah, really glad you found something." Autumn squeezes my arm. Her smile says she's proud of me. And it makes me want to cry. This is getting frigging ridiculous. It's got to be the sugar detox.

The conversation shifts to plans for the rest of the night. Autumn wants to join the boys, but Rajeev and Jeff say no, no female relatives allowed. Autumn fakes a pout and crosses her arms when they invite Matt to join them.

"Listen," she says, "wherever you're going there are sure to be women so why can't Jenn and I join?"

I mumble something about not being interested when Jeff cuts me off. "Absolutely not," he says. He claps Daniel on the shoulder. "Any ladies see this fella even saying one word to a fox like you and they'll think they don't have a chance with him." His words create an awkward moment, for obvious reasons.

"So, what's dessert?" asks Daniel.

"Homemade Apple Crisp with Breyer's French Vanilla,"

says Aunt Lucille, rising from her chair. Daniel grins. It's good to see such a genuine smile on his face. As dessert is passed, my happiness fades. Public dessert is always a sticky scenario. Do I eat and enjoy it heartily? Impossible, because I can't help but wonder whether people are thinking—*why does she do it? Doesn't she know this is what's gotten her here?* But if I don't eat it, there'll be similar thoughts anyway—*look at her, trying to pretend if we weren't watching she wouldn't have that whole crisp and tub of ice cream guzzled away in twenty minutes.*

Today adds another dimension. I wouldn't be eating it at home, not anymore. I've been doing so well, but I also know Aunt Lucille will take offence if I don't partake and don't explain why. But I'm not going to explain why, not yet. And I can't say I'm full. They know that's never stopped me before. I smile and accept the plate as it's handed to me. I eat it and it's good. It's so very good. It's so good I miss some joke Daniel tells about his boss and fake my laughter. I'm about to ask for more when I realize what I'm doing. If I'm going to be resolved, I should be resolved, damn-it. I take the final bite, but the joy is gone. The want is still there, but not the joy.

We stand, sing 'Happy Birthday,' snap some pictures, and it makes me eager to get home. I consider excusing myself to the bathroom, purging that pie, but I won't go down that road again—been there, done that—so I smile in the pictures, try to hide myself in the back but get ushered to the front when Matt says he can't see me. He dashes into the frame just as the light flashes. The evening is captured.

Daniel hugs me tight and kisses my forehead, "I'm glad you made it, cuz. We need to see each other more."

I smile back, "Have a great rest of your birthday, all right?" and wonder what it is we'd do if we saw each other more.

"You want to go see the new Channing Tatum movie next weekend?" asks Autumn.

"Sure," I reply.

"It was really nice to meet you," says Rajeev as he puts on his coat. I'm struck again by how cute his accent is, and by the fact that he bothers to specifically say goodbye to me.

"Yeah, good to meet you too." I send him my best smile.

"I hope everything goes well with the writing. I'd love to do something like that," he says again. I realize I never asked what he does, but it's too late now.

"You want a ride home?" Autumn's arm is looped around Matt's middle. "Matt's going to drop me off before meeting up with the guys, so it's no problem."

"That's all right."

"Ok, next weekend then." Autumn gives me a quick hug then heads out the door with Matt a step behind, his hand on the small of her back. Somehow, everyone is already outside as I'm putting on my coat. Aunt Lucille stands across from me, her smile too sure, her stance too casual.

"How are you really doing, dear?"

"I'm fine."

"You can't be fine. Your—"

"I'm okay. Really. I'm dealing."

"Anytime you want to come over, you know you're—"

"I know."

She stares at me. I'm not letting her speak. I'm not letting her say what she wants to say. "You know—"

"Thanks so much for dinner, Aunt Lucille. It was really good. Thank you." I step outside and close the door behind me. I only glance back once I've reached the sidewalk and see her standing in the living room window. Uncle Leo walks up behind her, puts his hand on her shoulder, and she looks up at him, says words I can't guess. He's not a bad man. I hear the words again though. I'll hear the words every time I look at him until the day I die. I wasn't meant to hear them at all—no one was, except for his neighbour. Autumn had stopped the music to put on a new album, one of my mom's favourites. It was in that inopportune moment that his voice, straining to carry over the melody, carried across the room instead, 'It's a shame, but it's a fucking curse of fatties, they bring it upon them—' and everyone in the room silenced. Uncle Leo paled. But the funeral reception carried on. No one said anything. Autumn pressed play and music flooded the room once more. Still, no one has said anything.

∽

I WALK THE WHOLE way home, all 7 kilometres of it. It should have only been about 6.5 kilometres, but I take a long way back, avoiding the turn off to my mother's cemetery. It takes me one hour and forty-seven minutes, probably the longest I've ever walked. I don't feel too tired at the end of it though.

In my apartment at last, I survey the space. I'm a bit of a slob. I'm doing so much else about my life I should do something about that too, so I pick up my laundry, stack papers and magazines, though what they need is to be sorted, and do the dishes. My apartment is presentable. Mom would be satisfied. She hated how messy I could be sometimes. I hate the way I'm thinking about her in the past tense. I know that's technically how I should think about her, but it seems a betrayal.

Tired from the walk and the cleaning, I plop down on the couch and think instead about how awesome my life will be once I've lost the weight. I go back to imagining Matt, his strong, glistening arms, his beautiful smile, and I envision those blue eyes gazing at me, adoring me, wanting me. I should think about some movie star or something, not my cousin's boyfriend, but I've just seen Matt so he seems more real to me, the me with barely an extra ounce of fat on her, that's beautiful, that, at long last, is happy with who she is. That me still couldn't get a movie star, but maybe she could get someone like Matt. My fantasy travels away from PG status and I realize how not okay that is. He's Autumn's boyfriend.

Needing a distraction, I grab my keys, grab my wallet, and head out the door. When I return I've got a carton of Breyers. I take the first bite and it's delectable. It's almost as good as that ice cream sandwich so many years ago. I hesitate as I lift the second bite but give in and let the cool creamy flavour slide over my tongue. I'm supposed to be resolved. I'm supposed to be focused. I plunge the spoon into my mouth then dip it back into the tub for another taste. I just had a long, long, walk. It's okay.

CHAPTER FIVE

When I wake up the next morning I feel like a failure. Eating a tub of ice cream was not okay. This whole mission to lose weight thing doesn't mean I never get to enjoy yummy food again, or at least I hope it doesn't mean that, but it probably means I shouldn't be eating a whole tub of ice cream before bed. I only intended to have a few bites, maybe the amount that would fit into one of those dainty little dessert bowls, a reward for my walk, but it was just so good.

I'm scared to step on the scale, so I don't. Instead, I go to my desk, open my laptop, scan my email for new assignments, and realize it's Saturday. No escape there. I consider calling Tammy but it's only eleven in the morning and she and Colin like to sleep in then do brunch. I stare at the screen. From what I know from the weight loss shows, food is the biggest part of the battle but it's still only part of the battle. I walked forever last night. I'm fit enough. I can be doing more. A search for gyms in my area reveals Fit4Life is the closest. I could go in, see someone, make this next step legit, but I call instead. The girl on the phone is altogether too cheery for my liking. I can just tell she's probably got a high ponytail with flowing blonde hair reminiscent of Rapunzel. It's probably natural too. Her breasts are most likely as perky as her voice and I bet she loves exercise, like really loves it. I say I've got the wrong number and hang up.

I'm just not ready. I'm not ready to stand beside that cheery woman who answered the phone. I'm not ready to put on my workout clothes and get sweaty with her looking on. Women like that don't even sweat. They glisten, and somehow it's sexy instead of repulsive. That's what Autumn does, she glistens. I'm sure Matt loves it.

I shake my head, stand up, then pace around my room. It's been less than a week! Less than a week and I'm in danger of giving in, giving up, admitting ultimate defeat. I stop as I see the picture of my mother and me above my bed, taken at my graduation five years ago. Her smile is wide and full of joy, and I know if she were here, if she had that wonderful thing called hindsight, she'd tell me I can't give up. She'd tell me to just do better. She'd probably apologize for not helping me do better, for accepting her own weight gain one day and, in that moment, accepting mine.

I was about eleven when she stopped trying to get me to eat healthier, stopped leaving those little hints from time to time, and just enjoyed food with me. Food had never been an issue for Mom, not until the hysterectomy she'd had after Billy. She'd been able to eat whatever she wanted pre-Billy and keep the voluptuous form that stayed Dad's eye. After Billy, different story, but she still loved food and so the pounds piled on. I love food too. That's my problem. I really love it, but I need to love my life more. I don't want to be dead before I'm fifty-five and there are other things too, things that matter right now. I want to look in the mirror and like what I see. I want a beautiful man, a man like Matt, to like it too. Maybe I'd even like to have kids one day. Time is a ticking, but it isn't too late yet.

I go back to my computer and enter a new search: Exercise Program for Beginners. The first suggestion adds 'at home' to the topic and I click on it. An article on WebMD is a guide for absolute beginners. After the second page it still hasn't told me anything about how to get started. I click back and try an article by Skinny Miss or some such thing. "5 Quick and Easy Moves for Absolute Beginners." Okay. This should be my thing. The first picture even has a woman who is far from trim. She's not fat but she's no model either. She's big enough that there's a chance she thinks she's fat. I like that.

The first move is a plank—the model for this is skinny. It's supposed to be easy, but I doubt my arms can hold myself up like that. I try it anyway—fifteen seconds. I feel I should be able to do anything for just fifteen seconds. My upper arms are shake and ripples run through my torso, making my fat jiggle. I forget to breathe and have to remind myself. When I come back to the computer, I've decided fifteen seconds are longer than one might think. I continue to read through the exercises and try each one, just once though—none of this repeat 2x repeat 15x. I have to know I can do it first, right? At the end of the article it talks about cardiovascular fitness and running so I click on the link: A 5km Plan for Absolute Beginners. In order to start you have to be capable of walking one mile. I don't know how many miles the walk was last night, but I know it's more than that. There's an inspirational video before the article and it leaves me tearing up once again. If that guy can do it, achieve all his dreams—and in nine months—maybe I can too. No, I *can* too.

If I'm going to run, I need running shoes. My little flats won't do. I don't want to deal with a store clerk so I order a pair online after researching what I should get. I know this is not the best way to buy runners, but it's better than nothing.

The shoes arrive several days later and I lace them up. I'm supposed to start with five minutes of walking—no problem—then three cycles of one-minute runs followed by one-minute walks. I'm huffing and puffing after that first minute, but I do the following two cycles and then finish with another five-minute walk, which turns into about twenty minutes because I decide I haven't been out long enough and it's a beautiful day anyway. For the next two weeks an additional walk run cycle is added every day. So I do it, and do it, and do it—day after day. On the rest days I do some of the bodyweight exercises I found.

I'm not perfect with my eating, I've bought a chocolate bar or two, but for the most part I stay away from temptation. I'm trying. In the third week I progress to cycles of two minutes running, with one-minute walks. Each week the runs increase until the seventh week has me jumping to a nine-minute run and I'm scared I'll kill myself, but I don't. When I'm supposed to jump to fourteen minutes in the eighth, I do that too. Then right in the middle of the eighth week I'm supposed to run twenty minutes all at once.

It's almost the end of June and summer is here in all its glory—the hottest day yet this year. I won't let that stop me. I even decide to run up the Citadel hill, a steep 200 metre climb. I set off feeling fabulous. About ten minutes in I feel decidedly less fabulous, but I won't quit. I pant along, watching a woman less than half my size jog by easily. She approaches the hill and I follow after her, watching as she gets smaller and smaller. I can't stop. I won't stop. I push myself harder and harder, wiping the sweat from my eyes with the back of my arm when things get so blurry I can hardly see. After a minute or two it seems like the wiping is not working because everything remains blurry. I don't think I'm running straight and I'm sure I can actually hear the beating of my heart—fast and furious. I stumble to the side of the road and flop down on the grass. The sky is blue and bright and waving above me. I try to get up but can't. My heart just keeps pounding. It's as if it's racing up the hill even though my body stays flat on the ground.

"Are you all right? Miss, are you okay?" A head hovers above me and I can't figure out why. There's no face in this head. Only a dark shape that blocks out the sun. "Are you okay?" I keep trying to breathe but it's not coming the way it should and I think—this must be what happened to Mom. This is it. I'm about to die. The head comes closer and I can see it's a woman, not much older than me. "Are you all right?" she says again. "Should I call the ambulance?"

"The ambulance?" I repeat and think of the two men who came that day. Blue eyes and the other one. How they couldn't move my mother. I won't let that happen to me. "No," I say. "No, please don't."

"Okay," she says, and I realize she's holding my hand. "Can you sit up?" I try and find that I can. As I do, relief floods through me. My heart is still racing but maybe I'm not going to die. "Good, good," she says. "That's good." She's sweet looking, this woman, and she seems genuinely happy that I'm not dead. I try to get up but she puts her hand on my shoulder. "Just sit here a minute, okay? I'll sit with you."

My heart starts to slow and my breathing becomes more even. "Why don't you try standing now?" she says. I do, and it's not like she can really help me up, but she tries. "How's that?"

"Good," I tug at my shirt, smoothing it out, and swallow. "I don't know what happened." She's probably thinking— you're a fat girl who tried to run up a hill, on a sweltering day, no less, what do you think happened?

But she just smiles. "It's a pretty warm day. Maybe you didn't drink enough?"

"Yeah, maybe."

She looks at her watch and what looks like worry clouds her face. "I'm going to be late, but are you okay?"

"Yeah, yes. I'm fine. Thank you."

She steps away then turns back. "You should go to the doctor. Just check. Make sure everything is okay."

"Sure," I say. "Yeah, I will." I pace in circles for a few minutes after she leaves. Instead of heading home, I make my way to a walk-in clinic nearby. I hate doctors but what just happened was scary enough to justify a visit. I haven't been to this clinic before. It's not too crowded, but the walls need a fresh coat of paint—they're grimy—and the air smells stale. The receptionist tells me it shouldn't be more than a half hour wait if I'm lucky. I'm not lucky, and it's almost an hour before I see the doctor. He's an old Middle Eastern man who smells of garlic, has a nice smile, and makes me feel decently comfortable.

"So, are we used to running?" he asks, while measuring my heart rate.

"I've been running for almost two months now," I say. "Well, running and walking …in intervals. Today was the first day I was trying to run straight through, and I was running up a hill."

"And did we eat today?"

"Yes." I say, a little perturbed at the way his speech creates a false connection between us.

"What?"

"A tuna fish sandwich. An apple. An omelette for breakfast."

"Water?"

"Maybe not enough."

"Everything seems okay right now." He sits. "Considering."

"Considering?"

"Well, you have high blood pressure, but your heart sounds healthy. Have we been trying to lose weight?"

"Yeah, for a couple months now. I've been eating way better. I started running, like I said."

"That's good." He nods and the way he does it, he reminds me of one of those bobble heads people put on their car dash. "So, exercise is fairly new to you?"

"Yes."

"Keep at it," he cautions, "but be careful. Especially as the weather gets warmer, make sure you're having a lot of water. You want to always stay hydrated."

"Okay."

"You may want to hire a professional, someone who can help you progress at the right pace."

"But I can do it on my own, too, right?"

"You can." he puts his hand on my shoulder. "Just be careful, okay? You have your own doctor I see. Maybe give him a visit if you're not ready for a trainer. Get his advice. We need to be careful with these things."

"Sure," I say, standing as he does. "Thank you."

Relief floods me as I leave the office. I'm not dying. It was hot and I didn't drink enough. I give myself two days without running then get back to the schedule. This time I run in the evening and avoid the hill. By the end of the tenth week I've completed the training schedule and a week later I'm running five kilometres. Well, I'm almost running five kilometres. It takes me over fifty minutes, so from what I've read I don't even know if you can call that running. I break to walk here and there but it's less than a minute at a time. It's making a difference though. I had to buy new pants. I've lost twenty-four pounds, which is actually a little disappointing with all the work I've been doing. It should come off faster, but it's better than gaining.

I'm still doing that initial strength training routine and wonder if I need more than that. It's scary though, because I'm not sure what is and isn't safe to try. I like the runs, or I liked them at first, but running almost every day gets a little monotonous. It shouldn't matter though; this isn't about fun. This is about looking good, feeling good, and living. But I also want results and I want them now. I want people to stop and turn. I want my friends and family to be wowed at my transformation. I saw Tammy three weeks ago, for the first time in almost a month, and she noticed something. She said I was looking brighter. But what does that mean? Brighter? I've avoided everyone else as best I could by saying that my new job keeps me super busy. I don't want to see them until I know they'll notice.

❧

TWO WEEKS AFTER SEEING the doctor I get ready for my run and don't feel too happy about it. It seems like all I do, day after day, is work on my writing assignments, cook healthy meals, and run—all of it alone. I see cashiers and strangers on the street, but that's about it. I may get out of the house, but I'm as alone as I would be if my weight were keeping me locked in.

As I'm tying up my runners, I think about Mom and how she would never have let me do this. She'd visit, and when she saw my resistance to take part in life she'd drag me out—it'd probably be to a restaurant, but at least it'd be somewhere. She'd get me laughing. She's fading from me and as I push through the run, ignoring the astonished looks I imagine I prompt as I turn down as many back streets and alleys as I can, I try to conjure her up. Mom laughing, the little snort that often accompanied it, the way she'd cover her mouth in embarrassment. Mom smoothing her hands through my hair before braiding it, the way she would mumble, 'so soft,' as she let the strands fall through her fingers. Standing in the kitchen, mixing up some yummy batter and humming. Putting on her eyeliner and scrunching up her lips as she did it. Curled up in bed reading to me and Billy—before Billy left to be with Dad. Scratching her chin, rubbing her forehead, telling me she loved me. I have to make myself think these things. It's a necessity. If I don't, the other images creep in to replace what she should be in my mind. No matter how often I try to do this though, the other images are still there—stronger, clearer—her body spread across the living room floor, the faint scent of urine, the paramedics pushing on her exposed dimply flesh, and my ineptitude.

I wonder now, as I feel myself getting stronger day by day, if that could have made the difference. She'd clearly already been on the ground for a while when I arrived, but that doesn't mean Mom died right away. Maybe if I'd been stronger, I could have pushed in deeper, reached her heart. Maybe she'd be here with me, running, or at least on the other end of the line, telling me how proud she is. Maybe.

I call up Tammy when I get home and ask if she wants to hang out tonight. She says sure, she and Colin are going to go out to dinner and I'm welcome to join. I ask if it could just be the two of us. Maybe she could come over—I'd make some snacks and we could watch a chick flick. She hesitates. She must be wondering if something is wrong, if I need her for some mourning reason. It's not been so long that I can't still imply the dead mom card with my tone, which I imagine I've done. It's legit though, I guess. She says she'll be there and asks what time. Seven thirty, I say, so the expectation of dinner will have passed. I hang up the phone and want to be hugged so bad my skin feels stretched with the yearning of it. I've never been touchy-feely though and Tammy knows this, so despite her propensity for hugs she won't embrace me when she walks in the door. Mom was the only one who did it unasked.

CHAPTER SIX

When Tammy breezes into my apartment she's like a breath of fresh air. It's cliché but true. She smells like spring. "New perfume," I state.

"Lilac breeze." The scent suits her. She stands in front of me and grins. "You look good!"

I reach forward and wrap my arms around her. I don't cry, amazingly. She takes a moment but then returns my embrace. She squeezes and gives my back a little rub. I step away, shrug, and head to the living room. "How's Colin?"

Tammy proceeds to tell me all about him, his Grade 5 students, and a comical incident at the science fair. I smile and laugh at the appropriate moments but feel disconnected from her words. Instead, I'm focused on her hair, its glorious sheen, her almost crimson lips, the folds of her blouse that mask the rolls I know lie beneath. She's as beautiful as she can be but more than that, her bubbly demeanour, her smile, her laugh, all seem genuine. It perplexes me. She is the way I imagine I'll be when I'm skinny, only she's not skinny, not even close.

Tammy's a more justified fat girl than me. Her love affair didn't start with a stolen ice cream sandwich eaten in a bathroom. She had legitimate reasons for finding happiness in food. Tammy was a skinny little girl once. And Tammy had a step-dad who shouldn't have been one. It sounds so stereotypical, so out of a TV drama, but it's true. He liked Tammy in a way he shouldn't have and Tammy, afraid to tell her mom, handled her fears with chocolate chip cookies and Twinkies and bags of ketchup chips. Food was there for Tammy. Not only did it provide that immediate comfort she needed, but as the pounds crept on, Step-Dad's interest slacked until he was no longer a problem. He even moved out. I guess without the appeal of a pretty little girl in the package, Tammy's mom was no longer such a great catch.

I feel heartless thinking of this so matter-of-factly, but I don't mean it that way, it's just the way she talks about it too, as a fact. And depending on how you look it, Tammy was lucky—he definitely did some bad things, things a little girl should not have to know about, but he didn't, well...let's just say it could have been a lot worse. And she's okay now. She's happy. With the help of a great psychologist, she worked through it all as well as anyone could, it seems. She has a boyfriend who loves her, adores her, really. It almost makes me sick sometimes, the way he drools over her like he thinks she's just the best thing since the internet...If I'm honest, it just makes me jealous. She's so happy.

"So," says Tammy, breaking me out of my reverie. "What about you? I like what you're doing with your hair."

I nod and touch the tendrils I took some time to curl. "Thanks. I've lost some weight too."

She nods. "Trying to be healthier?"

I note that she doesn't approve the weight loss or even comment on it. "Yeah. Cutting out some junk food, trying to exercise more."

"That's great!" She reaches forward and grabs for the sugar snap peas I have on the counter. She dips one in hummus. "Healthy snack?" She takes a bite. "Pretty good!"

Some days Tammy's energy, her vibrancy, annoys me, but today it's comforting. Today, her bubbly nature is contagious. Tammy is about my height and until recently I only outweighed her by a few pounds. Now I must weigh less. She looks better than me though. She believes in always looking her best. My mom used to say I should take a lesson from her. As I see her sitting here, more content than I imagine I've looked in months, I wonder if Mom was right.

∽

AFTER THE MOVIE, TAMMY leans back on the couch. "That was good." She moves her arm to the soundtrack that plays as the credits roll by. The motion reminds me of waves. It's hypnotic. When the music stops she sits up. "So, how have you been doing? Really doing?"

Sometimes I wish people would say the words they mean. I play along and answer with words I don't really mean, though I know this isn't what she wants. "Good, super good. I'm proud of myself for doing better, being better, you know?" I watch for her reaction, see if she'll call bullshit, though these aren't complete lies. "I mess up sometimes, but I've been really good with, uh, eating good, you know? I'm happy."

"That's good." She grabs some of the leftover popcorn. "But you have to enjoy as well. You can't let food rule your life." She crunches the kernels and looks less beautiful.

I want to say that's what I was doing before but I just nod. "I'm running too," I say. "And working out some— bodyweight exercises. They're pretty hard."

"Running? Like actually hitting the pavement, running?"

"Well, what other kind is there?"

"I don't know," she laughs. "I never took you as a runner. But that's awesome, really awesome." There's no condescension in her voice.

"Maybe you could try it with me," I say, hope in mine.

"Not me." She grabs a few more snap peas and picks up the hummus bowl. She scrapes around the edges. "Colin and I go for a walk through the park a couple of times a week. Sometimes we hit up the trails too. It's pleasant.

That's how I like my fitness. And I don't break a sweat."
She giggles.

I nod again, smile, then lean back and prop my feet on
the coffee table.

"Have you seen your Dad recently?" She asks.

"Nope. But I'm supposed to see him next week. We're
meeting for tea, to make up for a missed meeting last
month."

She nods. "And?"

"No." I cut her off, then stand. I was hoping to get
through this visit without a question about Billy. I know I'm
a miserable person for not visiting him, but I just can't. I
don't need people reminding me and making me feel worse.
"You want anything else to drink?"

She stands too and shakes her head, "I should get
going."

I don't want her to leave. "You haven't told me how
things are going with you," I say. "How is work?"

"It's really just same old, same old but I may be up for a
promotion."

"Oh, yeah, that's awesome," I say, wondering if my voice
sounds overly cheery. "Tell me more."

"I don't want to jinx it by talking too much," she says,
and makes her way to the door. She wants to leave me, as if
the way I am sucks away her joy. This may be completely
ridiculous. I don't know. I say the only other thing I can
think of. Something I should have said much earlier. "How's
your mom?"

"She's good," Tammy replies. "The surgery went well.
She's recovering. She's positive."

"That's awesome." I don't even know what it is but
there's something I want from her and I feel if I can just get
her to stay a little longer maybe I'll figure it out.

"I really have to go." She says, grabbing the door handle.
"But thanks for having me over. It was great." She puts her
hand on my shoulder. "We need to hang out more often. I

know I've been busy—with work, with Colin, but I miss you."

"I miss you too."

"Wing night next week? Colin has some great buddies." She winks.

"Maybe," I say, thinking she just doesn't get it.

I close the door behind her and go to pick up the now empty bowls and platters. My tiny apartment suddenly seems large. Besides Autumn, who is obligated to love me, Tammy's the only person I really have, and I basically had to manipulate her into coming to see me. She couldn't get out of here fast enough…though that isn't really true. She was here for a while. I debate going down to the corner store and getting some real snack food but instead I do squats and then lunges and then hold a plank for as long as I can, until my shoulders are burning and my arms are shaking and I know in only a few seconds more I will collapse. I pretend the tears are from the physical effort and tell myself I'm doing awesome.

I'VE BEEN SITTING ACROSS the table from Dad for only two minutes and already I regret being here. This meet up is two weeks later than it should be. Tea got postponed again. Some client emergency. He invited me to dinner twice in between but I declined. I haven't seen Evita and the girls since my mother's funeral and I'd like to keep it that way for as long as possible. It still makes me angry, that he brought them. It's not like they were mourning her. He should have just been there for Billy and me, instead of having his new family attached to him.

I tense at the way he smiles at me. It's pitiful. It's obligatory. "You're looking good," he says. "Have you lost weight?"

"Of course I've lost weight." My voice raises. "I've lost thirty-five pounds."

He smiles then nods some more, like what I've told him isn't momentous. "That's super," he says. "You're finally taking control of your life." The word 'finally' feels like a slap in the face, despite the fact that any outside observer would think he had nothing but goodwill toward me. "Food is just fuel," he says, holding up a bite of his croissant and popping it in his mouth. I don't know where he's heard that phrase, but I wish he hadn't said it. It's mine, it's been my mantra, and he's tainted it. He has no idea what he's talking about. He never has. One afternoon he walked in on Mom and me in front of one of our favourite movies, cheesecake pops and chocolate almonds by our side. It was just after Mom had lost a potentially big client. He shook his head and gave mom this look—'why do you do it?' he'd asked, 'Why?'

Mom shrugged and put her arm around me. 'It makes us happy,' she'd said, then turned the volume up higher.

Dad shook his head again and walked away. That was four months before he walked away for good. In the two months previous, the months I guess he'd been working up the nerve to make that final walk, he must have lost ten pounds. He wasn't like us. When Dad was stressed or sad or angry, he stayed away from food. If he was nervous, he'd say his stomach was in knots. When Billy's accident happened, and we were all there in the hospital waiting to see if he'd live or die, Aunt Lucille had offered Dad a freshly baked chocolate chip cookie. He threw his hands in the air. 'How can you eat at a time like this?' then stood and started pacing.

Mom grabbed Aunt Lucille's elbow and took another cookie. 'They're wonderful, Luce,' she said. 'Thank you.' Dad just didn't get it. He would never get it—the way those cookies soothed and comforted. He'd never understand how a bowl of chips could absorb nervousness, frustration, or fear.

I signal to our waitress. "Actually," I say, "can you bring me two brownies to go with my tea?"

She smiles, nods, and walks away. Dad tilts his head and purses his lips. "How's the new job going?"

"It's not that new anymore." I shrug. "But it's fine. How's your work?" I ask. "Busy as always?" He hates it when I answer questions meant for him; I find it efficient.

"Yes, it's busy," he says. "Home life has been taking a toll as well." I perk up at this. He almost never says anything negative about his new family. It's been seventeen years but I still can't help calling them new.

I keep silent, waiting for him to continue. Dad rubs his hand through his hair, and I notice he doesn't look as put together as usual. "Courtney dropped out of University. She's taken up with a musician. We're pretty sure he does drugs. She just won't listen to us. It's stressing Evita to no end." (Yes, my father's new wife's name is Evita, and no, she's not as exotic as the name implies. Her international experiences and connections started with the honeymoon to the Greek Isles Dad took her on. And yes, she's younger than my mom—twelve years younger—and kept her figure despite having sweet little Melinda and Courtney. Courtney was the main reason Dad finally moved out, I believe. Evita, his secretary at the time, was playing the pregnant mistress card.) He laughs. "My home is a battlefield." I thank the waitress for the brownies and keep listening, no longer really wanting to eat them, or at least both of them. Dad shrugs. "I guess all we can do is try to guide her and hope she makes some better decisions."

"She never was the brightest girl," I say. He scrunches up his eyes and says nothing. We sit for a few moments in silence.

"Have you been to see Billy?" he asks. He knows the answer, yet he always asks it.

"No."

It's clear he wants to say more—to chastise? To encourage? Perhaps he wants to tell me my visit will be what makes the difference. But it won't make any difference at all. Going there the night of the accident was bad enough. I didn't want to go. When Mom called, I told her I'd seen Billy once already that day and once was enough. But she was so desperate, rambling on about the rain, and a gravel shoulder, and how her baby might die. 'I can't go alone,' she pleaded to me. 'I need you there.' I didn't have a choice. She was too upset to drive, so I took a taxi to her place and we sat in the back together. I held her one hand as she kept the other tight against her chest.

I'd sat in the waiting room with all the family. I didn't want Billy to die. But at that moment I felt almost satisfied he was suffering, after how much he'd made me suffer. It was a sick feeling. When we were told he was in a coma, that there was nothing more we could do that night, I helped Aunt Lucille drag Mom out of the building. When I left the hospital, I told myself I'd never come back. I couldn't pretend I forgave him—being in a coma didn't change who he was. A couple weeks later Mom was dead, and it was so much easier to stay away.

My father and I are having a stare down as these thoughts travel through my mind. Finally, he sighs. "So, the weight loss. What sparked that?"

I have no idea what to say. I could tell him Mom, but that's only part of the reason. I could tell him it's because I want to get a sexy boyfriend who'll make love to me all night long. I won't go that far. How about just saying so that my own father will love me more? Or that so I'll finally love myself at all? I take a bite of brownie instead of saying any of these things and let politeness give me time. When I swallow, I answer. "I just thought it'd be good to get a little healthier. I put on some more weight," I pause, "after Mom. I didn't want to buy new clothes again."

He nods, satisfied with the least truthful answer, and

doesn't pry further, doesn't ask how I'm surviving without my mother, doesn't realize his daughter has essentially become an orphan. I watch him as he talks about the new election, as if I care. He's not looking bad for a man in his late fifties. I saw him and Evita running around the park by their house once. I watched from the bus window and wondered how different our lives would have been if he'd convinced Mom to go running with him.

He's still not too wrinkly, and though his hair is thinning, it's a full head of hair. I think of a family photo he sent out a couple of years ago. He definitely made a good trade when he decided to give up on mom and me and move onto Evita and their blossoming family. It was a great picture—they were all in white t-shirts and blue jeans. Dad looking handsome, Evita looking stunning despite being in a t-shirt, and the girls, the perfect picture of health and beauty with figures you could just tell were going to imitate their mother's. My mother had seen the photo on my kitchen table and held it up.

'He sent this to you?' she questioned, shaking the photo.

'Yeah,' I said, staring into the fridge.

'The nerve,' she said, letting the photo fall. She then came over and placed her hands on my shoulders. She kissed my cheek. 'So, what are you going to rustle up for dinner?' A flare of anger shot through me in that moment, anger for not keeping our family together, anger for letting that picture and the beautiful daughters in it exist, anger that she transitioned so quickly into asking what we were going to eat.

I bring my attention back to my father and the politician he thinks deserved to be the lead. I still can't focus on his words and so imagine what his original family's photo would look like. There'd be him, the same, and then me, big enough to be an embarrassment. We'd be standing around Mom's headstone perhaps, and then there'd be Billy. Billy…not an embarrassment exactly but also not someone it's fun to bring up in conversation. I realize we couldn't be around Mom's headstone. We'd have to be in Billy's hospital room, or ward room, or wherever he was. Mom couldn't even be in the picture. Maybe we'd hold up a photo of her—just as she was. Either way, it'd be depressing. I look at my watch before Dad has a chance to. "I really should get back to work." I sling my bag over my shoulder and pile my used napkins on my plate. I stand. "I have a big assignment due tonight." I don't. I finished it already, but it's all right for him to think I do.

"Duty calls." Dad smiles as he stands then clasps his hand on my shoulder. "It was really good to see you." He puts down a twenty to cover the bill. "You want a drive home?"

"I'll walk," I say. I'm not sure why, but when I pass Fit4Life I stop, then step through the door.

CHAPTER SEVEN

The woman who greets me at Fit4Life has to be the same woman I spoke to on the phone. She stands behind the desk, her hair in that ponytail I imagined. She's brunette instead of blond, but her eyes are even better than I pictured—a sparkly hazel—and her teeth are white. Her chest pushes against a too tight red tank top that hugs her slim waist. Her nose is a little too large for her face and slightly crooked—not Miss. Perfect after all—but her smile is warm and welcoming, and I feel bad for revelling in her imperfect nose.

"How can I help you today?"

I hesitate then stand taller. "I'm interested in learning about your membership options."

"That's great." She sounds genuinely happy. I wonder if she's taken acting classes. "We have a great offer I can tell you all about," she says, and ushers me to a little lounge area. It feels more like I'm in someone's living room than a gym. She talks to me as if we're friends but holds a clipboard in front of her and makes notes as she asks me about my goals, what led me to walk in today, and what role fitness plays in my life. She tells me about all the options the gym provides.

"I don't know how comfortable I am with group training," I say.

"That's completely normal." She lowers her clipboard. "I used to be nervous about it too. I felt so awkward and self-conscious bouncing around in front of everyone like that."

It surprises me that someone as beautiful as her ever feels self-conscious. "I have made a lot of progress," I say, "on my own. I've lost almost thirty-five pounds."

"That's great. So, tell me, Jenn, with how well you're doing, what can we offer you that goes beyond your current successes?"

I don't expect the question. What I expect is for her to tell me how, if I sign up with them, my results will be doubled, even tripled. "I think I could be doing better," I say. "I sometimes get bored or frustrated with my routine and I want to learn new ways to challenge myself." Just looking at her earnest face, I feel more motivated than I've felt in weeks. I didn't even know the words I'm saying are true, but as I say them, they are. "Yeah. I want more success, faster."

"I think you should start with a trainer. Four weeks, meeting two times a week. He'll be able to show you a ton of new exercises, introduce you to equipment we have here, assess your nutritional choices. After that you can either continue on or take what you've learned to develop your own fitness plan."

I'm hesitant. That kind of personal touch doesn't sound cheap.

"It's a great way to start. He'll also give you advice on what you should be doing the days you're not with him." She writes something on the clipboard. "So, I'm going to schedule you in for a physical, goal, and nutrition assessment. This is actually complimentary, and if you're not keen on training after that, there'll be no cost to you."

I smile at Mayhem—yes, that's her name—and realize as I've been talking to her I haven't felt like a fat girl, I've felt like an athlete. I shake her hand and agree to come back two days later to meet my trainer and have my first assessment.

"Come ready to get a sweat on," she says with a wave.

"I will."

✍

WHEN I WALK THROUGH my door back home, tendrils of
excitement continue to shoot through me. I may have just
made a decision that will change my life forever, that will
change the core of who I am as a person and how the rest
of the world receives and treats me. Years later, when I'm
sitting beside a man who adores me, with our four beautiful
children surrounding us, I'll tell them how I was nervous
but knew I needed a change. I knew if I wanted
transformation, I had to be willing to put in the investment;
so I did and if I hadn't, none of them would be here. My
husband will squeeze my hand and smile at me, so thankful
that I walked through those doors and then walked into his
life.

I realize it's a stupid dream but it's possible, so not really
that stupid after all. I sit back on the couch and think of my
mother's dreams. Did she ever think, when she was my age,
that her life would turn out the way it did? I feel again that
clasp of my father's hand on my shoulder before he walked
out of the café and try to think back to the last time I loved
him. I mean I still love him, he's my father, but I want to
remember when I enjoyed loving him, when I was happy to
love him, when love didn't feel like a burden or an
obligation.

One of my first memories is of my Dad, actually. I would
have been somewhere between three and four and just
learning to swim. I'm not sure where we were—maybe a
community centre, maybe on vacation and in a hotel pool.
The rest of the memory is clear. I slip into the water and
struggle and struggle. I know I can touch the bottom on tip
toe, but I don't let myself, and my arms flail and my feet flail
and the water gets in my eyes and there is my Dad, only
about six feet away but it might as well have been miles, and

he says, 'Honey, you can do it.' His eyes tell me he believes it with all his heart, so I do it. I kick and I pull my limbs through the water and before I know it I'm in his arms and he's throwing me up in the air, the water splashing all around us as he catches me, hugs me close, and whispers in my ear, 'You did it.' I'm filled with such pride in myself and such love for him I feel I'll explode, and I want to tell him this but don't know how, so instead I squeeze him tight, feeling safe, secure, and loved in my Daddy's arms.

I don't know that I could ever feel safe in his arms now. I can't imagine it. Every word he says, every kind expression or act that could be interpreted as love, I interpret as obligation or guilt. For the first time in…ever maybe, I wonder if this is fair, if I'm partly to blame for what our relationship is. Most of the time when I think about my father, I think about how he rejected me, how his choices told me I was unlovable, how I wasn't good enough to be his daughter, how he needed a new, better version. When he sat me down and told me he was leaving, that although he'd always love my mother he wasn't in love with her anymore, that they hadn't been happy for a long time, the words I heard were—I don't love you anymore. I haven't been happy with you for a long time.

I saw the way he looked at Mom, how he'd make little comments about what she ate, or ask if she'd seen the new advertisements for the gym that just opened up down the road. He never mentioned her weight, never, but I knew it disgusted him. I knew we disgusted him. Long after Mom had given up trying to get me to eat healthy Dad still suggested I take extra salad or failed to invite me when he and Billy would go out for their 'boy's nights,' which, I learned from Billy, often involved watching sports and indulging in wings, fries, and burgers. The few daddy-daughter dates in my late childhood involved excursions to the park, to the skating rink, and, once, rock climbing. If we went for a treat, it was to some health place that served frozen yogurt, rather than Dairy Queen or McDonald's like I wanted.

When Dad told me Billy had decided to come live with him and I could choose whether I wanted to live with him or Mom, that I'd visit whoever I didn't live with every other weekend and some Holidays, I knew he was saying I'm rid of you. We both knew there was no chance I would leave Mom. I'm not sure what was worse when it came down to it, Dad's desertion or Billy's. Billy and I hadn't been close for years, but I basically pretended he didn't exist after he went to Dad and Evita's, just like he pretended Mom didn't exist as she stood there crying while he packed up his belongings.

She promised him she'd call every night and read him stories over the phone whenever he wanted. He seemed excited to be leaving and told her that was okay, Evita was a great story reader and she even did voices. This made Mom cry harder. Billy adored Evita, and he adored Courtney and Melinda when they came along. One time Mom and I were at one of Billy's soccer games. We were coming over to congratulate him for scoring the winning goal when one of his teammates asked, with a laugh in his voice, 'Hey Billy, isn't that your Mom and sister stomping over to say hello?'

Billy glanced our way then pointed in the other direction where Evita stood with the girls, smiling and holding her hands. 'No,' he said, 'my Mom and sisters are right there.' He trotted over and gave Evita a big hug as she tousled his hair. I'm not sure I'd ever felt so rejected.

Mom just smiled this sad smile, put her hand on my shoulder, and led me to the car. 'Never mind,' she said to me before opening the door. 'It's just a phase.'

WHEN I WALK INTO THE club two days later, my hair's pinned up in a ponytail and I'm wearing a snug black t-shirt, black yoga pants, and a bright purple headband. I can feel the skinny girl inside of me. She's waiting to get out. She's bursting. I go to the front desk and smile at Mayhem. She smiles back, asks how I'm doing, and says if I just take a seat in the lobby my trainer will be right with me. I stroll over to the lobby…well, in my mind I'm strolling. It probably looks more like a clumping shuffle. I wait for a minute or two and my confidence level peters out like the air from a balloon on a cold winter day. Beautifully fit people, people who are already where I want to be, stroll by, and the road to get to where they are seems impassable. Just as I'm debating whether to get up and leave the building, never to enter its doors again, I hear my name. I look up and there he is, just as toned and perfect as I remember. "Matt?"

"I was wondering if you were the Jennifer Carpenter I was meeting with today," he says. His smile could end a war.

"Yeah, I…hi, Matt," I hope I don't sound quite as stupid and flabbergasted as I feel.

"Well," he says, "it looks like I'm your trainer." He seems genuinely pleased by this and I can't help but imagine the beautiful babies he would make. He sits down beside me and we exchange a couple of pleasantries about Autumn and my family before he gets down to business.

He's already seen my chart. He knows my general goals but starts digging deeper. I feel too vain to tell him the whole truth of why I've embarked on this journey, so I stick to generalities—I want to be healthy, I want more energy and strength, I want to feel comfortable in my own skin. I throw in some of the deep truth as well, that seeing my mother die was one of the hardest things I've ever experienced and it's still hard every day knowing that she should be here, could be here, but she's not because she didn't take care of her health. I tell him I don't want to follow in her footsteps, and as I say these words out loud for the first time, I realize how true they are. This isn't just about weight loss. It's not only about feeling beautiful or getting the guy. It's about staying alive.

Renewed purpose trickles into me. I may not like my life all that much but I still want it, even as it is. Of course, the life I'm working towards will be an entirely different one...I pause in my explanations. Matt waits for me to continue and when I don't, he says he knows I can experience the success I desire, that I can be filled with energy and vitality and know that I'm treating my body the way it deserves to be treated. It sounds so hokey, or it would sound hokey if anyone else were saying it, but I soak the words up like they're an elixir.

Next he asks tons of questions about my nutrition and tells me about all the macro and micronutrients to power the wonderful machine that is my body. He closes his file. "Next time we meet I'll have some sample menus made up for you. It looks like you've not been doing too badly food-wise these past couple of months." He smiles and I'm sure my heart skips a beat. "But still," he says, "there's definitely room for improvement."

Next we move onto the physical assessment. He takes my measurements and I want to die of embarrassment and shame, but I stand there and smile, trying to act casual.

I say something perky. "Like you said, lots of room for improvement!"

"Absolutely." He grins back and I feel myself melting. I imagine he's a passionate and tender lover, not that I know what any kind of lover is like. Still, I envy Autumn more than words can describe and have a brief moment of thinking it wouldn't be so bad if she got hit by a car.

When he asks me to step up onto this professional looking doctor's scale, I laugh. "Are you sure? I might break it."

He shakes his head. "Not a chance." I step up and the number is way better than it would have been a couple of months ago but worse than it was this morning. I should expect that though. I'm wearing clothes and haven't just, uh, emptied myself. I don't say this of course. I simply step off of the scale once I see he's written the number down. He pulls out this device that looks like a large game controller. "Hold either side," he says, "this will give us an estimate of your body fat and muscle mass." He explains how muscle weighs more than fat and how we want to make sure I'm losing fat, not muscle, etc. etc. It's so hard to listen to his words when I'm lost in his eyes and I wonder if this ridiculous attraction will be an aid or a stumbling block to my weight loss journey. "A good goal would be for you to be somewhere between 23-26% body fat," he says, "which means you'll have to just about cut your current numbers in half." He writes something down then looks up. "We'll aim for muscle mass in the high twenties."

"Well, that shouldn't be too hard."

"You'd think that, but at the moment your body has more muscle to carry around the extra weight. It's inevitable, you will lose muscle mass as you lose weight. We want to prevent that as much as possible through strength training."

My head spins with all the numbers but I like the way he says 'we.' He thinks of us as a team. He has a stake in my success.

Matt suggests a weight range he thinks would be a healthy goal. I silently pick the lowest number in that range. It's exactly one hundred pounds down from where I started. One hundred pounds in one year. I can do this.

Next it's time to test my physical strength and endurance. Matt says it won't quite be a workout, but it'll give him a good idea of where I am and what my exercise plan should look like. It's hard, beyond hard, and I make it worse by pushing through each exercise with everything I have. I don't whine, I don't complain, I work like my life depends on it. I work to see his smiles and hear his words of surprise and encouragement. I start sweating pretty quickly and this makes me want to stop. I don't. I just hope I don't stink. At the end, I'm grinning through the pain and trying to control my breath as best as I can. Wheezing is not attractive.

Once I've stretched he sits back, his face all business. "You did good," he says. "I'm impressed." He leans forward, resting his elbow on his knee, and stares right into me. "Are you ready to do this?"

"Yes, of course," I stumble over my words. "That's why I'm here."

"It's not going to be easy." His tone makes me feel as if what I'm about to embark on is crucially important, and by accepting this mission, I'll be a hero. I nod, terrified and excited and, I'll admit, aroused. "But it can be fun." The grin covers his face again and I literally feel my body relaxing. "I'm going to need you to work for me when we meet—just like you did today—and follow my guidelines for exercise and eating when we're not together. If you do that," his grin grows, "I fully believe you can reach your goal. In seven and a half months you can be a new person." I nod slowly. "So, are you ready to do this?" He stands and raises his hand for a high five. I meet it.

I walk into the women's change room and collapse against the wall, finally letting myself pant. I don't even know if I can make it home, my legs feel so weary. I close my eyes and breathe deeply—in and out, in and out. I picture the woman hiding inside of me, the beautiful, energetic, sexy woman. The type of woman who would make Matt stop and stare. I push myself up and open my locker. Coincidence or fate, I don't know. But I'm sure there's no one better than Matt to get me to my goal.

CHAPTER EIGHT

When I wake the next morning my legs ache. I stand and the pain shoots up the back of my thighs. I bend to pick up my shorts and the muscles in my arms and back feel like they've been beaten with a baseball bat. It's two more days until I'm supposed to head back to the gym, but I can't imagine feeling better by then. I can't imagine this kind of pain is normal.

After making a healthy breakfast of egg whites, zucchini, and peppers cooked in coconut oil, I decide to go for a walk for some active recovery. I've read about that and remembering the concept makes me think maybe my pain isn't so abnormal after all. I throw on a pair of yoga pants I bought at the start of this journey and am pleased that they're not as snug as I remember. I head to Point Pleasant, a large park on the southernmost tip of the Halifax peninsula. On a shady, barely used section of the trail a boy of about seven stands, staring at me. "Are you alone?" I ask.

He continues to stare, his gaze reminding me of a deer stuck in headlights.

"Shouldn't you be in school?"

He runs toward a side trail and I shrug it off. I'm not going to chase him. I continue to walk but am unnerved by how much the boy looked like Billy around that age. He even had on a motorcycle shirt similar to one Billy used to have. I remember Billy in that shirt, on a day like this, when I'd gone to pick him up at the playground near our house.

On my fourth birthday, when Mom and Dad had told me I was going to have a baby brother or sister, I was so excited. I thought of Billy as mine, a perfect little birthday gift. But by the time I went to pick him up that day at the park, nine years later, I thought of him as less than perfect. When I called to him, one of the other little boys asked Billy, 'Is that your sister?'

'Yeah,' he said. The boy laughed and some of the others joined in.

'She's the elephant!'

Billy looked from me to the boys, 'Did you say sister? I thought you said sitter.' He started laughing too. 'That elephant's not my sister.' It couldn't have hurt worse if I'd been kicked in the gut.

'Come on, Billy,' I'd said again. He'd waved to the boys, saying he'd see them tomorrow, and trotted over to me. Neither of us said anything on the way home. When I asked for a second helping of macaroni that night, he held his arm up like an elephant's trunk and looked at me with this little smirk on his face, almost like he expected me to be impressed. I ignored him but have never forgotten that moment—the first of many like it.

Part of me was relieved when Billy decided to leave with Dad. That may have been the best thing about the divorce. I finally felt like I could breathe in my own home, like I could walk the halls without the fear of Billy stomping behind me. When I got to high school I really felt free. We'd never be in the same school again. It's amazing how much someone pretending you don't exist can make you feel exposed. Not that I really blamed him. It couldn't have been fun to be called Elephant's sister, to be asked when he was going to turn into an elephant too, even if he was the one to turn that comment into my nickname. When he began to put on some pudge around age eleven, he joined the soccer team and started lifting weights. He wasn't going to end up like me.

❧

AFTER THE WALK, I TRY to shake the thought of Billy from my mind but can't. The last time I spoke to him was on his twenty-second birthday. I showed up at the apartment he shared with a couple of roommates. I had called beforehand to wish him Happy Birthday and see what he was doing to celebrate. He said he was just taking the day off, hanging around at home and then going out with his buds that night. I'd felt bad about not trying harder with him over the years, for letting his teasing get to me so much. I was his big sister after all, so I spent the afternoon making what I remembered was one of his favourite cakes. Not that I imagined he ate cakes that much anymore. He'd kept the weight-lifting up and become pretty ripped over the past few years. But it was his birthday. I knocked on his door and waited. Hearing loud music coming from inside, I knocked until the music stopped. A guy in dirty jeans with hair all down his chest answered. 'Yeah?'

'I'm here to see Billy.'

'Billy, some delivery's here for you,' the guy drawled.

'I'm his sister.'

The guy laughed. Actually laughed.

Billy came to the door, a friend of his beside him, presumably to see what the delivery was—or what caused the laughter. 'What are you doing here?' Billy had asked.

'I brought you a cake.' I held it up, smiling. 'Your favourite.'

'I'm not going to eat that shit,' he sneered, 'you want me to get all blown up like you?' I stood, mouth open, cake in hand, not knowing what to say.

The guy who opened the door chuckled, the other one said, 'Harsh, Billy, harsh. Besides, the cake looks awesome. You make it yourself?'

I stood there, nodding like an idiot, oscillating between

wanting to throw the cake in Billy's face and wanting my brother to take back his words, to say he was sorry, to say he missed me, that he'd been stupid all these years, that he loved me.

The second guy reached forward and took the cake from me. 'It really looks awesome.' He smiled. 'What kind is it?'

Billy leaned against the wall, watching the exchange. I tried not to let my voice tremble. 'Peanut butter chocolate layer cake.'

'Awesome,' the guy said again. He looked at the cake with what seemed to be admiration then held it up like a prize. 'This will be so sweet to have with the fellas before we go out tonight.'

'Thanks.' I nodded again, and we all stood there awkwardly. 'Well, I guess I'll be off,' I said.

'Yeah,' said, Billy. 'See you around.'

I turned and shuffled down that hall as fast as my legs would take me. I was hoping he'd step out the doorway before I got to the elevator, say sorry, say something. I heard the door close and my hope turned into one of the most intense feelings of hate and disgust I've ever had. He was the embarrassment, not me, I thought to myself. 'He's the embarrassment,' I said out loud, trying to convince myself. The reflection I saw in the elevator mirror—round face, blotchy red tear-stained skin—told a different story.

I sit at my desk remembering it—the way he stood against the door, like it was a burden to even look at me. I don't know who I feel more disgust with, him, for being the way he was, or me, for putting up with it and just running away like that.

That was the last exchange we ever had. When it comes down to it, I feel slightly more disgust with myself. But only slightly. I push the memory, the sadness, aside. I open my laptop, choose an assignment, and start working.

❦

AUGUST IS JUST AROUND the corner and the heat's so intense I decide I can't wear the t-shirt and pants I usually wear to my sessions with Matt. I push out a breath of air and pull on a pair of Capri leggings and a tank top, hoping the flapping of my arm wings don't disgust him. I step in front of the mirror and for the first time I see it—the person before me is not fat. Not really. She's overweight, yes. No one would call her slim or skinny or even trim, but she's not exactly fat. Okay, some people might call her fat, but no one would call her obese. I take a step closer to the mirror and grab a stool so I can get a better view. I turn one way and then the other, amazed at how I missed this transformation.

Yesterday couldn't have been much different but yesterday the fat girl was looking back at me. My jeans slid off me the other week and I had to rummage through my closet for a smaller pair, but I still didn't see it. I don't even know how much weight I've lost. I promised Matt I'd stop my obsessive daily weighing. He asked me to get rid of the scale. I hid it in the closet instead. I thought about it often, but I'd been good. I hadn't checked despite the urgings. I can't help it this time. I take the stool to the closet and get the scale down from the top shelf. I strip down naked, close my eyes, and step on. When my eyes open, I rub them in disbelief then crouch down to make sure they're not lying to me. The scale wavers then settles back where it was. I do the math. I've lost sixty-two pounds. Sixty-two pounds. I step off the scale and want to call someone, but of course there isn't really anyone to call. I've been staying away from Tammy more and more. At first it was too hard to watch the way she and Colin indulge. Now I'm way lighter than her and wouldn't want to make her feel bad, though I know that probably wouldn't happen. She's happy just as she is.

I don't want to tell Autumn either, although she'd be psyched. I asked Matt not to tell her about our training. He wasn't comfortable with the idea but agreed. I ran into them once at the grocery store and it was pretty awkward. She noticed the change in me and when I was resistant to talk about it, saying I was eating better, going for runs, I felt like I was betraying all the work Matt's been doing with me. She got all interested at first—the trainer in her—saying things such as 'that's so great, I could really help you out, assess your running, your eating. I mean obviously you're doing great already, but I'd love to help.' And when I said no, I had it covered, she seemed hurt and then concerned— 'You're not just starving yourself, right?' Her brow furrowed. 'If this is going to be a sustained change, it's important that you—'

I cut her off, said I was fine, and in a bit of a rush, then headed in the other direction. I hated the way she assumed I was stupid enough to starve myself. Even more, I hated the way she looked so cozy and perfect next to Matt. They looked like a couple out of a magazine.

I know it's awful the way I'm lying to her when all she wants is to help me, to see me healthy and thriving. And I know she'd be hurt if she knew all the money I'm ladling out at that gym for Matt's training when she would have done the same thing for free, but there's no way the motivation would have been the same. When Matt pushes me I want to succeed for him. If Autumn pushed me, I'd probably cuss her out.

I couldn't even tell Matt about my amazing weight loss. Then he'd know I'd broken our no-scale-until-deadline-day rule. That was one nice thing the bloggers I read had that I didn't. An anonymous world of fans willing and eager to hear about every little success. Not that this was a little success.

I put my clothes back on and return to the mirror. "You lost sixty-two pounds," I say to the woman staring back at me. "No one would call you elephant now. Maybe pudge face, maybe stocky, but not elephant." I smile my biggest smile but it seems hollow. The woman I am waiting for, the woman I know is somewhere deep inside me, isn't the one looking back. Instead, the woman looking back seems sad. She can't really be happy until it's that skinny woman looking back at her. Still, as I walk to the gym, I'm pretty sure I am standing just a bit taller, walking just a bit lighter. How could I not be? I have just gotten sixty-two pounds of fat off my back.

❧

I HAVE A SLIGHT GLEAM of sweat when I enter the gym. Matt greets me in a black tank that accentuates his perfectly sculpted arms and hints at the pecs and abs just below the surface. He's glistening too.

"Today's boot camp style. You want to go to the Commons?"

"Sure."

He hits the button for the crosswalk. "I thought with it so sunny and beautiful it'd be ludicrous to stay inside," he says as we walk the block and a half to the city's huge green space in Halifax's urban core.

"Yeah, for sure." I look over at him, he smiles at me, and I wonder how happy he and Autumn really are. He seems pretty glad to see me. It could just be his job to look happy. It probably is. At the same time, Autumn doesn't tend to take her relationships very seriously. She's had at least a dozen over the years, none lasting more than a year, most only making it a few months.

With the sun glaring down on us, the workout is noticeably more intense than it would have been in the air-conditioned gym. But with Matt standing beside me I work hard and find myself translating his words of encouragement into words of affection. After we've stretched, I lie back in the grass and stare at the massive clouds floating across a blue sky. Matt lies down beside me. "Don't you need to get to your next appointment?" I ask, my gaze still on the clouds.

I hear the rustle as he shakes his head and takes a deep breath. "I had a cancellation. No one else for another hour." I glance over and catch his eye. He puts his hands under his head and grins at me. The dimple in his right cheek is so evident at this angle. Attached to his smile—there just for me—it's one of the sexiest things I've ever seen. "Let's just chill," he says. He looks up and, a few moments later, so do I. If I were to keep my eyes on his body much longer my thoughts would travel to an entirely inappropriate—again. "Did you ever make stories out of the clouds?" he asks.

"Stories?"

"Yeah."

"No." I focus on the shapes transforming before my eyes. "But one time my mom and I found a ton of animals in the clouds."

He looks over at me and I catch his eye before he returns his gaze above. "That's where you start," he says, "or where you can start. But then you let the story develop as the clouds transform, let them become your guide."

I nod.

"You see the one up there that looks like a horse?"

He points and I try to follow his direction. I don't see anything that looks even remotely like a horse. "Yes," I say.

"We'll start with that. Chancer was a mighty stallion, but he'd never felt like he had the shot he deserved. When he was still a young foal an attack by a lion had injured him and it took years before he was as fast or strong as all the other horses. See the lion head there, up above him."

"Mm-hmm, I murmur, though the only thing I see looks a little like a rabbit.

"Well, now Chancer is just as strong, just as able as all

the other horses—maybe stronger—but no one can see it. They all think it's too late for him.

"Chancer's the only one who knows how capable he really is. Then one day…" Matt pauses as the clouds shift across the sky, "a young princess sees Chancer running through a field. She's from the human realm and so knows nothing of his past. All she sees is the most beautiful and regal stallion she's ever laid eyes on, so she calls out to Chancer and he soars up to her." Matt stops again—he laughs. "And I guess they merge and turn into a frog." He waves his hand back and forth as if he's wiping out the images. "The stories don't always turn into much." I laugh too, and for some reason, I want to cry. I don't though. Matt stands and offers me his hands. I take them—firm and strong. "I should probably use this as a lunch break," he says. I nod, savouring the moment my hands rest in his. "Hey," a grin spreads across his face, igniting that dimple, "did you get Autumn's message about the barbecue at Crystal Crescent this weekend? She said you didn't call her back."

"Oh," I shrug, "yeah. I've been meaning to. I'm not really a huge beach fan though and I guess the barbecue wouldn't really be plan approved."

"Ah," he shakes a finger, "you shouldn't eat on plan all the time. Besides, you've been doing great. One indulgence won't do any harm. Plus, play a lot of beach volleyball when you're there. That'll be a great workout."

"I don't know," I bite my lip, wanting to say yes, but dreading what it would mean. The idea of wearing a bathing suit in front of Matt and Autumn and all their friends terrifies me. They're probably all unbelievably fit.

"Just come," he says. "Please." And there's that dimple.

"Okay."

"Give Autumn a call." He starts to walk away from me, backwards. "I'll see you Saturday. Great job today!" I smile back at him and the thought of him seeing me in a bathing suit, as I am now, makes me want to crawl inside a hole. It was bad enough wearing today's outfit, but a bathing suit? It might not be so bad if I find a reason to keep my shorts and a t-shirt on the whole time. I could just say I don't know how to swim—though Autumn knows better—or that I dyed my hair and don't want to get it wet yet. That would work. On the way home I stop into the grocery store and pick up a packet of dye.

THE NEXT DAY I HEAD TO the Halifax Shopping Centre to get a new outfit for the party. I'm walking by one of the plus-size stores when I notice some girls coming out of a store across the hall. One of them doesn't look that much smaller than the woman I stared at in the mirror yesterday morning...at least I think she doesn't. I look up at the sign. I've been in the store before, last winter, to buy a scarf. I take a deep breath and cross the threshold. A lady who is folding t-shirts greets me with a smile.

"Can I help you with anything?".

I shake my head and walk past her then stop and turn back around. "Actually, I'm looking for a pair of Bermuda shorts...something suitable for the beach." She finishes folding the shirt she's working on and tells me they've got a few options. She doesn't tell me I'm in the wrong place and point across the hall like I imagine she might. She asks me my size and I tell her I'm not sure. "I've lost weight," I say, hoping she doesn't look surprised that this is the result of *losing* weight. She doesn't.

"Hmm," she assesses me with her hand to her chin. "I'd say somewhere between a 12 and 14? Do you like these?" She asks, pointing to a light peach pair.

"Sure," I say. She picks out a 12 and then grabs a 14 in a light blue after I nod that it's fine.

"Anything else you're looking for?" With her help, I pick out a couple of cute t-shirts and she starts a fitting room for me. I pull on the 14s first and they slide on with ease. They're a little loose—not that Bermuda's are supposed to be tight. I take them off and pull on the 12s. These are snug, snugger than they're supposed to be, but I can walk. I do a couple squats and they don't rip. The tightness will remind me not to eat that much.

The t-shirts all fit and I choose the loosest one so it masks the muffin top (who am I kidding—tops) that the shorts squeeze out. The effect is not great, but it's the best I've ever seen on my body. I unbutton the shorts and step out of them, revealing a bright pink line where the waistline indented against my skin. I rub the area, knowing I'll be uncomfortable in them, especially if I eat anything at all, but I fold up the Bermudas anyway and smile at the salesperson as I place them on the counter. It makes sense to buy them tight. I still have more weight to lose. It's cost effective. While walking past the food court on the way out I see a group of women, probably in their early twenties, laughing over platters of hamburgers and fries, Chinese food, and pizza. They're all slender. They're all beautiful. They have no idea how easy they have it. My mouth salivates as I take my gaze away from the women and onto the food. I want some so bad it almost hurts.

CHAPTER NINE

When I get home, I call Autumn and there's something a little funny to her voice. She asks how I am, and I say pretty good. "I bought a size 12 today."

"Oh, that's awesome." Her happiness doesn't seem as genuine as I'd expect, as if her thoughts are elsewhere. "You sure you don't want me to help you out—assess your training or something?"

I sigh. "I got a trainer."

"Oh?" She pauses. "I could have. I would have—"

"I know," I say. "But I just didn't want…" I sit down on the couch. "I didn't want to risk messing anything up with us, you know? It didn't always go so well in the past."

"Yeah," she says. There's a pause. "Okay, I'm really happy for you. You must feel so much better."

I want to say, yeah, absolutely, but I'm not sure I do feel so much better, at least not yet. All I can think about at the moment is how delicious that pizza looked and how amazing the aroma of orange chicken felt as it teased my nostrils. So, I say, "I have way more energy and I didn't even really realize they hurt, but my knees and back feel better. I guess they were just achy before. Now they're not."

"Yeah," she says, "that often happens. That's great."

"So anyway," I say. "I'm calling because of the message you left me about the barbecue."

"That was over a week ago. I thought you hadn't gotten

it."

"I've just been busy," I say.

"Mm-hmm." I can almost hear her disbelief.

"I'll come."

"Oh." Autumn's voice perks up. "That's great." She gives me the details and says she's looking forward to seeing me, that Daniel is too. He'll be there. I agree to all of this, saying the appropriate things. She's silent then and I want to end the call, but I can feel she has something else on her mind. After another pause, she says it.

"Billy's been improving. Quite a bit. He's having regular conversations now and going on short walks around the ward. He'll be going home in a month or two."

"How can he be walking?"

"I mean in a wheelchair."

I nod then realize she can't see me. "Oh, so how can he be going home?"

"He'll be going to stay with your dad until he can be on his own."

"And when will that be?"

"We don't know." I realize that I'm not a part of this 'we' she speaks of. She's quiet for several moments, and I am too.

"I should probably get going."

Autumn lets out a loud puff of air "I shouldn't be the one telling you this. I don't know what's up with you."

"What—"

"I know you and Billy never got along, but he's still your brother, Jenn. I shouldn't be the one to tell you this stuff." I try to tune her out but it's not easy. "Listen. I love you but someone has to say something. It's despicable that you haven't even gone to see him, not once."

"You're right," I say once she's finished. "It's despicable and I'm despicable. But everyone loved Despicable Me, right? So that's what I'm going for." She doesn't laugh at my joke. From the muffled silence I think maybe she's crying and I wonder if Matt is there waiting to comfort her, if Matt is there to hear what she thinks of me, if he's now thinking the same thing. "I really do have to go," I say. "If I'm still invited I'll see you at the barbecue."

"God, Jennifer," she says. "Of course you're still invited. I'll see you Saturday."

"Yeah," I say. "Saturday."

∽

I ARRIVE AT DANIEL'S five minutes early and see a number of cars in the driveway. It's a thirty-five-minute drive to the beach and not even possible to go by bus. I did check though; a hot sticky bus ride seemed preferable to being stuck in a car with some of the guys from the Halloween Party a few years ago. I tell myself they won't even know who I am. I was covered in a sheet and almost sixty pounds heavier. Still, I feel myself bristling, my defences on ready. When I knock on the door Daniel opens it.

"Hi." He looks at me like I'm a stranger before recognition sets in. "Jennifer?" he asks, then laughs. "Jennifer? Wow." He takes a step back, his hand still on the door frame. "What happened to you?" He lets out a short whistle.

I'm not sure what to say. It's so obvious what happened. "I changed my hair."

"Well," he laughs again. "It looks great!" He gives me a quick hug then ushers me in. I nod hello to some of his friends—a few I've seen before, others are new. One girl is slightly bigger than me. It's always a relief when I'm not the fattest person in a group and it hits me—even now, when I go out, there will be many places where I won't be the biggest one there. Not even close.

Rajeev comes over, straight toward me, a smile on his face. "Jennifer, hi!" He barely does a second take. "That's quite the colour," he says of the auburn, almost red hue. "It looks nice on you."

"Thanks." He asks me something about the writing job but I only half hear him as I scan the room to see if Matt has arrived. When I don't see him I draw my focus back to Rajeev. "What was that?"

"I was asking if you like the work so far? The writing."

"Yeah. It's pretty good. Not too challenging but interesting. Gives me a lot of flexibility. A lot of time to do other things."

"Oh yeah?" he says. "And what have you been keeping yourself busy with?"

"Oh, well, I started cooking a lot more. Trying out new recipes. That's fun."

"I love to cook!" Rajeev's face lights up as he says this. "It's my pass—"

"I'm sorry. I'll talk to you later." As Autumn and Matt breeze through the door, I walk away from Rajeev and head toward Matt, realizing I should head toward Autumn instead. As far as Autumn is concerned, I've only seen Matt two times.

"Jennifer, you look so good!" Autumn's voice is shrill with excitement, unlike on the phone the other day. "Turn around." I do a little turn for her, my cheeks warm. "You've done amazing," she says. "Wow. Do you see this, Matt?" She rests her hand on his shoulder and looks up at him with an intimacy that makes me imagine a train bursting through the room and catapulting her right out the other side of the house. Maybe this isn't another one of her ditch it and forget it relationships...The thought sends a tremor of jealousy through me. I love her, I tell myself. I love her.

Matt smiles, but it's restrained. "Yeah, you look great, Jenn. You must be working really hard." He's looking at me like I'm a jerk for lying in front of Autumn like this, for making him lie, and I guess he's right; I am a bit of a jerk. He's clearly not the type of guy who is comfortable with lying, but he's keeping his word to me and that means something.

"My goodness!" Autumn exclaims again. "You must feel like a whole new person." I shy away from her words. I don't want this attention, not now anyway. Not when I'm only halfway there. Rather than feel the success Autumn clearly sees, I'm reminded of how horrible I must have looked to prompt this excessive reaction. Autumn gives me another hug. "I'm really proud of you, Jenn. Your mom would have been proud too."

"Mom didn't have a problem with me," I say. "It was you who never thought I was good enough." Shock and hurt flash in Autumn's eyes and I instantly regret my words.

"I," Autumn shifts her gaze from me to Matt, "that's not true, Jenn. I just wanted to see you healthier, happier, I never—" she stops mid-sentence. I know I should apologize. I should say that's not what I meant. But it's too hard to get the words out.

"Anyway, I still have a long way to get where I want to go." I take a breath. She looks so hurt, but it's true that Autumn's brand of encouragement to get healthy throughout the years felt like a slap in the face. Still, her intentions were good. "Maybe we could go for a run together sometime or have a workout. That'd be fun."

"Yeah," her words come out slowly, "that would be nice. Any time you want some help I'd be happy to. I mean I can't believe you're paying for someone else to—"

"Gotta keep people employed, right?" I say, smiling, though it feels forced. "Help the economy and all."

"Sure." Autumn nods. She doesn't deserve this from me. Yes, her efforts to help me change generally caused more emotional harm than good, but she's never treated me like a pariah, the way so many others have. If I'm honest, my resentment doesn't come from her, but from my jealousy of her. She's always loved me, loved me so much she never wanted to see me end up like my mom, loved me so much it killed her to see how miserable my fat made me, even though I tried to pretend it didn't. She looks up at Matt who smiles down at her and glances back at me with an expression I've never seen on his face before. I feel small, and not in a good way.

"Well," says Autumn, "I'm going to go see if Daniel needs help packing anything up." She places a hand on my arm. "I'm proud of you, Jenn. I know that took work." I smile and don't know what to say. I watch as she walks away, her perfect ponytail swaying in rhythm with her perfect hips and feel a little less bad. She'll get over this.

I end up in a car with Rajeev, Daniel, and two of their friends, a girl named Sammy and a guy named Andrew. Andrew seems like he may have spent too many years indulging in the Ganja. I'm not sure if he's high now—it seems to be more a perma-state. Sammy is cute as can be. She has long red curly hair, freckles, and hazel eyes. She's plump, but not fat, still attractive. She's one of those girls who, though somewhat overweight, is perfectly proportioned. No visible rolls or anything, and I realize this is partly because all of her clothes fit properly, unlike the Bermuda's digging into my flesh. You'd probably call her sturdy before fat—the type of woman who looks like she was born to work on a farm and carry babies.

I learn from her conversation with Rajeev, however, that Sammy is a consultant at a big firm downtown and her business is expanding into publishing. She's thinking of applying for an editor's position. This makes Rajeev think of my illustrious career writing short stories and articles. Of course, I'm fully to blame for Rajeev thinking my job's a big deal. I've made the gig sound a lot more interesting and important than it is.

"Have you ever considered writing a novel?" asks Sammy.

I laugh, then realize how rude that sounds. In her world novelists are a reality. "No," I reply. "I haven't ever really thought about it. In my job the general plots are given to me—I fill in the details."

Sammy nods. "And do you like that? Or do you wish you could create your own stories?"

"I like it all right," I say. "It's a flexible job with decent money."

"But do you like the work? The writing?"

I have to think for a moment. I haven't thought much about the actual writing. I've viewed it as a means to an end, but as I consider the question, I realize I do like it. It's interesting and empowering to take a one or two sentence topic or plot line and turn it into anywhere from a 1000—10 000 word story. It's a relief to step outside of my own life for those few hours I spend at my desk every day and create lives for others.

"I do like it," I say. "I like it a lot." Sammy nods. Daniel and Andrew are having their own conversation in the front seat, and Sammy turns to Rajeev. I learn through her questioning he's a defence lawyer who is just starting out. His focus is helping society's underdogs—my word, not his. "What made you choose that direction?" I ask. "Wouldn't you make a lot more money in divorce law, or something like that?"

He gives this knowing smile that makes me feel like a greedy ten-year-old. "Well, then I'd be rich in body," he says, his accent getting slightly stronger, "but not very rich in soul." Sammy seems impressed or at least satisfied by this answer. I feel a little sceptical and wonder if the job is just a stepping stone and the line one he uses to make himself feel better about it.

WHEN WE GET TO THE beach, spirits are high. People laugh as they set up the volleyball net, prepare the fire pit, and lay out towels and blankets. I get to work as well but feel as if I'm slightly outside of myself. I'm used to being on the sidelines, watching everyone else enjoy life with hardly anyone stopping to invite me in. Today I don't even need an invite. It's just assumed that I'll be a part of it all. Andrew tosses Sammy and me some blankets and expects us to set them up as he and Daniel start hauling rocks for the base of the fire pit. He grumbles at the bottles and half melted cans he removes from the pit. "People have no respect."

Sammy speaks with me about the weather, what an awesome day it is—perfect for the beach—and asks if I'll take a dip with her after we finish setting up.

I shake my head, "I didn't bring my suit." She gives me a curious look and I gesture to my hair, "fresh job," I say, "I don't want the colour to run."

"Ah," she says, "you can still go in. Just don't go under." Such a simple solution. I clearly didn't think my dye job through.

"Yeah," I shrug, "but I still don't have a suit."

"You'll dry," she smiles.

The water does looks great. "Not today," I say, the edge slipping into my voice before I can catch it.

"Okay," her brows furrow, "no problem. Maybe next time. So," she grins at me, "got your eye on any of the fellas out there today? There are some cuties!" I scan the guys over by the pit and the volleyball net. "Autumn's maybe got the best of the lot," says Sammy and it's like she's taken the words out of my mouth. I nod. "But Darren's pretty hot."

"Which one is he?" I ask, although I can guess.

"The one in the orange board shorts."

I guessed right. He's equally as toned as Matt though there's more bulk to his muscular frame. He's got dimples in both cheeks and short, tight curly hair.

"Do you think it's racist to say he reminds me of a black stallion?"

I shake my head. "I wouldn't tell him that though."

"If I ever got him in the bedroom," she says, "I don't think I'd be able to help myself." She's giggling and her cheeks get a crimson flare. I nod, wondering what it would be like to touch those pecs, those abs. When the me I'm meant to be is finally released, would a man like Darren even look twice at me? "We made out last year," Sammy says, "briefly, at a party, but he started dating this girl Suzanne shortly after and nothing ever came of our little encounter. I've only seen him once since then but Suzanne's not here today." Sammy smiles. "I wonder what the deal is." She's got her gaze focused on Darren and when he turns our way, he gives her an enthusiastic wave. She waves back and I hope I'm successfully hiding my shock at her words. I can't help wondering if he was drunk when this encounter occurred. Sammy's pretty and she seems nice and smart, but I can't imagine a guy like Darren would even consider a girl so obviously below his league. If he were to approach me with that kind of interest now, I'd think all he wanted was a quick and easy lay.

As Sammy and I settle in on the towels while the guys put up the volleyball net, I watch Darren. He seems friendly and easy-going, much like Matt. A chubby little kid from up the beach kicks a soccer ball and it lands right in the middle of Darren's back, leaving a sandy circle. He picks up the ball with one hand, rubs his back with the other, smiles, and says to the kid, "Nice kick, that packed a wallop," then tosses the ball back to him. It's not what I expect. I'm not sure what I expected exactly, but it wasn't that. Some of Daniel's other friends, who are lugging the coolers over to the fire pit and are decidedly less fit and attractive than Matt and Darren, whistle at a group of women strolling by in string bikinis.

Sammy shakes her head. "Who does that?" I shrug and keep my eyes on the women. They're not fit looking like Autumn and some of her trainer friends but are slender as can be. They scoff, as if they're insulted, and I wish that just once I'd have a guy whistle at me without it being a mockery. I draw my attention back to Sammy, who is asking me something about Rajeev.

"What's that?"

"I asked what you think of him," says Sammy.

"What I think of him?" My gaze drifts over to Matt, who threatens to throw Autumn into the water.

"Yeah."

"He seems like a nice guy." I'm not sure what else to think.

"You think he's cute?" asks Sammy.

"I don't know." I remember thinking he was kinda cute the first night I met him. Today he seems a little too soft around the edges, literally. After all the days I've spent gazing at Matt's muscles it'd be hard to settle for less. I know Sammy wants more though. "He's got a great accent."

Sammy smiles. "I think he might be into you."

I laugh. "Rajeev? Into me? What have you been smoking?"

"What's that supposed to mean?" she asks, looking offended for me.

"Oh, I don't know." I shrug. "I just have no reason to think Rajeev is into me."

"Well," says Sammy, "I've known him a long time, and he doesn't usually chat up girls he doesn't know well, and he's been chatting you up. He's very selective. Maybe a bit shy. You two only met once before, right?"

"Yeah," I glance over to where Rajeev plays soccer with some of the other guys and a few kids. He picks up a little girl he just helped score and tosses her in the air.

"Great shot!" he says with a huge grin. The girl's mother (I assume it's her mother) watches nearby, ready to pounce if need be.

"I guess he still has a bit of learning to do about our cultural norms," laughs Sammy. "But he's a sweet guy. A good guy. If he makes a move," she gives me a smile, "be open to it."

"Maybe," I say.

"You've got your sights on someone else?"

"Maybe." I can't help it, my eyes trail back to Matt, water glistening on him like he's some kind of Greek god.

Sammy smiles. "Well, I won't pry." She stands. "You sure you don't want to come in?" I shake my head and watch as she joins Matt, Autumn, and a few others who splash in the waves. I lie back on the towel and let my head rest in my hands. The sun feels amazing and I'm taken back to that afternoon before the stolen ice cream sandwich when Autumn, Daniel, and I had lain on a dry patch of lawn after running through the sprinklers. I was in my favourite bathing suit, a Little Mermaid two piece, and the sun felt like a warm hug, just like it does today. As far as I was concerned, my body was all it was supposed to be.

I roll onto my back. I want that feeling again—being happy in my own skin—and I will have it. My upper arms, torso and thighs may be covered today, but the time is coming when I will lie on the beach in a bikini, unashamed, letting the sun warm me. The next forty pounds will be harder to get rid of than the first sixty. I know that's how it works, but I'll do it. I'll do whatever it takes and I'll come back next summer, splash in the water, then lie on the sand, proudly baring my skin, happily indulging in my own glorious existence. If it can't be Matt I'm experiencing it with, a guy equally as good will lie beside me. Maybe even Darren. I'll be worth a guy like him. I smile as I wriggle my toes in the sand. It will happen.

WHEN THE GROUP COMES back from the water, Matt shakes his hair like a dog, spraying Autumn, who has just finished towelling off. She squeals and swats at him, then hollers as he scoops her up as easily as if she were a doll, tosses her over his shoulder, and marches back to the water's edge. At the last moment he sets her down and she punches his chest. He grabs her wrists, stopping her, and lifts her arms around his neck. She melts into him for a kiss that leaves me squirming with desire, desperate to be the one in his arms.

"It's nice, isn't it?"

Rajeev plops down beside me. "What's nice?"

"Young love." He smiles, a wistful expression on his face, and holds up his smartphone like a notepad. "I'm collecting orders for dinner. What'll you have? Burgers? Hot dogs? Sausages? And how many of each?"

"None," I reply, still looking at Matt and Autumn. They walk toward us, fingers interlaced.

"None?" Rajeev leans toward me, blocking my view of the couple. "You're not hungry?"

"I'm going to have the veggies," I say, "with hummus."

Rajeev stares at me, and the look in his eyes makes me want to slither away. "This is a barbecue, and I know you eat meat."

"Autumn's hummus is awesome," I say, as Matt and Autumn walk back into view. Matt grabs a towel and rubs it through his hair. Drops of water glisten on his chest.

"I made the sausages myself," says Rajeev. "An old family recipe. Try one. For me?" He grins and leans back, catching my eye. "I promise you won't regret it."

"I said no," I say, as the smell of the cooking meat makes me want to say yes. This guy just won't give up, so I stand and head over to the group of people tossing around the volleyball. It's something I've never done before, but I've done so many things I've never done before in the past few months that I feel emboldened. Besides, I have to show Matt that all the hard work he's been putting in is working—I'm fit now.

We only play for about fifteen minutes before Daniel calls us over to eat and although I'm a little winded—manoeuvring on the sand is harder than I thought—I could have kept going. I load up my plate with celery, carrots, tomatoes (but only a few—they're loaded with sugar) and a generous scoop of hummus. As I'm crunching on the hummus dipped carrots, I tell myself that I'm making a positive choice for my future, that the scent of the fatty meat mixed with sweet barbecue sauce is the scent of misery, mockery, and failure. It doesn't matter that the sculpted people around me are having some—they've already won their battles. Maybe one day I'll taste those foods again but today the only taste I want in my mouth is that of success. When Daniel tries to tempt me with some of the remaining hot dogs, I tell myself he's only asking because that's what he's used to—Jennifer the handy garbage compactor who's happy to finish off the family's leftovers. "I'm full," I say, "throw it to the birds." Daniel shrugs and Sammy sidles over to me.

"I wish I could be happy with veggies," she says, "my pants have been getting a little tighter than I'd like with the stress of the office transition and all, but I just love my meat." Her eyes sparkle and her smile is sweet and slightly self-deprecating.

"It just takes discipline," I say, and watch her smile fade. "But I also really like the hummus," I add, trying to make up for my words. "Have you tried it? Autumn makes the best I've ever tasted. It makes discipline that much easier!" Sammy shakes her head. "Try some of mine," I say.

She dips a carrot. "Yeah, it's great. Maybe that'll be my seconds."

"Good idea," I say, and wonder if the words come out wrong.

❧

BY THE TIME THE SUN starts to set everyone is more mellow—full of food and sunshine. The couples cuddle in their beach towels and blankets and we singles spread throughout, talking softly or simply watching the sky. As the oranges meld into purples and blues I try to think back to the last time I sat before a sunset. It was with Billy, one day when Mom had taken us to this same beach. I hadn't gone in the water that day either, afraid to let the teen boys who played with their Frisbees and soccer balls see my rolls. Billy had had a grand time. He and Mom made sandcastles and splashed in the waves while I read or listened to music on my Discman.

When the sun started to set, Mom had fallen asleep. Billy joked she looked like a beached whale and I punched him, but then he got quiet, transfixed by the sky, and I sat beside him until the last light faded and we decided it was time to wake Mom. It's one of the few good memories I have of Billy—just sitting there, not talking. I felt connected to him in a way I probably never will again.

Rajeev, who is less than a foot away from me, breaks my reverie. "It's beautiful, isn't it?"

"Sure," I say, and notice a girl a few feet in front of me snuggle into her boyfriend's arms. That's what I want. Someone who accepts me and is happy to be with me— kinda like Billy and I were that day, but on a whole other level. This time next summer I could be that girl. I could be in the arms of a guy who wants me.

"Do you want to go for a walk?" Rajeev asks, leaning over so only I can hear his question.

"No," I say, annoyed that he's interrupting my thoughts again. "I'm fine here."

CHAPTER TEN

The following week when I show up for training, Matt isn't his smiley self. He's not rude exactly, but I'm certainly not feeling the love. "Everything okay?" I ask him.

He shrugs. "Why don't you start warming up on the elliptical." It's an odd request. We usually go through the warm-up together, going over exercises that are specific to the workout I'll be doing that day.

"So, what have you got for me?" I jog over to him when my five minutes are up, trying to counter his sour mood with enthusiasm.

"Sprints."

"Okay." I paste on my best smile. "I'm ready for you."

"Jennifer," Matt rubs a hand across the back of his neck, "I think maybe it'd be better if you got another trainer."

My mouth drops a little. "Sorry?"

"I really don't like this whole lying to Autumn thing, acting like we barely know each other, like we haven't been spending an hour together twice a week for the past couple of months." He's speaking faster than normal, like the words taste bad as he spews them out. "I haven't talked to her about it because of my professional beliefs and keeping to your requests, but I really don't like it."

"Oh." I plop down on a bench. "Well, if it's that big a deal to you we can tell her. I mean she knows I have a trainer now, so..."

"It's not just that," says Matt. "I didn't like the way you

98

treated her on Saturday. She loves you and is trying to support you and you, well…" I can tell he's trying to find the right words, the professionally acceptable ones. "You weren't very kind to her."

"I know," I say. "I felt bad about that. It's just reflex, I don't know, we've had some tensions in the past about my weight and about her trying to change me. It just slipped out. I didn't mean to—"

"Jay is a great trainer." Matt cuts me off. "I'm sure he can help get you to where you want to go."

My pulse starts to race. I've never been dumped but I imagine this is what it feels like. "I don't want Jay as a trainer," I say. "I want you. I've been doing so well with you. You inspire me." Matt shifts from foot to foot and it looks like he's struggling. "We work so well together," I say. "And it's been fun, right?" He continues to stand there, staring at me. "I'm sorry about Autumn, and about making you," I pause, "withhold the truth from her. That wasn't cool. I get that, but I don't think I can do this without your support. I don't even know Jay, and this is only going to get tougher, right? To get to my goal?"

I don't mean to but I start tearing up. He sits beside me and sighs, then reaches his arm across my shoulder. "Okay, okay," he says. "I'll train you. Don't cry." I nod but the tears keep coming. He rubs my back, and it's the best thing I've ever felt. "We'll let Autumn know," he says. "Maybe we can even all work out together sometimes, off the books, of course. She'd like that."

"Sure," I say, "that'd be great, really great." Matt withdraws his hand and jumps up. I join him and wipe the tears away with the back of my hand, realizing this might be the first time I've ever manipulated a man with my womanly wiles, even if that wasn't my intention.

"Ready for the sprints?" he asks. I nod and follow him to the track. The image of myself lying on the beach with a guy like Matt, his arms wrapped around me, floats in my head. It drives me to keep going. But who am I kidding? As much as I know I shouldn't be, it's not a guy *like* Matt I'm thinking of, it is Matt.

During the workout, I push myself harder than I have in weeks. I sprint toward that dream. I know it's likely I'll hurt tomorrow, but a huge protein shake waits in my locker, so I'll down that, spend some extra time stretching after our session, and then I know I'll be all right.

❧

ON THE WALK HOME from Fit4Life my phone rings, showing a number I don't recognize. "Hello?"

"Hi, is this Jenn?"

"Yeah, who's this?" I ask, but I think I know.

"Rajeev."

"Hi."

"Hi."

"Uhh…how'd you get my number?" I ask.

"Oh, I hope you don't mind. I asked Daniel."

"No, that's, uh, that's fine. What's up?"

"Well, it's short notice but Sammy called me earlier. She has these tickets to a book launch for Miriam Toews at her firm and she asked if I wanted them. There were two."

"Uh huh?"

"I know you're into writing so I thought you might want to come. There'll be free food and drinks."

I cringe at the thought that he thinks food will be a draw for me, but it does sound kind of interesting. "Uh…when is it?"

"Oh, sorry. Of course. It's tonight. At six. Should only be about an hour, maybe two. What do you say?"

"I don't know."

"It'll be fun." I can almost hear his convincing smile through the line. "And you don't want me to have to go by myself, do you? I'm not sure anyone else would be interested."

I'm just the nerdiest person he knows, I think. "Okay," I say. "Why not?" It's not like I have anything else to do tonight.

"Great. If you give me your address, I can pick you up."

"Okay. I'll text it to you."

"Great."

I JUMP WHEN MY APARTMENT buzzer sounds at 5:30 that night. I expected Rajeev to just text me to come down. I give a quick glance in the mirror then head to the lobby. He stands grinning in a blue dress shirt and slacks. A faint scent of cologne wafts toward me as I approach. It seems the way I'd imagine a date, but obviously not. We're going to a literary event. Of course he wants to look nice.

"I like your hair like that," he says. I let it curl in waves around my shoulders. I wanted to look nice too.

"Thanks."

"You ready?"

"Yeah."

He opens the car door for me then trots around to the other side. He chats casually on the drive, mentioning some stuff that's going on in the political scene and I have to admit I don't know much about it. This doesn't faze him.

"I've only actually read one of Toews' books," he says, clearly changing the subject when he realizes politics are not my thing, "in a first-year lit class. I don't know much more about her."

"I've only read one too."

"*A Complicated Kindness?*"

"Yeah."

"Me too. It wasn't my usual choice, but I liked it."

"Me too." I know I'm not contributing much to the conversation but I can't help it. I don't know what to say. This is foreign territory and I can't quite figure it out. Sammy's words repeat in my mind: she thinks he might be into me. But Rajeev said it himself, he only invited me because no one else wanted to go with him. "Have you ever been to an event like this before?" I ask.

"No, I don't really know what to expect." He glances over. His smile really is cute.

"Me neither."

We park a few blocks away and are mostly quiet on the walk. He opens the door for me when we arrive. Probably a cultural thing. I find myself looking over at him during the event. He seems so engaged. It's weird. He's a lawyer. He works with the down and out, and yet he's riveted by this white author who is clearly anything but down and out, whose books have nothing to do with his life—or at least the one book we've read. He's engaged in everything, really. I can't imagine him bored. He's even engaged in me. He looks over then, a smile on his face. "She's so down to earth," he whispers. I nod. "But yet she writes with such eloquence." I smile and try to focus my attention so I can listen to the author, really listen to her, the way Rajeev is. Based on the way she writes, she must have known turmoil, but I find myself wondering if she, in her skinny jeans, has ever struggled the way I have.

After the talk's over, Rajeev heads to the book display.

"Do you want one?"

"I'll maybe get it from the library or something," I say.

"No. It's alright. My treat." He smiles like it's a pleasure to be standing beside me and I shrug. "I'll take two," he says. He exchanges cash for the books and slips them into the bag the woman at the table hands him.

Once we've found Sammy, who clearly doesn't have time to chat, and thank her for the tickets, Rajeev leads me back out to the street. His hand just grazes the small of my back a time or two and I can't tell if it's on purpose or just a reflex as he tries not to lose me in the crowd.

"Do you want to grab something to eat? Some appetizers or something?" he asks when we step out into the evening.

"No," I say too quickly. "I'm not really hungry."

"How about a walk then? There's a great park nearby and it's a beautiful night." I feel a little weird about the prospect of just walking with him. I'm not sure a guy has ever asked me to go for a walk before but he's right—it is a beautiful night. And walking is better than nothing. I know if I go home I'll just veg on the couch—no calories burned there. I nod and he directs me to a little side street. We're far from my neighbourhood and as we head down what's basically an alley, I have no idea where we'll come out. We step into a park I'm not familiar with. Street lamps light a trail around a small lake.

Rajeev breaks the silence. "So, what did you think?"

"It was really nice." I glance at Rajeev, then look away, bringing my focus onto the glistening water, the crickets chirping, the warm evening breeze, and tell myself this isn't a date, though it sure feels like one, and it sure feels nice. "I didn't know what to expect, but I liked it."

"Yeah," he says. "I really admire people who can do that. Take words and just make them so," he looks into the night, like he's searching for the exact word, "important. That scene she read, about the sister playing the piano piece like that. It was incredible, perfectly painted, but better than a painting because I could feel it, almost hear it, not just see."

"Yeah."

He's quiet a moment. "The reading she chose…It had me thinking of my father." I glance over and he seems far away, then he meets my eye and a sad smile emerges. "He died two years ago. I was over here when it happened, which was…weird. Hard."

"I'm sorry," I say, hoping he doesn't ask about my

mother. "How did it remind you of him?"

"It was after the piano scene, when she talked about suffering—something about how it's passed from one generation to the next. My father did very well for himself. We weren't rich but we were well off. His father though, was a poor merchant man. My grandfather suffered some hard times—poverty, abuse, imprisonment—and it was like my father could never let go of that," Rajeev kicks a rock out of the path, "even though it wasn't his life. It was as if he was always afraid that what he had would be snatched away. He didn't know how to be happy. He didn't know how to enjoy what he had. He always wanted more, needed more, but having more only increased his suffering.

"When I was a boy I resolved I would never be like that."

Quiet surrounds us, broken only by the crickets continuing song, our footsteps on the soft dirt and the soft thwack of a duck jumping out of the water and shaking off its wings. Although I want to hear what he has to say, the intimacy of it all makes my palms sweat.

"My father was angry and disappointed that I chose to study the type of law I did," says Rajeev. "When I told him my dreams, I thought he would be happy. I'd be protecting—defending—people like my grandfather. But my father said he didn't pay to send me to Canada so I could squander my future away. He sent me so I could get a good job, a high-paying job, and never want for anything. In our last conversation he said I shamed him."

I take a deep breath. I know what it feels like to have a father who's ashamed of you. "That's awful."

Rajeev shrugs. "It's sad. For him." He tosses the bag of books from one hand to the other. "My mom is proud of me. She gets it."

I nod. Then my mouth opens and the words are out before I can stop them. "My mom just died. Well, not just. Several months ago."

"I know."

"You do?" Again, the words jump out.

"Daniel mentioned it that first night. He said usually your mom would have been there, and that she made these killer desserts. He said it was one of the first times he'd seen you since her death."

"Oh." For some reason, I'm surprised Daniel would bother to talk about me. But I guess, really, it's my mom he was talking about.

"How are you doing with that?"

"Oh, great." I laugh. "Super."

"Don't." He stops walking and turns to look right at me, into me. It's the most uncomfortable I've been all night. "Don't do that." He shakes his head and continues walking.

I'm speechless and fall a step behind. "It's hard," I say, catching up to him. "I miss her. We had a fight a couple of days before…We planned to meet up, to make up, you know? But she never came. I waited and waited then found her back at her house. On the floor. I tried…" My voice trails off.

"You don't have to talk about that." He takes a few steps. "You two were close?"

"Pretty close."

"That's nice."

"Yeah," I say, again, perplexed that I'm even talking about this to a guy who is practically a stranger, "it is."

CHAPTER ELEVEN

Just minutes after Rajeev drops me off, there's a knock on my door and I figure it must be some Mormon or something. No one else would show up unannounced at 8:30 pm on a Tuesday night. I'm in a tank top and underwear because of the heat so I throw on a robe and look through the peephole. The person is turned away from the door but I can tell from the ponytail and physique that it's Autumn. I open the door and start a smile that stops midway as she barges past me. "Well, hello." I close the door then follow her to the living room where she stares out the window. I walk toward her and when I'm a few feet away she whips around.

"So," she says, her voice loud but even.

"So?" I return.

"What's your explanation?" I sit on the couch, hoping she'll reciprocate by sitting on the armchair across from me, but she stays standing, her arms crossed. I wait for her to continue and we end up having a stare down. Finally, she sits. "Why exactly have you had my boyfriend lying to me for the past two months and why, perhaps even worse, have you been lying to me?"

"I don't believe either of us ever lied," I say.

"Come off it!" she yells, then brings her voice down to an even level, though no less intense. It reminds me of when she went off at those high school boys. "A lie of omission is still a lie and you know it. So what's your ploy, anyway? You meet my boyfriend and decide you want to get some one-on-one time with him? Is that what this whole weight loss thing is all about?" Her voice rises again. "Don't think I haven't seen the way you look at him." She takes a deep breath and continues. "And here I thought you were trying to live a better life, to get your health on track, to not end up like your mom."

She stops, as if she wonders for a brief moment if she's gone too far. I don't know and I don't care because I realize in addition to being mad about the lying, Autumn is actually somewhat concerned about my supposed plot. Autumn must think there's at least the slightest possibility that I could pry Matt away from her. It's the biggest compliment I've ever had. "Well?" she says.

I put my head down before responding and try to contain my wonder and joy that Autumn sees me as a threat. Me! I look back up at her and give a slight smile, one that's meant to soothe. "You've got it all wrong," I say. "This," I gesture to myself, "this mission to lose weight, to be healthy, it has nothing at all to do with Matt. You were right. It's about being happier. It's about," I take a deep breath, "no one having to ever see me the way I saw Mom." I can actually see Autumn soften at these words as she relaxes into the couch. "I didn't pursue Matt," I say, and it's true. "I was completely shocked when I showed up for my first session and he was the trainer. I didn't even know he worked there. I wouldn't have told you I was training no matter who my trainer was." This is true, too. She tries to say something but I raise my hand to stop her. "I love you, Autumn," I continue, "but you know we've had some bad experiences when you've tried to train me in the past. Really bad experiences."

There's nothing she can say to that; she knows I'm right. "Listen, I know it wasn't the best idea to have Matt keep that from you, to keep it from you myself, and I'm sorry, but I needed to do this on my own. I needed that." I watch

Autumn take in my words and I'm pretty sure she's still roused by the sense of righteous indignation she stormed in here with, but I'm also pretty sure she's wondering if she overreacted.

After a few moments she shrugs her shoulders and lets out a little laugh. "Sorry." A flush creeps across her cheeks. "I'm sorry for the rampage, for accusing you, for—"

"It's fine." I wave a hand. "I understand."

"It's just so weird," she says, "so shocking, you know? I mean the beach party—here I am thinking you two hardly know each other and—"

"I know," I say. "Matt was pretty upset about it. He wanted me to get another trainer because he hated lying to you. He's a good guy."

She nods. "He's not like the other guys. He..." Her voice trails off, gets tender.

"Are we okay?"

She laughs, and there's something behind it that I can't pick up on. "I guess I really overreacted." She tucks a stray tendril of hair behind her ear, a soft smile on her face. "I didn't mean to."

"Sure you did." I wink. "That's who you are, an over-reactor."

She picks up a pillow and tosses it at me.

"I'm not trying to steal Matt," I say, testing to see if she'll brush it off, say something that implies I couldn't steal him even if I tried, and she just had a moment of insanity.

She smiles at me. "I know. I know you wouldn't do that to me." She gives me her amazing grin. "But if you lie like that to me again," her face goes serious. "I'll cut you." She pulls her finger across in front of her throat, like she's slashing it, then laughs. "Okay?"

"Okay." I know my mind shouldn't go there, it's not anywhere I've let it go before, but I wonder if I could steal Matt away. Not that I would. I'd never intentionally hurt Autumn, but I just wonder if I could. Matt is basically the man of my dreams—let me correct that, the man I didn't even think I was good enough to dream about.

Autumn plops down beside me on the couch. She hugs me. I return her embrace, but my thoughts keep rolling. Autumn rarely stays with any guy more than a year. She and Matt must be pushing nine months by now. The expiry date for this relationship is coming up soon, and though I'd never do anything to speed it along, would it be so wrong to be there when it dissolves, ready and waiting to let Matt fall into my arms?

Autumn pulls away. "So, what were you up to when I barged in?"

"I'd just put in *The Princess Bride*."

"Shall I join you?" Before I have a chance to answer, she curls her feet up under her and pulls a blanket over. She tucks it around the both of us and I press play.

"You want me to rewind it?"

Autumn shakes her head. As the adventures ensue, I'm distracted. I can't stop thinking about the fact that Autumn actually thought I was a threat—to her. My mind reels with possibilities. I barely laugh at my favourite scenes. I barely see them. When the credits roll, Autumn yawns, stands, stretches, then gives me a hug goodbye. I lock the door, walk to the bathroom, then stand in front of the mirror and look at myself, lingering rolls and all. I examine my face. I flip my hair and twist it between my hands, taming the curl. I scrutinize my eyes, my lips, my teeth, then pull away from the mirror and smile. For the first time in my life I feel like a viable woman.

❧

THREE WEEKS LATER I rush around my apartment, getting ready for Labour Day weekend outing to Mount Carleton Provincial Park in New Brunswick. It'll be Matt, Autumn, and me—with most likely a few others along for the ride. Autumn's determined to be part of my weight loss journey. She had me over to her apartment earlier in the week for a ridiculously healthy and ridiculously good dinner and wants to introduce me to some non-gym related fitness.

When she tried to take me on as a project in the past she told me a healthy weight and fit life wasn't about being able to succeed in the gym but about being ready for the type of life I couldn't live when my weight was holding me back. So, I guess this weekend is about a life my old self couldn't enjoy—a two-day, one night, over thirty-seven-kilometre hike with a peak elevation of eight hundred and twenty metres. When Autumn first told me about it, I laughed.

'No really,' I said, 'what are we doing?'

She looked at me with that aggravating grin of hers. 'That's the hike,' she said. 'We can do it. You can do it.'

I shook my head, 'I don't think I'm there yet Autu—'

'You are there, Jennifer, and Matt thinks so too. We'll both be there to cheer you on.' When she said that, that Matt would be joining us, my decision was made, but I didn't want her to think that was my tipping point.

'Well, who else is going?' I bit my lip. 'Will I be the only one dragging you two powerhouses behind?'

'You won't hold us up,' said Autumn, placing a hand on my shoulder. 'Matt's told me of your progress. I don't think you'll have trouble at all. But,' she said, 'we've invited several other people. Some of Matt's friends and then a couple of the gals from my club.'

'So,' I said, laughing again. 'It'll be me and a bunch of trainers? I think you may have unrealistic expectations of my abilities.'

'Not at all,' said Autumn, 'I have perfectly realistic expectations. And it's not a race. So, you'll come?'

'I'll come.' She flung her body against mine—one of her signature tackle hugs. 'Sweet.' She hugged me again. 'Sweet, sweet, sweet. Be ready Saturday morning at four-thirty a.m.

We'll pick you up. Bring a sleeping bag, proper attire, but don't worry about anything else. Matt and I have the food, tents, and camping gear covered.'

I look at the huge hiking backpack Autumn dropped off the night before, already half filled with my share of the load. She said I could put in whatever else I wanted—clothes, necessity toiletries, etc., but warned me to travel as light as I could. After lifting the bag I knew why.

Despite the nagging fear that I won't be able to complete the whole thirty-seven kilometres and they'll have to carry me out on a stretcher, I'm looking forward to the hike. I weighed myself before getting dressed and was surprised to see another eleven pounds had fallen off me. Though really, it's more like they've been grunted off—Matt upped our workouts and says I'm ready for that next level. I bought a belt last week to help keep my pants and shorts up. I don't want to buy a whole new wardrobe until I'm at goal weight (though I have picked up a few more items). This morning I needed to use the belt on those Bermuda's I'd bought for the beach. When I come back from the hike I hope to step on the scale and see two more pounds gone, making me three-quarters of the way there—seventy-five pounds. Two pounds in two days would be somewhat ridiculous and most likely water weight, but a girl can dream. I make my final decisions on what I'll take and what I'll leave behind and head down to the lobby to wait for Autumn's text.

When I approach the van they've rented for the weekend, I expect to open the door to a crowd, but only Rajeev looks back at me. We go through a round of greetings and Matt pulls out onto the main street, in the direction of the highway. "Are the others meeting us there?" I ask.

"This is it," says Matt. "Three others were supposed to come, but they all pulled out."

"Chickens," says Autumn.

"Give 'em a break." Matt smiles over at her and the

green monster inside me jumps. "They all had other things going on."

Autumn winks at him. "I still say they couldn't hack it." She looks back at Rajeev and me. "Not like us." She holds up her hand and Rajeev gives her a high five. Seeing Rajeev's arm in the air, I wonder if he'll be able to hack it. He still has that somewhat soft look to him—not that he's fat or anything, or even overweight, not at all. But he doesn't have the sculpted muscles to carry him through that Matt will rely on. I might even be more ripped than him. Annoyance creeps in that he's here—that he's the only other one here. It feels like a set up.

About half-way through the drive, after a bathroom break, I bunch up a sweater and prop it against the window. "I didn't sleep well," I say, "excitement, I guess. Anyone mind if I try to take a nap?" It'll be another three hours to the trail entrance. I know I won't sleep, but as much as I can, I'll fake it. I'm not in the mood to join in the small talk. Rajeev spent the first couple hours of our drive grilling me on a plethora of things. He seems disappointed that I haven't read the book he got us yet, but I have more important things to focus on. I think back to Daniel's birthday dinner when I was flattered by Rajeev's interest in my life, and to the book launch and that intimate conversation—how it was so unnerving, but also nice. That's the word that comes when I think of him. He's nice, really nice, but today he feels like a nuisance. I know we'll be paired off. It's not like I was hoping for romantic moments with Matt by a waterfall or in front of a sunset, but I hoped to at least spend some one-on-one time with him, let him get to know me outside of training.

Autumn can be super close and clingy to her closest gal pals and I was counting on her running off with them from time to time, allowing Matt and me some private time. Although she and Rajeev are friendly enough, I highly doubt they'll be going off together. Such is life. I'm not where I believe I need to be to be worthy of Matt, anyway. I squirm against the window, trying to get comfortable, then sigh. I'm not where I need to be, but I will be.

While the others talk, my mind slips back to the last time I went camping. It was shortly before Dad left. I think he planned it to make him feel more like a father or something. With me, an overweight and under-active eleven-year-old, and Billy, a kid with barely the attention span of a house fly, it didn't go so well. Thinking back on it, I realize Dad showed some pretty impressive patience at all my complaining and all of Billy's darting off into the woods— Billy just had to look at that flower or this rock or see if he could catch that squirrel.

We didn't end up setting up camp at the top of the ridge like Dad wanted. We didn't set up camp at all. We turned back after an hour and a half of trekking, just thirty minutes from our destination. Dad didn't yell when I refused to go further and Billy said he didn't care. He just turned around, said, all right then, and led us down the trail and back out of the woods. I felt proud that I'd succeeded in ruining the trip. I knew something was going on, the way Dad was staying out late and how he rarely touched Mom anymore. I sensed he was about to ruin our lives, so I was happy to ruin something he wanted.

On the way back Billy chased a butterfly right off of a small cliff. He just sprinted out, and it was almost like he was frozen in air for the millisecond before he fell. I stood there, jaw wide open, as Dad bolted over to the edge faster than I'd ever seen anyone move.

I've heard Dad tell the story half a dozen times. He gazed out over the ledge and saw nothing but a dry, rocky, creek bottom. It was the single most terrifying and confusing moment of his life. And then he heard Billy's voice. 'I almost caught it.' Dad looked down to see Billy, arms wrapped around a rock, legs dangling below him, a big grin on his face. Relieved beyond belief, Dad started laughing at Billy's smile then had to stop himself in order to reach down and pull his son back into the arms of safety. That's the way Dad always said it, 'into the arms of safety,' like they weren't just his arms or something. He liked to add that it wasn't the first time Billy's adventurous spirit had gotten him into trouble and it wouldn't be the last. I'm guessing he stopped telling the story after Billy's accident got him into the worst trouble of his life.

CHAPTER TWELVE

When the van stops I shake myself out of my reverie, smile, and stretch as if I've been having a peaceful and energizing nap. I pretend to wipe the sleep out of my eyes, while really making sure none of the tears that threaten to escape are evident. I've heard the camping story so many times but something about rehashing it in my own mind, in light of Billy's situation, is different. I hate thinking about Billy. By this point, I don't know who I'm angrier at—him, for being such an ass all those years and for being a stupid idiot who rides in the rain after a night of drinking, or me, for still not going to visit him. Even Tammy went to visit him—and he'd been almost as rotten to her as he was to me. I justify staying away by telling myself it wouldn't make a difference. He wouldn't want to see me anyway.

Mom used to plead with me to come with her when she was still alive. But I just couldn't. I couldn't see him like that. It was bad enough being there that first night. I can't go again. I can't pretend I am the loving, concerned sister. It's not like I don't love him. He's my brother. I was glad he didn't die when he fell off that cliff and I'm glad he's not dead now. I just don't want to see him.

I'm only half paying attention as Matt talks about the trail. He tells us what to expect on the hike in, how long we'll go before stopping to build camp, and how to pace ourselves. Several minutes up the first ascent Autumn sidles up beside me. "Hey," she smiles. Once glance and I can tell it's her fake one.

"What?" I ask, not slowing my pace.

"How you doing?" She continues beside me, seemingly oblivious that she's cramping us along the slight trail.

"I'm fine, Autumn."

"Yeah?" She sends another one of those fake smiles my way.

"Yeah," I reply, hating the way she does this, instead of just getting to the point. I increase my pace, feeling my heart rate increase with it, and she follows right along. When she speaks, she doesn't even have to catch her breath.

"So how many years have I known you now?" She smiles again.

"I don't know Autumn, twenty-seven?"

"Yeah," she nods, "and in twenty-seven years I have never known you to sleep in a moving vehicle."

I turn to her and almost trip over a raised root. "What's your point?" I keep my eyes glued to the root-filled path.

"Well," she says, "I know you weren't sleeping for the past three hours," she hesitates, "or at all, though you were doing a pretty good job of pretending to. Then you were clearly in another world once we stopped, and you've been basically mute since we started hiking. What's the deal?"

"Can't I just be in my own mind for a bit? Do I have to be gabbing constantly?" I send her a slight glare and feel like a bitch for doing it. I return my gaze to the path before I can see her reaction.

"I'm just concerned," she says. "And by your tone I'm guessing my concern is justified." She lowers her voice. "At first I thought it may be Rajeev. Nervousness or something—he's cute—it would make sense."

I look over at Autumn again and roll my eyes before remembering to watch my footing. "It's not Rajeev."

"Okay, okay," she says, "will you tell me what it is?"

I sigh and take a deep breath, trying not to reveal how

winded I'm getting. "It's nothing, Autumn, really, though thank you for your concern. I was just resting, okay?"

Autumn's quiet for a moment and she's forced to fall slightly behind me as the trail narrows and we start clambering over some large rocks. When it widens just enough for her to squeeze in beside me again, she does. "Is it Billy?"

I resist the urge to whip my head toward her and keep focused on the ground in front of me. "What?"

"Well," she says, "that's the only other time you've ever gone camping, right? With you and your dad and Billy? He loves telling that—"

I shake my head. "You know me too well." I'm partly annoyed and partly touched that she can read me like this. She's silent for another moment before speaking.

"You still haven't gone to visit him, have you?" She says it as a statement, not a question. I shake my head. I can tell she's holding back, wanting to say something, but instead we walk in silence. Autumn was the first one to get to the hospital. She'd seen Billy all bloody and dirty with grit and gravel. She'd looked into his eyes before he'd slipped into the coma. He was still in the coma when Mom died. He stayed that way, basically a vegetable, for two months and eighteen days.

When he woke, someone would have had to explain why his mom never came to visit. I wondered how that conversation would have gone—Billy, the mother you wish wasn't your mother is now dead. Her fat killed her, just like you always hoped it would. Except the person wouldn't have said that last bit because no one else knew that was Billy's hope. It was just the three of us the night Billy called Mom a fat fucking piece of lard and told her he hoped she'd suffocate on all that fat in her sleep one night, 'and maybe kill that little tub of lard beside you while you're at it, roll over in your sleep during one of your precious little sleepovers.'

I try to remember why he said it, besides the fact that he was an ass. I think it was because Dad was taking Evita away for a five-year anniversary trip and the girls' grandparents weren't comfortable with Billy staying with them for the two weeks, which meant he was stuck with us. He'd begged and begged but they'd said no. Mom had smiled when he'd said that to her. Smiled in a way that made me want to hug her and kick Billy in the throat. 'You don't realize it at the moment,' she said, 'but you don't really mean that. And I love you, Billy, no matter what you say.' Billy stared at her for a moment then knocked his bowl of ice cream to the ground, went to his room, and slammed the door.

I try again to picture what the person would have said to Billy when they told him he'd slept through his mother's death. I try to hear what he would have said back, but then realize he wouldn't have said a thing. Dad told me that when Billy woke up, he couldn't speak. He didn't remember how to make his mouth form words. All he could do was make these warbled noises. 'You should go visit,' Dad said. 'He can hear. He can understand.' I told Dad I just couldn't handle it. I didn't have anything to say anyway. What was I going to do, go in there and start cussing him out? Tell him what I really wanted to say?

I up my pace again and get a few steps past Autumn. Matt is ten to fifteen feet up ahead and Rajeev's about the same distance behind. Determined to get out of this little window of confidence I push even harder, but when I'm still a few paces behind Matt, Autumn puts her hand on my shoulder and stops me.

"Slow down, Jennifer," she says. "This is no race and you don't want to get worn out too soon."

"I'm just trying to get a bit of a workout," I say, sending her as equally a fake smile as she'd been giving me.

She keeps her hand on my shoulder, slowing me down, until we're too far away for Matt to hear her whispered words. "He's speaking again."

I process that information. That means Billy definitely knows about Mom, would have been given the details. Has anyone tried to explain why I never showed up by his bedside? What could they say? Not that it matters. He probably never even thought to ask.

I look back to see Rajeev gaining on us as Autumn matches my slowed pace. "He's doing really well, actually," she says. "He doesn't remember anything from the day of the accident, or why he was out in his motorcycle in such a storm on his birthday, and he's pretty shaken up about your Mom. But he's doing well. It'll be a few more months of rehab before he can function normally—that rod in his leg means he has to build up the strength to walk again. But after that they should be sending him home."

I take a few steps then ask, "Back to his roommates?"

"No," says Autumn. "I think he's going to move back in with your dad."

I nod.

"I know you and Billy have never gotten along very well," she says, her voice soft, "but I really think you should go visit him." I take in Autumn's words and think about the meaning. If he doesn't remember anything from the day of the accident, he doesn't remember the birthday cake, what he said to me…He doesn't remember why I never want to see him again. "He's asked about you."

I turn to Autumn. "What did you say?"

"It wasn't me he asked," she says, offering no more.

"I'll think about it," I say, just as Rajeev catches up to us.

"Think about what?" he asks, smiling brightly through his laboured breathing.

"Oh," I say, "whether I want to go for a swim tonight in that brook Matt was talking about."

"I'd be up for it," says Rajeev, his smile growing broader. "I could use a dip."

⊱

AS THE TRAIL WIDENS and the path evens out, the four of us walk in a little cluster, chatting easily now that we don't have to worry about catching our breath. I breathe deep the air whenever a breeze comes our way and feel my body relaxing for the first time in weeks. I hadn't even realized I was tense, but from how my muscles release as I soak in the beauty of the mountain views, the wildflowers along the path, and the sound of the singing birds, I know it's been a long time since I've felt this good.

I forget about viewing this hike as exercise, wondering how many calories I can burn, and view it as what it is—a hike with friends. I stop even thinking about a way to spend quality time with Matt and am happy enjoying everyone's company. Surprisingly, it's Rajeev who has the majority of my attention—all of our attention, really. He tells us stories of the explorations he used to take as a child in rural India. Stories that involve little old men and nosy grandmothers, snakes, and even a tiger once—though he admits the tiger story actually happened to his father, not him, "It just comes across better as a first person telling," he says with a chuckle. At one point he has me laughing so hard my side hurts. The hours pass quickly and before long Matt tells us that our camp site is just around the next bend.

"So," says Rajeev, sidling up behind me on the now thinned out path, "are you ready for that dip?"

"I don't know," I say, "I didn't bring a swimsuit."

"Seems to be your regular excuse." He winks. "That's all right. Just jump in as is—the sun should dry you."

I'm quiet for the next few steps, considering—it is blistering hot. My clothes would mask what I want to hide. Is it a roll of fat, is it fabric, who could tell?

"Hey," he calls out before I can respond, "this one here forgot her bathing suit again. What do you say, Matt?

Should we all just dive in?"

Matt's laugh echoes through the woods. "Grand idea!"

As Autumn and Matt spring ahead, Rajeev stays beside me. "So, what do you say? You jumping in?"

"Maybe," I mumble as Matt and Autumn, running like gazelles, start struggling with their shirts. Matt reaches the water's edge a few paces before Autumn and sheds his shorts, socks, and shoes before doing a cannonball and splashing Autumn, who hops on one foot, trying to get her boot off.

"Jerk!" she yells. She frees her foot, tosses her clothing to a nearby rock, and dives in beside him. Her bright fuchsia bra and panties accent her toned body as she surfaces, the water trickling down her tanned skin. I expect Rajeev to be ogling her, but he's looking at me, smiling at me.

"So," he says, "you ready?"

I want to say no. Seeing Autumn reminds me how far I have to go. I felt pretty good standing on the scale and looking in the mirror this morning, but all that confidence is blown away by her perfection and even the thought of stepping in fully clothed, allowing the water to cling to my body and reveal each and every one of my bulbous flaws, seems too much to bear. As I'm thinking this, beads of sweat work their way down my back. The breeze hasn't visited us for a while, the sun is strong, and my shirt is damp with sweat, anyway. It doesn't matter if I'm not perfect. It's too hot for insecurities. "Okay." I decide and bend to take off my boots.

Rajeev peels off his shirt and starts working on his belt. When he's finished undressing, he stands in his boxers and looks my way, his head slightly angled. "It's okay you know," he says. "Underwear's just like a bathing suit. It'd be much easier for you to move."

"Oh," I say, touched at his expression—soft and concerned. "I'm fine."

"You sure?" He smiles. "Hey, if you're shy I'll turn

away." He turns his head, pretends to cover his eyes, then peeks through with a little grin. I notice how dark his almond eyes are, how a hint of mystery hides behind them, how they're focused. They don't flit around like most people's do when he looks at me; he doesn't avert his gaze.

I laugh. "Nah, I'm wearing whites." It's a lie I fear will be exposed the instant the water hits my light green tank top, revealing the navy bra underneath, but I say it anyway—I could be referring to my underpants.

"All right," he shrugs, "well, come on then."

I follow him to the water's edge and try to tell myself none of these people are here to judge me. Autumn saw me in bathing suits before I lost any weight. Not in years, but still. Matt's seen me at my worst, sweaty and panting, and Rajeev, well, why should I care what Rajeev thinks of me? He's not an image of perfection like Autumn and Matt. His stomach may be almost flat but there's no definition. I mean he's nice, he really is—and cute and funny and smart—and that's important, but I don't need to care what he thinks of me. He's not the guy I've done all this work for. If I'm going to be my ideal, I want to be with my ideal as well. I want to know I'm good enough. That's worth waiting for.

"Be careful," Matt calls, as I tentatively put one foot in the cool water, "it gets deep surprisingly quick." Rajeev jumps in and then comes up with a spurt, shaking his hair like a dog. I haven't jumped in the water since I was a kid and first realized my splashes would be bigger than everyone else's. I take a few steps into the cool pool and it feels amazing. I tiptoe to make sure I don't end up falling and making that splash after all.

Rajeev paddles over then stands. "You all right?"

"Yeah," I smile, "I just like taking it slow, and I don't want to fall in at the drop."

He comes closer, then offers his hand. "I'll guide you."

I hesitate and feel a weird twist in my stomach at the sight of his outstretched hand and wide smile. I take hold and he leads me, grasping my waist as I stumble into the water and gasp, shocked at the intense current that shoots through me as I fall, the water colder than I expected, and Rajeev's arms stronger than I imagined. "It's cold," I spurt, at a loss for words at how good it feels, his arms around me.

"Yeah, it's awesome," he says, still holding me, his eyes locked on mine. I look away and he releases me. "Just swim around a bit," he says, "enjoy it." I tread and watch him dive underwater. Moments later Matt hollers. His hands fly up in the air. He sinks into the water as if pulled under. When the guys emerge they're laughing and splashing each other. Calling out threats.

Autumn swims over to me as Matt wrestles Rajeev under. She rolls her eyes then yells to the guys, "Just don't drown each other, all right?" She returns her gaze to mine with a knowing smile. "Boys." And there's something about that smile, coming from my cousin who has always made an effort to include me in her life even when I haven't deserved it, even when I've said no to her invites time after time, who, despite my bad behaviour, invited me to be a part of this beautiful day, that makes me hug her. It's awkward in the water and we start to sink as our treading legs entangle. Autumn laughs, spurting water out of her mouth, and grasps my hand tightly.

CHAPTER THIRTEEN

Once the refreshing cool of the brook becomes frigid, we make our way over to the rocks and lie in the sun to dry out. It's quiet, and as I contemplate how far I've come, how far I still have to go, how weirdly nice it felt to have Rajeev's arms around me, but how much I want Matt's to be, I wonder what thoughts are keeping the others silent. We all have our secret musings and though I'm curious, it's also nice to lie in such quiet, yet not be alone. Matt sits, stretches, and grins a half sleepy grin at the rest of us. "Well, I'm ready for some dinner." We all agree.

I set out to collect brush for the fire as Matt prepares a barbecue station. Rajeev and Autumn go back down the trail to pick some blueberries Autumn saw on the way up, so I gather the twigs and small logs as fast as I can. This may be my only chance for some one-on-one time with Matt. I shuffle back to camp, weighed down with an armload of wood. Matt smiles at me, looking impressed. I dump the pile beside a small hole he's been digging out and dust the dirt and wood chips off of my damp shirt. "You should change," he says, "you'll get a chill."

"I guess," I say, though I doubt I will. It's sweltering out. "Thanks." I sit on a log and look up at him.

"Well?" He raises his eyebrows.

"I'll wait till the others get back." I smile. "How else can I help?"

He motions to the brush I've collected and we arrange wood for the fire. "Did you enjoy the hike?"

"It was amazing," I say, trying to get the sticks exactly right. "One of the best days ever. I owe it all to you." He looks over at me, his head cocked to the side. "Well," I say, "I never would have been able to do this four or five months ago. Not a chance. Not without your training."

Matt's silent as he finishes building and lighting the fire. He sits down beside me. "You know," he says, "you shouldn't think your success is because of me. Not at all. You're the one who did this. I only provided some guidance, some motivation; any good trainer could have gotten you the same results."

"I don't know about that," I say, inching closer to him on the log. "You know how to motivate me. I don't know that I could have done what I've done without you." I laugh, "I never had much success with Autumn."

"That's different," says Matt. "It's the whole family dynamic thing—it seems like you two are almost more like sisters than cousins. Maybe the tension of sibling rivalry got in the way."

"Maybe."

"Anyway," says Matt, "you've learned a lot, you've been incredibly focused and motivated, and you'll reach your goal before you know it. You need to know that it was you who got you there so it can be you who keeps you there. You can do this without me, without anyone."

"Why would I need to?"

Matt leans back. "Well, I can't be your trainer forever."

"I don't see a problem with that." I smile.

"I don't want to become a crutch for my clients," he says. "I want to help them get past their restrictions and show them how they can take control of their lives— whether it's overcoming stubborn weight, or an injury, whatever. My goal is to get them to the point where they know enough that they can train themselves."

"That's not a very good business model." I nudge his arm with my elbow. "Is it, now?"

"It's working just fine."

"Anyway, I'm not just a client, am I? We've got a relationship going here."

"I have relationships with all my clients," he says. "True concern and interest is part of where the motivation comes in." He takes a deep breath. "But yes, we have more than that, you're Autumn's cousin. You may be my cousin one day." He looks at the fire as he says this, nudging it with a stick and smiling softly. "I wouldn't want to keep taking money from you."

I'm silent. I want to clarify what he means. I want to tell him he better watch himself—Autumn's bound to break his heart. She breaks all the guys' hearts. I also want to shake him and make him see I'm the one for him—or that I will be in just a few months. "What do you—?"

"We found loads of berries!" says Autumn, trotting into camp with a smile. "Though I think Raj may have ruined his dinner eating two out of every three he picked."

"Oh, don't you worry," says Rajeev. "This is bottomless." He rubs his stomach and smiles like a mischievous little boy. "What?" He sets down his container of berries. "Nothing's on the grill yet?"

"Just about to." Matt stands, giving my knee a squeeze as he does. His eyes tell me that little interchange was our secret. I'm less than thrilled at the confidence.

⤸

I TRY TO PUT MATT'S words out of my mind and enjoy the rest of this night. After dinner we sit around the fire chatting as the roaring blaze settles into glowing embers. Matt and Rajeev are full of stories. After all the tales Rajeev entertained us with on the hike, I'm surprised he has any left. Matt has some winners from his days as a budding soccer pro and Autumn gets Rajeev to tell some tales about Daniel that neither of us have heard.

Besides laughing at the boys and asking for more stories, Autumn's almost as quiet as I am. I try to read her expression in the dying light, but it tells me nothing. Maybe he already proposed. Maybe she suspects the proposal...but she wouldn't say yes. She goes through men faster than most people go through toothbrushes. There's no chance— she sidles closer to Matt, leans her head against his shoulder, and snuggles in as he lifts his arm and wraps it around her— is there?

I'd never once thought Autumn and Matt would be forever. If she were going to settle on a guy, surely he'd be the one to pick, but Autumn doesn't settle on anyone. That's why I'd allowed myself to hope, to dream...

My throat tightens, and then I'm craving a chocolate bar like it's heroin. Well, like I imagine a heroin craving would be. Somewhere along the way, Matt became what I was working towards, who I was working for. Not just the idea of him, of someone like him, but *him*. The realization smacks me in the face—for the past few months I've been transforming myself for him even more than I've been doing it for me. Yet if I understood him correctly, and if Autumn says yes—if she already said yes—what am I even doing this for?

Terrible images of me blowing back up again, those seventy pounds creeping on and then bringing more handfuls of fat along with them, float through my mind. The vision expands and I see Autumn walking down the aisle, looking more beautiful than she ever has, as I stand beside her, rows and rows of fabric needed to cover my monstrous frame. In this vision I stare at Matt, who watches Autumn with joy. Unlike the other bridesmaids I don't walk down the aisle. How could I? As big as I am, I would barely fit. No, I'm already at the front, waiting as everyone else enters. The scene changes. Autumn and Matt have children and live happily ever after. I pull myself further and further away from the only family left that's ever been kind to me, that's ever loved me. I have to pull myself away from them though, because how can I stand it—Autumn married to the man I love? Not that I love Matt, but I could one day, I thought maybe I would, and maybe, just maybe, he could love me back.

I know I'm being ridiculous, ludicrous even, but the images keep coming and I have to get away. Now. I practically jump to standing, right in the middle of Rajeev's story, a story I couldn't retell if my life depended on it. He stops talking.

"You okay?" Autumn's eyes widen.

"Yeah, I…yeah, my leg, it's cramping or something. I think I just need to go for a walk."

"It's pitch black," says Autumn.

"There're stars." I motion to the expanse above us, an expanse I notice for the first time. It's incredible. But I pull my gaze away, back to Autumn. "I'll stay on the path." I swallow, trying to keep my voice calm. "I'll be fine, really. Just a few minutes."

Matt throws a log on the fire. Rajeev fiddles with it and a renewed blaze shoots up. It lights Autumn's face. She's staring at me, trying to read me I'm sure, and the guys sit back, waiting for her move. "Walk around the camp," she says. "You'll get eaten by a bear if you—"

"I'll go with her." Rajeev stands, the fire illuminating his grin. "If I can handle a tiger, I'm sure I can handle a bear." He reaches down and grabs the knife beside Matt's leg. "Just in case." He winks.

"The tiger was your dad." I rack my brain, trying to think of a reason he'll accept, but can't. "You don't need to come." This is the last thing I want—Rajeev beside me. Rajeev with his endless questions and intense stares.

"Decision's been made," says Rajeev. "Either you walk

around the camp, as Autumn suggested, or you let me escort you. No one's letting you go off into the wilderness alone." He says this rather gallantly, and with the knife held up in the air and the cocky Indiana Jones smile he's wearing, he almost looks sexy in the firelight. Almost.

I don't want to walk under the stars with Rajeev, but if I have to stay and watch Autumn and Matt cuddling for one more minute, I may burst—literally combust. "Fine." I wave an arm and take off down the path. Rajeev falls in step behind me.

"Slow down," he says, catching up to me. "You've got a cramp now, but if you trip and fall you may have worse than that." I slow my pace but say nothing. "So, what's going on?"

"I have a cramp," I say, tempted to increase my speed again.

"You could shake your leg a few times and that would probably solve your problem." He rests his hand on my shoulder and I shrug it off. "I'm not buying it, Jennifer."

"Well, maybe I just wanted to be alone," I say, stressing the final word.

"You came on a thirty-two-kilometre hike with three other people to be alone?"

"I thought there'd be more than three people," I say, "and it's thirty-seven kilometres."

"So," says Rajeev, keeping a light tone to his voice, "you thought it'd be easier to feel alone in a crowd."

"I don't know," I don't even try to hide my exasperation. "Let's just walk, okay?"

"No." Rajeev takes hold of my arm and pulls me over to a large boulder. "Let's sit."

"My leg," I protest.

"Nothing's wrong with your leg."

I'm glaring at him, though I doubt he can see it in the dark. He sits on the boulder and gently pulls me down beside him. I scooch away until I'm as far over on the rock as possible without falling off. I know it's childish, but I want as far away from him as possible.

For once, he's quiet, and the silence unnerves me. I'm eyeing him, but he gazes straight ahead. Finally, he leans back, takes in the sky, and sighs with what sounds like contentment.

"Look up," he says, without looking at me. I don't. After a moment, he glances over. "Look up," he says again. I oblige and try not to be awed by what's before me. As my eyes adjust, I realize I've never seen so many stars in my life. Incredible barely describes it. "What do you think, when you look up at that?"

"Huh?" I whisper.

"What do you think?" I can feel Rajeev's eyes on me as he asks the question and then sense when he turns back to the sky.

"I don't know," I say, "that it's really beautiful?"

"Anything else?" he asks, a smile in his voice.

"I don't know." I continue to look up. Amazed. "I don't know."

"Do you know much about the stars?"

"Not much."

"It takes years for the light from even the closest star to reach us—with the exception of the sun, of course. The light from some of the stars we're seeing could have been travelling to us for millions of years."

"Millions?"

He laughs. "Could be tens of millions, even hundreds. So the thing is, we're not really seeing the stars as they are. Some of them may not even exist anymore. They may have burned up long before we were born. So, when we see them, it's like we're looking into the past."

"Okay?"

"Sometimes it's like that in life too. We look into a past that no longer exists, looking as if it's real. We hold onto things in our life that there's no reason to hold onto anymore because, unlike the stars, they don't bring us beauty, they bring us pain."

I'm partially following Rajeev, but I tell him I'm not. "Well," he says, "I can see that you're holding onto things that were. Just like my dad did. You're holding onto past pain, past fear. You don't need to."

I go rigid at these words, like a cat on the defensive. He has no right to make assumptions about my pain, my fear. The pompous jerk. I keep silent despite my developing rage at his intrusion in my life, despite his philosophical ramblings. We have a long walk tomorrow and if I speak, I'm pretty sure I'll say something I'll regret.

"I don't know if it's issues related to your weight, your family, or something else, but whatever it is—rejection, loss, fear—it's burned up now. It no longer exists. Yet you treat it like it does, like it's real, the way you probably imagined all those stars up there were still real."

I stay silent and hope he thinks I've stopped listening.

"You're very…" he pauses, "distant, and guarded, and it seems like your eyes are closed to some of the beauty, the goodness, the joy that is life. It's like you're holding onto these old hurts and using them as an excuse to create new hurts, to keep people away."

My pulse races, my hands clench. What do you even say to that? And from a stranger? But I have to say something. "You don't know what you're talking about."

"I do." Rajeev sits up and looks over at me. I sit up as well. "I like you, Jennifer. I was going to ask you out during this trip, on a proper date, not a last-minute thing like before, but I don't think I will." He pauses. "Not yet anyway. I don't think you're ready."

"Ready?" I snap. "What is that supposed to mean?"

"What do you think it means?" His voice is even, curious.

"You mean 'cause I'm not skinny enough for you yet? You thought by now I would have lost more?" I stand and look directly at him. The cocky bastard. "Well, I wouldn't have said yes to you, anyway. Not ever. I've got my sights set on better than you." As soon as I say the words, I hear how ridiculous they are. That's not what he was saying, I'm sure it's not.

He shakes his head and stands so he's only inches away from me. "Of course that's not what I meant. You know that's not what I meant." We're so close I could lean forward and our chests would touch. "You can be happy, Jennifer. You have everything you need to be happy, right now. You just have to believe that. You just have to let go of the things that make you think happiness comes in a certain package. It doesn't."

It's dark, but in the starlight I can tell he's looking right into my eyes. Something in his gaze makes me nervous and scared and angry and excited and, most of all, ashamed I've just behaved like I have. I turn from him. "I don't have to listen to this. I'm heading back."

I step onto the path and, only three steps in, my toe catches on a rock, hurtling me forward. Rajeev grasps me from behind and prevents my fall. I maneuver myself out of his grasp without a word and continue toward the campsite. It takes my eyes a moment to adjust to the light from the fire. When they do, I see Autumn curled up on Matt's lap. They're not making out but they probably were seconds before. I walk past them, fuming. "I'm exhausted," I say, and crawl into my tent.

I hear the three of them whispering as I set up my sleeping bag and lie down, but I can't make out their words. They must be talking about me, talking about how it was a mistake to bring me along. I try not to think about or make sense of what Rajeev was trying to tell me. Yeah, I'm not happy. I've never been very happy, but I have good reasons for that. He doesn't know what my life has been like, what I've gone through, the way the world treats people like me.

He was right about one thing though, I do need a certain package to be happy and I'm going to get it.

It was stupid to get so concerned about Matt implying he was planning to propose. He hasn't yet. If he had, Autumn would have told me. There's no way she'll say yes. At least she probably won't...not based on her track record. So this could actually be what I was hoping for. Autumn turns Matt down and I'm here to pick up the pieces of his broken heart. After wanting to marry her, he'd be even more in need of comfort than if it'd just been a normal breakup. Of course I don't want to see Matt in pain, but that's out of my control.

I roll over, trying to find a better position on the hard ground. No one ever tells you that when you lose pounds and pounds of fat, you also lose pounds and pounds of cushioning. I stare at the top of the tent, barely able to discern it in the dark. But what if she says yes? Autumn seems different with Matt. She doesn't complain about him or joke about him like she did with the others. She used to love to say the last guy, Tommy, was all brawn and no brains. Matt certainly has brains. And he's kind. Matt is probably the best thing that ever happened to Autumn. So many of the guys didn't seem to really see her, just the package she comes in. Matt sees her.

I can't think about that though. I won't think about that. I'll just be pleasant and encouraging and wonderful, and when Autumn turns Matt down, it'll be my shoulder he cries on. It'll be me he'll grow to love. A part of me realizes I'm likely being delusional—if Matt was truly heartbroken, which he probably will be, the last thing he'll want is to be around me, Autumn's cousin. But—I roll over, trying to get comfortable—grief makes people do weird things. I just need to be ready when the time comes. I need to be someone Matt notices, which means I need to pick up the pace. I'm far from where I want to be, where I need to be. He may propose soon. No more sulking, I tell myself. Only focus. No more cheating on snack foods. I can probably amp up the fitness too—add another workout to my week or up the intensity. But it needs to be more than that. The woman I envision is kind and sweet and focused, in addition to being perfectly fit. That's who I want to be. That's who I will be. That's who Matt deserves. It's time to fake it until I make it.

Autumn unzips the tent and crawls in. "You still awake?" she whispers.

I keep silent and try to make my breathing even. I'm definitely not in the mood for girl talk tonight, but starting tomorrow morning I'll be the best cousin she's ever seen.

CHAPTER FOURTEEN

The next day, as we do the shorter, but still ridiculously long hike back to the trailhead, I'm chatty as can be—despite my aching muscles and sore feet. I smile, I laugh, I treat Rajeev like nothing happened the night before, and I do my best to seem like I'm enjoying every moment. At first it's forced, but after a couple of hours I find I really am enjoying myself. When I see Matt and Autumn holding hands or teasing each other, I tell myself I'm glad they're both happy and when they're not any longer, then I'll get my chance.

We crash at a motel rather than camp again, all of us opting for an early night. In the morning, once we're on the road, Matt glances back at me. "How about we cancel tomorrow's training session so you can give your body a break? You went hard this weekend."

"Are you kidding?" I say. "No way. I'll be there. And I don't expect you to go easy on me, either."

"All right, all right." He laughs. "It'll just be upper body then, and no arguing."

"Works for me!"

It's nice, not lying to Autumn about Matt being my trainer. We talk freely on the drive home, all of us tired but in good spirits. When I step out of the van that night, Autumn leans out the passenger window. "Jenn," she says, in that nervous, forced happy tone she gets sometimes. "Mom and I are going over to the home on Wednesday—at

135

five o'clock. We could pick you up on the way if you want."

I bite my lip, holding back frustration that she's using my rosy disposition today to bombard me. "Wednesday?"

"Yeah."

"Oh, sorry." I shake my head as if I'm legitimately disappointed. "I have plans."

"Okay." She leans back in her seat as Matt starts up the car again. "Maybe next time."

"Yeah." I smile and wave. "Maybe next time." I try to shake the invite off as I walk into my apartment lobby and wait for the elevator. It seems different now—not going to visit Billy when he doesn't even know why I'm not there, doesn't remember that last day. But at the same time, he was a jerk my whole life. He knows that. Why should I have to be the bigger person? I step in the elevator and push the button for my floor. The me I'm working toward—the me who isn't bitter, who doesn't begrudge others' happiness, who is joyful—I doubt she'd stay away from her brother this long, no matter what he'd done or what a little ass he was. But I'm not her yet. Maybe that'll be one of the first things I do when the scale tells me I've made it. Maybe then I'll go visit Billy. There'll be no way he can say any of his old quips then. He'll see that he was wrong about me all along—I'm not a failure, not an embarrassment—and I'll be able to forgive him whether he forgives me or not. Maybe.

I walk out of the elevator, up the hall, and open my apartment door. Suddenly I feel tired; the pack I'm wearing massively heavy. It slides off of my shoulders and I plop down on the couch. Going downhill today was almost more tiring than going up. My legs actually started shaking. Though I'd never admit it out loud, a wave of relief flowed through me when Matt said we'd focus on the upper body tomorrow. Exercise is the last thing I want to think about. What I really want is to lie on this couch all night with a bag of chips, some cookies and veg in front of the TV. Of course, there are no chips anywhere to be found in this apartment. It's necessary because of moments like this when I'd likely eat the whole bag.

I ate a few chips last night. Baked blue corn chips. Autumn's choice of course, though they weren't bad and apparently they're better than the real thing health-wise. I'm tempted to run to the grocery store and grab some, but no matter how healthy they are, eating a bag would probably wipe out the whole week. So instead I stand, head to the bathroom, brush my teeth, and take a nice, long, hot shower.

I know I should wait until tomorrow morning to get the most accurate reading, and I'll check again if I'm not satisfied now, but after towel drying my hair as thoroughly as I can, I toss the towel toward the rack and lift one foot then the other. I close my eyes, scared to look—this is becoming a habit of mine—but finally open them and gaze down at the scale in wonder. Seventy-five gone. Seventy-five gone. Seventy-five gone! I want to shout it from the rooftops. I want to run naked through the streets proclaiming my glory. I'm so happy I could scream.

I step off the scale and catch a glimpse of myself in the mirror. The woman I see is better, much better than what I'm used to, but a far cry from sexy. She's still somewhat roly-poly—the muscle definition barely shows through the layers of fat, the stretch marks scream of imperfection. I turn away and shut off the light. Seventy-five pounds is amazing, but I've got a long way to go.

FOR THE NEXT FEW weeks I'm on fire. I'm so focused I can hardly believe it. I'm so focused I barely have chocolate or chip cravings. I weigh or portion out almost everything that goes into my mouth and cut back from the daily minimum suggestions in Matt's guidelines, though I know he wouldn't approve. Slow and steady is what he believes in, I won't keep it up forever, but I'm on a roll! I know food is fuel. I just want my body to fuel itself from my fat stores a little bit more than it has been. It's not like I'm starving myself. I'm just eating less and adding in mini workouts in addition to my sessions with Matt and my own scheduled workouts. Five minutes here, five minutes there, of intense activity—burpees, jumping jacks, tuck jumps. And it's making a difference. I've lost eight more pounds and am down another size. My goal weight is pretty much the lowest of the healthy weight range for my height, taking into consideration my muscle mass goals, and so I'm already within my medically ideal weight range. My doctor would approve, though I haven't even been to a doctor since I collapsed on Citadel hill. My doctor's not nice like the walk-in-clinic one. He's a badgering old man and I certainly don't need him giving me his outdated recommendations.

I walk into the gym feeling spry and excited about today's session. I splurged on some new gym clothes, even though I know I'm probably a full size or two from where I want to be, but it's all part of faking it till you make it. I'm going to look as good as I can. I want Matt to see how well I'm doing, how much he's helping me. I need him to see. Ever since the hike he's been bringing Autumn up in conversations more and more, but that doesn't mean he's blind to me.

I've been practising my sexy walk and as I sashay over to the training area, I notice a few of the guys in the free weight section glance my way. I'm tempted to look behind me to see what hottie they're gawking at, but quickly decide I'm the hottie, whether it's true or not. When I get to the training area I turn and see no other women in this part of the gym. It *was* me! I hold in my squeal and do an inner happy-dance. When Matt walks out of his office I'm beaming, and I can tell from the way he smiles back at me that he thinks I look good.

At the end of our session, as I'm going through my stretches, Matt hops up on the window ledge across from me. I feel his eyes on me and try to go through the routine with as much sex appeal as I can muster. Even the attempt is so new to me that I fear it's having the opposite effect and I just look ridiculous…and then I feel miserable for even trying—he's not single yet.

"Jennifer," says Matt.

"Mm-hmm?" I don't look up, as I stop trying to look sexy and simply focus on the stretch.

"Have you weighed yourself lately?"

"I'm not allowed." I lie with a smile.

"We should maybe do that before you go." Concern leaks from his voice.

I relax the stretch and look up. "I thought I wasn't scheduled in until the end of the month."

"I know." He steps off the ledge and comes toward me. "I'm worried you're losing weight too fast. We may need to assess your caloric intake—up it a bit. You know, if you lose too fast your body will start eating its own muscle. You did good today, but I think you could have done better."

"Oh." I look toward the floor then back at Matt. "Well, it eats its own fat too though, right?"

"Yeah—"

"And I didn't sleep well last night, so that's probably why."

"I just want to make sure you're doing this safely," he says, helping me up. "So it's maintainable, so when you start eating for maintenance your body doesn't think it needs to put on extra pounds in case you go into starvation mode again."

"I'm not in starvation mode."

"I just want to make sure you're not. You're looking a little too slender for my liking," he says with a teasing tone. I'm frustrated, but glad that he's noticed. "Seriously though," he takes hold of my upper arm and gives it a little jiggle, "I'm sure you had more muscle tone a few weeks ago. Losing it at this point, instead of gaining, it's not a good sign."

I follow Matt to the scale and step on. He adjusts the lever then stares at it a moment too long. He returns his gaze to me then motions for me to step off. "You've lost a lot."

"Yeah," I say. "But if my calculations are right, I'm still pretty much on pace, like I have been."

Matt tilts his head back and forth, as if he's searching for the right words. "You're already where you should be, weight-wise. Really, you don't need to lose anymore, just tone up. And if the weight keeps coming off, I wouldn't want to see any more than half a pound a week, maybe even every two weeks, accepting the fact that some weeks you'll lose nothing."

"I'd barely make my goal weight in time!" I say, my voice raising more than I want it to.

"You've made your goal weight range." He speaks slowly, annunciating each word. "You're already at a perfectly healthy weight. You don't need to lose anymore. You could, but you don't need to."

"I've still got this." I grab a hunk of fat from my middle and squeeze it to show him. "That's not healthy."

"It's fine," he says. "Curves." His smile is so wonderful, but I resist its charms.

"Autumn couldn't grab onto a hunk like that."

"You're not Autumn."

"But—"

"Autumn has been working out and eating well her whole life. A lot of what you grabbed there was probably loose skin. You've got to give it time to firm up, and if you lose too fast, it may never."

"Matt—"

"Have you been following my food guidelines? I think you should up your intake a bit."

I meet his gaze. "I've been going under, under the minimum."

"Every meal?"

"Pretty much."

Matt lets out a long puff of air. "Jenn," he says, a mix of concern and frustration in his voice. "You're supposed to eat meals in a wide caloric range. The minimum shouldn't be eaten more than three to four meals a week. That keeps your metabolism guessing. You may be losing now, but if you don't up the intake you're going to plateau big time, and maybe gain."

"But—"

"If you don't up your food intake, I can't in good conscience keep training you."

"But I'm so close to where I want to be. I'm almost there."

Matt steps toward me and puts his hand on my shoulder. "Listen, Jenn, it's not healthy, this obsession with a specific number. I don't even know what number it is you're working toward. You're in the range we talked about now. You told me that your goal was health and fitness. You're there. There's no way the few extra pounds you think you have on you are going to raise any health concerns. But starving yourself? That will."

"You don't understand, okay?" I'm trying to keep the desperation out of my voice. "This is important to me. It just is. I do have a goal," I plead, "a specific number." Despite not wanting them to, the tears start coming. I don't want Matt to stop training me—I can't let that happen. And I don't want to keep lying to him, but I can't eat more. I can't see the scale stop yet, or even go up. "I've worked so hard."

"Jenn," he puts both hands on my shoulders now, "calm down. I'm just asking you to eat enough food to support all this work you're doing, to make sure you continue to lose at a healthy rate and don't plateau, don't start putting weight back on again. You need to trust me, okay?" I stare at him. "You're holding too much stake in this idea you've got in your head, this image, this number. What's it for, Jenn? You're healthy, you're a good healthy weight, and you're strong. That's beautiful. That's all you need."

"I just…you don't understand," I say again. "I need to reach my goal. I need to be the woman I'm supposed to be." I feel stupid as I say this. I know he won't get it, but I have to tell him. I have to make him understand.

He pulls his hands away and looks at me like I'm a question. "You are the woman you're meant to be. You always have been. Weight doesn't change that." He looks at me a moment more. "Being some arbitrary weight can't make you happy, can't change your life. You're the only one who can do that, and what you've done these past months, all the work you've put in, that was always inside of you. You've always been whatever person you're trying to be."

We're having a bit of a stare down and as much as I want him to, as wonderful as I think he is, I know he just doesn't understand. He probably never will. He's never been fat. He has no idea what it's like to be fat. He has no idea of the cruel world I was living in—the world I still live in. I may not be fat anymore, but I'm far from the ideal. I want to be perfect. I'm not even where I need to be yet, hell, where I'm destined to be, and already I can see the difference in the way people look at me, how they respond to my smile, how they don't shy away from me, how they no longer avert their gaze. I'm one of them now, better than many. There are probably some who wish they were me. People seem happy to be around me now, rather than just waiting for the moment when someone better comes into view. I smiled at a woman and her child on the bus the other day, a pretty woman, and she started chatting to me, making small talk. That's never happened before. Matt has no idea and he never will. I felt my ribs the other day. My ribs! I turned this way and that and I could see their outline in the mirror. It was incredible. I'm almost there. Being some arbitrary weight can't make me happy, he says, can't change my life. He has no idea.

I end our stare down by looking away. I'll tell him what he needs to hear. I can't risk angering him or, even worse, losing him. I need him to help me through these last seventeen pounds, and I need him to still care for me, still be there with me when I've made it. Once he sees me as my perfect self and knows all that I've gone through to get there, realizes it was largely for him, maybe then he'll understand.

"I'm sorry, Matt," I say. "You're right. I know you're right. I guess I just got a little obsessed." I shrug my shoulders and offer a self-deprecating laugh. "I've been working so hard, you know? And I felt like my results were slowing. I wanted to amp things up a bit. But if you say that's not safe, that's not the way to do things, then I'll believe you." He nods his head, not quite looking at me. I reach my hand up, touch his arm. "We okay?" I ask, smiling sweetly, as beguiling as I can muster. "You still my trainer?"

He grins when he makes eye contact again. "For now," he says, "until you get to that arbitrary goal you have." His tone teases, almost mocks when he says the word 'arbitrary.' "Or until I decide you've gone far enough. This goal you have, you may not get there. It may not be possible while still maintaining health and strength. But for now, you have strength to gain, and I'll help you gain it." He pauses. "After that we'll just be friends, okay?" I smile at this, and warm to the touch of his hands as he places them along my arms. His face is so close to mine. "We'll be family." All the warmth washes away.

CHAPTER FIFTEEN

Back at home I stare in the mirror and try to see what Matt sees—a healthy, strong woman who doesn't need to lose any more weight. I can't. I can almost see her, she's there, but she's hiding behind at least eight to ten pounds of disgusting fat, maybe more. Matt may think he knows what he's talking about but I know my body, and I know what's been working for my body. If my metabolism needs to be tricked, needs to never know what's coming, then that's what I'll give it. I'll stick to the minimum meal guideline in general but then throw in some even lighter calorie meals and days. That will give these last pounds something to battle with. Those pesky little fat cells will have no choice but to let go.

I GO THROUGH THE NEXT week like a machine—workouts, writing assignments, carefully monitoring every morsel that enters my body. I look forward to weigh-in day with excitement, to that moment when I'll know I've proved Matt's theory wrong. I'm tempted to do my own weigh-in a day early but decide to wait until after my scheduled training session, that way I won't have to hide the cocky expression I know will be plastered across my face. Not that I want to feel cocky about it...I'm sure Matt thinks he was giving me the best advice. I'm sure he meant well.

When I get to the gym I feel ready. I'm going to give it my all. I'm going to work as if my life depends on it. After the warmup we start with squat jumps, and despite pushing as hard as I can, I'm not going as high as I usually do. Each time I squat, it's harder to get back up. In the weight room, I can't even make my regular reps, which is especially bad since this is the day I'm supposed to up them.

"That's enough for now," Matt says as I struggle through a dead-lift. "How about we move onto sprints?"

"Yeah, sure." I paste on a smile and wipe the sweat from my brow. After the first three I'm struggling to catch my breath. By the fifth, I feel as if my chest is about to burst. I stop at the end of the sixth, knowing I can't go on. I stoop over, bracing my arms on my knees, my head dipped between my legs, willing the spinning to stop. Matt places his hands on my back and bends so our faces are only inches apart.

"You okay?"

I nod and smile, too out of breath to speak.

"You've been eating, like I said?"

I nod again, even though it's a lie.

"Okay." Matt stands. "Well, lets end the workout here for today."

I shake my head and wave my arm. "I'm okay." I push out a grin. "I just needed a little breather."

"Nah," he says, "you've done well, but I think your body is telling you you need a break. Maybe you're coming down with something. Whatever it is, you're done for today." I give in, knowing I can do my own HIIT workout once I get home to make up for it...after a nap, perhaps. "I have something I want to show you, anyway."

I smile and nod as my breath starts to even out and follow Matt to his office. He closes the door behind us then heads to his desk. He grabs a box, holds it behind his back, and smiles like a four-year-old boy on Christmas morning. Just as I'm about to question him, he whips his hand around to reveal a beautiful diamond and sapphire ring. It's not too big, not too small. Like the proverbial bowl of porridge, it's just right, and I'm breathless again.

"Well," Matt's voice is excited, eager for my approval, "what do you think?"

"It's, uh…" I look up at him, into his waiting eyes, and see the hope and excitement and iota of fear that lives there. "It's perfect." It's so perfect I'm afraid Autumn will be swept away by it, but I quickly comfort myself—there's no way. They've barely even been dating for a year and Autumn was talking just last week about branching out, starting her own gym. She's also talked about doing that backpacking tour of Europe she's always dreamed of. She wants to travel the world. When we were teens, she couldn't talk about her dream of travelling Europe without talking about all those sexy, accented men. Meeting them won't be much fun if she's married.

I reassure myself—things will work out perfectly. Autumn's already thinking of quitting her job, taking that trip, returning to open a gym, and this ring will be the perfect incentive. She'll turn Matt down, quit her job, leave for Europe, and I'll be here to pick up the pieces. My smile becomes genuine and I whisper. "Absolutely perfect."

"I know," says Matt. "It is, isn't it? I got one with the sapphire in it 'cause of her birthday. I knew it was kinda risky, but I didn't want something too standard, too much like any other ring, you know? I wanted something unique, original. Just like Autumn." I nod. "So, you think she'll like it?" He looks to the ring before looking back at me. "You're sure it's not too out there?"

"No," I say. "She'll love it. How could anyone not?"

"I'm going to propose tonight. I have this whole thing planned, I…" he pauses, "well, I'll let Autumn tell you all about it afterwards. She'll want to."

"Of course." I offer a tight-lipped smile. "Sounds awesome." As I see how hopeful he is, how expectant that she'll say yes, my eagerness for him to be mine is overshadowed by the pain I know he'll soon feel. No one deserves that kind of heartbreak. I have to try to lessen it in some way. "Matt, have you and Autumn ever actually talked about marriage? Does she know it's coming? Is this something she wants?"

"Well," he says, closing the box and securing it back in his desk. "We've talked about marriage hypothetically, dreams for the future, you know? Not in concrete terms."

"So, what if she's not ready for it? I mean I'm excited for you, I really am. And I know Autumn cares for you, but she's always been a lone wolf, despite usually having a guy on her arm. She has her own dreams, her own goals, she's—"

"I know," he says, "and I won't take any of that from her. I'll be part of her dreams. We'll be part of each other's dreams. Like we are now. Those other guys," he shakes his head, "they didn't get Autumn. They treated her like she was some prize. They didn't see the true treasure she is. Trust me, Jenn, what Autumn and I have, it's different. I'm not worried." He laughs. "Well, maybe a little worried, a little nervous. But that's normal. Nerves, you know. Excitement." He stops. "You don't think she'll say no, do you? She didn't say anything to—"

"No." I cut him off. "We've never talked about it, about you, in that way."

"Good," he says, then stares into my eyes again, his smile almost bursting. "I feel like this is the first day of the rest of my life. I just had to tell someone. And I should have made you promise before showing you." He laughs again. "Not a word of it to Autumn, okay?"

"I wouldn't dream of it." He leads me out into the training area to go through my stretches. It's a shock that he's proposing so soon. but it will be okay. At the rate I'm progressing it'll be just a few weeks before I've reached my goal. He'll need some time to grieve, to mourn, and during that time if he's a decent guy, which I know he is, he won't even be able to notice my body, the intricacies of it. Still, I'll call the salon Autumn frequents when I get home and make an appointment for tomorrow. Starting now, I'm going to focus on not just being the best I can be, but looking the best I can look, in every way possible. I'm already amazed at the difference just spending some extra time on my hair and makeup can make. Once I get some professionals to show me how it's done, who knows, I may be irresistible. I smile at the thought. Who knew—me, irresistible? Not even Cinderella's transformation will compare to mine.

I GET HOME. I TAKE that needed nap. I finish up some edits for an assignment. I make the salon appointment. And then I bounce around. I need to make up for those missed sprints. High Intensity Interval Training—I love it. It's ninety seconds of work, thirty rest, for five rounds. It's intervals on steroids. After a quick warm up, I launch right into it—full burpees with a wide squat and pike jump. When I finish that round, I'm panting heavier than during the sprints and my head feels woozy. The thirty second rest goes by far too fast, but when the buzzer sounds, I transition right into lunge jumps, propelling myself in the air and landing in an opposite lunge each time. I don't even make it half through the set when I have to stop—my legs burning and my chest tight. I tell myself I am powerful, I am strong, I can do this, and manage two more jumps before the buzzer goes. I'm just starting squat jumps with a kettle bell when the room spins and I collapse to the floor, the kettle bell landing just past my right ankle. I roll to my hands and knees and pant there, like a dog, then propel my body forward and puke into the wastebasket against the wall. I stay on my hands and knees, gulping for breaths, my heart racing. I gaze at the little bit of food that came out of me.

My mind travels back to that on the hill when I couldn't get my heart to stop racing, and how scared I was that my mother's fate was about to be mine too.

I concentrate on my breathing and after a few minutes I feel my pulse returning to normal, like it should. I'm living in a different body now. I don't have to have the fears that plagued me all those months ago. Fat isn't clogging up my arteries and stressing out my heart. This reaction still worries me though, and I think maybe Matt was right, maybe I am coming down with something, but then I figure, ah well, this just means I'll have even less in me to take to the scale tomorrow morning. Bulimic thoughts dance through my head but I push them away. I'm never going down that road again—I tried it for two weeks in junior high and quickly decided I liked my food too much to see the way it looked coming up.

This little collapse and fainting spell are nothing—a virus, lack of sleep maybe. I'll take some extra vitamins. I'll go to bed early to give my body its needed rest. I'll kick whatever bug is bugging me. There's no other explanation for how tired I am.

Since going to bed early means I won't be burning any calories, I skip dinner and, after watching a couple of episodes of one of my favourite sitcoms, crawl under the covers at seven thirty. I lay in bed for over an hour, my limbs restless, and in that odd state between sleep and wakefulness images of Autumn and Matt, married, happy, with four perfect little children following them around, float through my head. I comfort myself with the knowledge that Autumn's got bigger dreams. She will turn him down, and then I'll be there. It's going to be me, Matt, and our four perfect little children. With those thoughts in my mind, I drift into a deep sleep.

❧

I WAKE THE NEXT MORNING and try to hit the snooze button. I'm not ready to face the world. After slapping it several times, I realize it's my apartment buzzer coming through my phone and not my alarm that's roused me. I climb out of bed, reach for the phone, pick up, and my voice groggy, ask who it is. Autumn's voice bursts through the intercom and I pull my head away to buzz her in before hearing what she has to say. I grab a sweatshirt and pull it on over my tank top. I shrug and don't worry about the short shorts I have on. I could actually wear them in public now—my legs wouldn't shock and appal. My hand grasps the doorknob just as Autumn knocks. When I open it she pushes through and is so squealy and twirly I can hardly make out her words, but as I watch her, my memory of the day before races back in—this isn't the behaviour of a woman who just crushed a man she cares about. Not at all. Autumn finally sets her bag on the coffee table and plops down on my couch, holding out her hand with the sparkling, perfect ring on her finger.

"Matt proposed?"

"Yeah, he proposed!" she squawks. "Did you not hear a word I just said? And he told me he showed you the ring." She laughs. "I'd be mad I wasn't the first to know if I weren't so happy."

"And you said yes?"

"No," says Autumn, letting her hand drop. "I said no but wanted to keep the ring anyway." I sit back and stare until she laughs. "Of course I said yes. Isn't it beautiful?" She fawns over the ring and the room seems a little off centre. I squint my eyes and look again. "Here," she says, opening the bag, "I brought celebratory cupcakes!" She laughs. "It's a day for indulgences."

"No."

She opens the bag and brings out two large cupcakes, setting one in front of each of us. "Don't worry," Autumn laughs again, and I can't figure out what's so funny. "They're made with honey, coconut oil, and some oat flour too—tons of nutrition in these babies."

I push the cupcake aside. "But Autumn," I lean forward, "how can you? Why did you? What about your dreams? You can't just give them up. You were going to quit your job, tour Europe—"

"I'll still do that," she says, "just a little further down the road. We've got it all planned out. We're both going to work a little longer, save up for the wedding and the trip. We'll take a three-month backpacking honeymoon and then come back and open up a studio together. We'll focus about three years on the business, and then come the babies!" She laughs again. "Jenn, I couldn't be happier. I never thought I'd find a guy like Matt. So many of the others…well, you know. But he's the whole package, isn't he?"

"Yeah." I nod, dumbfounded. "Sure is." Autumn un-peels her cupcake then takes a big bite. "But Autumn," I rest a hand on her arm, "how are you going to run a business if you have kids? How will you get and keep clients?" I'm grasping here, and it's disgusting. I know it's disgusting, but I can't stop myself. "You're not thinking this through. No one wants to take fitness training from a tubbo."

"Jenn," she says, pausing just before taking a bite, "I won't be a tubbo. I'll be pregnant, and then I'll be a mother getting rid of her baby weight. People will understand that. Women will probably be inspired by that. My dream isn't to train Olympians or something. I want to train real people, normal people, with life struggles and commitments that get in the way of their fitness goals. I want to show them how they can work through all that."

"Autumn," I lean back again, "it seems like you're rushing into things. I mean how well do you even know

Matt? Really know him? At first you thought some of the other guys were gems and then—" I know I shouldn't be saying this, I know I shouldn't be thinking what I am—but it's not fair. Autumn's had everything laid out on a platter for her—most beautiful, great grades, popular. She's hardly had to work for anything. She doesn't deserve Matt. I deserve him. I've worked so hard to be someone good enough. She was just born that way.

"Jenn," she snaps, then softens, "you're supposed to be happy for me. You're supposed to be excited with me. Training's a job anyway, just a job. People will still want me to train them. And this," she wags her hand, "this is life. This is what life is about. Aren't you happy for me?"

"Of course, of course." I look away and then down at the cupcake. I love Autumn. I do. I want her to be happy. I just never thought…I look back up. "I just need to know you're happy and sure, really sure, not just excited. Not just swept up by a beautiful ring and the idea of this life you've always wanted." I lean forward again and place my hand on her knee. "I love you, Autumn. I only want what's best for you." And I do. I really do.

Autumn's quiet a moment. She seems to assess my words, then she bounds off the chair and onto the couch beside me, grasping both of my hands in hers. "Matt's best for me," she says. "I know it. And you're going to be my maid of honour."

I swallow at her words and remember the person I want to be, the person I'm meant to be, the person who takes joy in the happiness of others, without bitterness, without resentment. Not the person who was just trying to dissuade her cousin from marrying the man she clearly loves. I see it now. This is different. It's always been different with her and Matt. I just didn't want it to be. I smile. I return her hug. I eat the cupcake and listen, trying to focus as she goes on and on about the plans and details, as she tells me how excited Aunt Lucille was, how she offered to cover the cost of the dress, and how Uncle Leo said they'd be covering a heck of a lot more than that.

After all of this, she sits back and stares at me for a moment, like she's seeing me for the first time today. She smiles. "You're looking amazing, by the way. Not that you didn't look good before. You've always been beautiful. Your goal though, you must be there?"

"You've been talking to Matt?" I try not to let my annoyance come through.

"No. Not about that. I can just see it. Why, what did he say?"

"Nothing." I wrap my arms around my middle, feeling self-conscious at her assessment. "I don't look great yet. Not like you."

"What do you mean?"

"What do you think I mean? Come on, Autumn."

"What?" Her eyes widen.

"You're perfect."

She laughs. "Perfect?"

"Yeah. And it's so easy for you. Always the beautiful one, always the—"

"It's not easy," she says. "Yeah...I guess, I mean, people think I'm beautiful. But that's hard too. It's certainly not easy. Do you have any idea how much I work out?"

"Yes, but—"

"And the time I spend on my hair, my skin regime, just to live up to people's expectations of how I look?"

"You don't even need to—"

"Even one pimple used to terrify me—the way it marred what everyone told me was a perfect complexion. And the way men view me as an object, a conquest? It's..." she shakes her head. "I don't know. I know you've always thought you were judged by your looks, that it's been hard for you." She pauses. "I've been judged too."

"It's not the same th—"

"Maybe not, but it still sucks sometimes. All those guys,

153

all those jerks…Matt's the only one who seemed to really see me, you know?" I stare at her, amazed that I've never considered most of what she's telling me. I know about the guys. They did treat her like a trophy, but I never thought about the rest of it, the expectation. "All you've done, all the weight you've lost, what really matters is how much healthier you are. How you were able to take that amazing hike with us. How you had a goal and how you stuck to it."

"I guess."

"Anyway," says Autumn, offering a slight smile. "I've probably taken up enough of your morning." She stands and so do I. We hug. "See you soon?"

"Sure."

When Autumn leaves I try to shrug off her words, not wanting to accept or think about them. She's still lucky. She shouldn't compare her situation to mine. I'd looked at Autumn in the past sometimes, trying to figure out what life was like inside her head. I'd imagined it was a constant stream of happiness, or at least contentment. The only time I've ever seen her truly sad or worried for more than a few minutes at a time was when her father was sick. But even then she was showered with love from the people around her, so many people. When my mom died Autumn was almost the only one who did any showering.

I return to the couch and sink into the cushions. I feel even more tired than I did when I went to bed last night. It's a different kind of exhaustion though. I'm drained. Positively drained, and after a few minutes of sitting there, absolutely spent, I realize I'm crying. The tears leak out unobtrusively.

With Matt's announcement yesterday and Autumn's visit today, I'd forgotten my weigh-in. I've done amazing this week, and the way I feel right now, I need the boost the scale is sure to give me. I peel myself up from the couch and head to the bathroom. I've already eaten—that cupcake— but I step on the scale anyway. It was a light thing. It couldn't have weighed more than a couple of ounces. I look at the scale, step off, then step back on. I step off, pick up the scale, turn it over, pop the batteries out and scrounge through the drawer for new ones. I step back on. The batteries were fine. I'm up four pounds. I step off. I grab my face wash and hurl it at the window. The lid pops open and peach tinted cream makes a Rorschach against the glass. I turn to the mirror, and based on the reflection I see, it might as well have been forty pounds.

I've practically starved myself the past month and I gain four pounds? It doesn't make sense. I rack my brain, trying to think if I'm forgetting something. Did I have a big cheat I can't remember? Did I miss a workout?

No. I was perfect. I. Was. Perfect. I head to my kitchen and open the cupboards, the pantry. I slam the doors shut. Not a sliver of junk. They might as well be empty. What's the point of trying, if this is what I get? I pull on a pair of pants and grab my purse.

CHAPTER SIXTEEN

When I step out the front door of my apartment's lobby, the sun beats down on me, letting me know I'm ridiculously overdressed. No matter. I book it to the corner store and pick up a large bag of regular ripple chips and a tub of vanilla ice cream. Back home, they feel so good going down it makes me bawl. And as I'm eating and crying and wiping the tears and snot with my arm, not even half-way finished, another feeling creeps upon me. I propel myself to the bathroom with the urge to bring it all back up. This is a legitimate urge. My stomach rolls. But I don't let myself have that relief. Instead, I lie on the bathroom floor, writhing in agony, and only part of the pain comes from the trash I've just stuffed into my shrunken stomach.

After the ache starts to subside and I become aware of the cool tile, after my eyes fully adjust to the bright light above me, I realize Matt may have been right. His guidelines were based on portion sizes and despite telling myself I'd never count calories, I've been counting like a madwoman. His recommendation worked out to about a 1200 a day minimum, with days when I went high above that to compensate for the workouts. 1200 has been my maximum. Many days I've barely swallowed 850 calories. It doesn't make sense; with those numbers I've barely eaten enough the whole week to gain four pounds. It must be what he said—my body's holding onto everything it can to survive.

My determination has gotten me this far, my determination is what I've been so proud of, and now it's my blind determination that's put me on the bathroom floor, writhing in pain. All for a number on a scale. A scale! I've never felt so stupid in my life.

I seem to lose sense of time as I lie there on the cold hard floor. It could be twenty minutes, it could be sixty. Slowly, the pain in my gut fully subsides and with it goes the feeling that everything I've been working toward is pointless. It's not pointless. This is just one minor setback.

It's my chime from my phone that gets me to roll over, get off the floor, and stand. I go to the kitchen where it sits on the counter and open the new text. It's from Tammy—*Taboo, 10:30 tonight. Please, oh, please. I miss you! xo*—I'm not even sure of the last time I saw Tammy. Maybe thirty-five pounds ago? I'd been coming up with reasons to avoid her barbeque's and dinners out. At least this was after dinner. I look at the clock. My appointment at the salon is in forty-five minutes. If I don't go, I'll probably spend the whole day moping in this apartment, wallowing in self-pity, and finishing the bag of chips and tub of ice cream. *Sure thing,* I write back. *I miss you too.*

I jump in the shower and am in and out in seven minutes. I don't need to worry about my hair, and luckily I shaved yesterday. On my walk to the bus stop, I try to silence the thoughts swirling in my mind. Matt loves Autumn. Autumn loves Matt. Matt is going to marry Autumn. Matt is not going to marry me. As I say these words in my mind, I know they all make sense. I know it was ludicrous for me to think Matt and I would end up together, for me to let myself feel about Matt the way I did. It was ludicrous for so many reasons. He's practically perfect and I'm...me. If I'm really honest with myself, I'm not even sure I felt that strongly about Matt, not really. I think maybe it was the idea of him I was so attracted to, what he represented.

It seems so clear now, anything I thought I saw from him, any indication he returned my feelings in some small way, must have been the trainer client relationship. By the time the bus arrives I've made a decision: I'm not going to think about it, any of it, at all. Matt may have been my biggest motivation in transforming myself from the monster who people stared at and whispered about to the girl who cute guys happily give up their seats on the bus for, but he wasn't my only motivation.

I smile back at the cute guy then stare straight ahead, pretending to be engrossed in the music my earphones signify I'm listening to. It doesn't matter that the batteries died on the walk over and there's no sound. Things aren't always as they seem and sometimes that's a good thing.

I walk into the salon with a sashay that's almost become natural. No one turns their head in shock to see me there, to see someone like me spending that kind of money on her appearance. The ladies are polite and friendly and helpful. They walk me through a white hall and into a secondary salon area. They introduce me to my stylist and sit me in a tall white swivel chair.

"I want the whole deal," I say. "Hair and nails and skin and makeup, and I want you to show me how to be my best me, to look like a natural beauty."

"But you already are," the stylist gushes. "Of course," she adds, "makeup can pronounce the natural beauty you already possess. If a person hasn't got it already," she bends down and whispers like she's sharing a secret, "there is not a whole lot we can do." She says it like this information is only for a private club of beautiful women and, naturally, I'm a card-holding member.

୭

I GLIMPSE MYSELF IN a store window as I leave the salon. My hair is gently curled, my eyes look larger and more alert, my skin appears flawless, and I'm walking like I'm somebody. Somebody who isn't afraid to catch her reflection in a public space, who is actually pleased by the little confidence burst. I'm not where I want to be, where I will be, but in these clothes it's hardly noticeable. I look good. A bikini would tell another story, but I'm not wearing a bikini tonight. Tonight, I'll look fabulous. I'll be fabulous. And no one will know any different.

Rather than catch the bus home, I walk down Spring Garden Road, eyeing the shops. I step into a boutique I've never even thought to enter before, with a mission to pick out a new outfit for the club. Taboo is a mix of swanky upscale dress and casual attire. Upscale is definitely what I'm going for. I try on seven dresses before finding the perfect one. The tight ruching around the torso hides the flaws and bulges that still linger on my frame, and it's a size six. A six! Not wanting to take the dress off, I stand, turning this way and that, admiring my figure in the mirror until at last I peel out of it and pick a few other outfits that show off my new shape. As I'm walking to the bus, I see a shoe sale and decide a new dress deserves a new pair of shoes. A sexy pair of shoes.

On the way home I cringe at how much money I just spent, but my work is going well, and it'll be worth it—I can take on a few extra assignments, no big deal. When I think back to who I was, how miserable I felt just ten months ago, it's mind boggling. A large credit card bill is more than worth how amazing I feel in my new look. At this moment, I barely care about those four extra pounds. With everything going so right, for a moment there's a part of me that even thinks Matt will somehow be mine, but then I think of the joy in Autumn's eyes, how excited Matt was to show me the ring, and I know that's not true. I don't even want it to be true.

From my seat on the bus I watch the city go by, then watch as a man around my age jogs up the street. His chest glistens, his muscles are perfectly cut, his jaw is chiselled. He catches my eye through the window and I can't be sure, but I think he smiles at me. I turn from him, my smile growing large. Matt may have been my goal, but perhaps he's just what I needed to get where I'm going. Matt's not perfect, after all, and he's not the only guy out there. I glance back again to the jogger, but he's almost out of view. I've never believed everything happens for a reason, but maybe it does. It's a comforting thought. Maybe Matt was the motivation I needed to do all this. He thinks I could have done it on my own, and maybe I could have, but that's doubtful. I was at a stalemate before training with him. I was bored with my workouts and frustrated with my slow progress. He changed that.

I think back to my reflection in the change room mirror. I looked damn good in that mirror. Damn good. Those four pounds this morning could have been anything—water weight, some fluke of my upcoming period. I have noticed that my weight loss seems to slow in a monthly pattern. But I'm not sick, so the fatigue, the dizziness, makes me think I haven't been giving my body what it needs. Starting tomorrow I'll go back to Matt's calorie mix-up schedule, keeping to his guidelines but still adding in my extra turbo workouts here and there. That should do the trick. Tonight though, tonight I'm going to celebrate how far I've come. Tonight, I'm having fun. Tonight, I will get my first taste of what it is to be the skinny girl. I laugh out loud at the thought, and don't even care that a couple people on the bus glance over at me. And I'll be Autumn's maid of honour. I'll wear a beautiful dress—Autumn isn't the type to make her bridesmaids look grotesque so she shines—and who knows, maybe I'll even meet my Mr. Right at the wedding. Maybe.

∞

AS I'M GETTING READY later that night, I push Matt's smile from my mind. I'll still see the smile, and I'll smile back as we go through our training sessions, though maybe he's right and it's almost time for me to handle things on my own. When I put on the dress and add my new heels, I'm even more amazed at how good I look. No, at how sexy I look. Me. Sexy. Me—an object of desire. Me, a woman who will turn heads.

Noticing the dress' cut, I decide I need a little something to accent the empty space where the neckline plunges. I search my jewellery, wondering the last time I even opened it. I so rarely wear jewellery. When I looked as hideous as I did, I didn't see the point. As I'm scrounging through, searching for something that will work, I come across a box I took from Mom's house. Most of her stuff went into storage since I wasn't ready to go through it and couldn't bear to just get rid of it all. She kept her best items in this jewellery box though, and the guy at the storage depot looked shady.

I carefully lift the box and carry it over to the bed, set it down, open the cover, and pick out the top item. I close my eyes and see my mother: her smiling face, the tilt of her head, the sparkle of these dangly diamond earrings against her jawline. They were one of her prized possessions. Just possessions, though, she'd say, but if you're going to possess something…she'd tilt her head, letting the light catch the jewels, and laugh.

I don't know how much time passes as I lay out the items, remembering them on her, remembering her. I haven't thought much about Mom these past few months.

I've been too focused on me. I hold up a necklace I think may work, turn toward the mirror, and clasp it around my neck. It's perfect. It's beautiful. Mom would agree. Staring at my reflection, I wonder what Mom would think of this woman who is staring back at me. Of course Mom wanted to lose weight—she would have liked to be the woman she once was, but not at the cost of no longer enjoying life.

That was always her problem, our problem, we bonded over food. It was how we connected. I can't help but wonder if what I've accomplished would have been possible if Mom were still living. I was able to push Tammy and the temptation she brings out of my life easy enough, but I couldn't have done the same thing with Mom. She wouldn't have let me. And Mom needed her food—more and more after Dad left. She didn't talk about it much, but the divorce devastated her, the affair. Despite her efforts at beauty, despite her joyful demeanour and positive attitude, I know she didn't believe she would ever attract another man. Food made her feel good. It was the one thing that would never judge her...really the one thing. Even I judged her. Not to her face perhaps, not even always consciously, but I did.

All at once I want her to be here, helping me try on her jewellery, but I'm also somewhat relieved she's not. I couldn't have told her about my feelings for Matt, about my hopes. She would have been so disappointed in me. I couldn't have told her about the way I turned down Rajeev, or the reason—that he wasn't good enough for me, perfect enough for me. What would that have said about how I viewed her? How would that have confirmed her thoughts she wasn't good enough for any man—not anymore at least?

Mom always told me, when I'd come home from school crying or even when Billy had been the cause of my tears, that true beauty was something that was inside us, that was determined by our character, our goodness, our resiliency, not by a number on the scale, not by a pant size. I never believed her then and, looking into the mirror, I can't believe her now. Beauty may be in the eye of the beholder but…I don't even know how to finish that thought. I close the jewelry box, put it back in the drawer, and glance at the clock. I need to leave. I'm already going to be late. Tonight is about fun. Tonight is about being sexy. It is not about thinking about dead mothers and their long dead words. Tonight is about my new life.

CHAPTER SEVENTEEN

I spot Tammy and a few of our girlfriends—her girlfriends, really—before they spot me. They see me, but glance over and then look away. It feels good not to be recognized. They're all dressed up—hair and makeup done—but none of their effort hides how overweight they are. None of them are as big as Tammy, but they all have some serious weight to lose. I feel pity for them, knowing I was once there, remembering how horrible it was. It's like they can't even see what I see—they're all smiling and laughing and seem to be having a great time. They can't be though. Not really. No one can be happy carrying all that extra fat on their bodies. I never was. When I used to come out with them, I didn't bother with the big charade. As long as my hair was combed, and I was wearing clean clothing, that was enough—I knew no one would be looking my way, anyway, and they never did. Well...almost never. Some of the other girls would get hit on from time to time, dance with a few guys, or get offered a drink—mostly by the chubby chasers or guys who were chubby themselves.

One night a guy actually came over to me. The scowl I wore whenever anyone looked my way not enough to scare him off. The rest of the girls had gone to dance or get their drinks refilled and I was sitting at the booth alone.

'What's your name?' he'd asked me.

'Why do you want to know?' I replied.

'I don't know.' He perched on the stool across from me.

He wasn't bad looking—for the standards I had then, anyway. 'You seem interesting.'

I'd rolled my eyes at that, taken another sip of my drink. 'I'm not. Just your average fat girl.'

'Why would you say that?' He stood. 'And why are you looking at me like I'm out to attack you?' He'd had a nice laugh and a friendly smile. He didn't seem like a creep, so he must have had low self-esteem to be talking to me.

'Look,' I sighed, 'I'm just here to hang out with my friends, have a little fun.'

'Are you having fun?' he asked. 'You sure don't look like it.'

'I was having fun,' I said, speaking a lie, 'until you came along.'

'All right, all right.' He took a step away. 'I'll leave you alone.' He started to walk away but turned back. 'You know though, you bring it upon yourself.'

'Bring what upon myself?' I snapped.

'Rejection.' He gave me one last smile. A small one. Then turned and walked away, for good that time.

I'd blown his comment off with a long swig of my drink, but it stayed with me, and it comes back now. I stand for a few moments near the bar and watch Tammy and the girls. They're laughing, they're talking, they look happy, relaxed, confident even. They look like they're good friends having fun. It doesn't seem like the act I always imagine it to be. It looks real. I, on the other hand, despite knowing I'm more appealing than any of them, had to go to the restroom the moment I came in the door to make sure the ruching on my dress was properly concealing the bulges my tummy taming underwear makes on my thighs and waist, to double check that my makeup and hair look fabulous. That's what tonight is about for me—looking fabulous. Is there something wrong with that? No, there's nothing wrong with that.

Yet, as much as I enjoyed the result I saw in the mirror, it's not until I down my first drink, standing at the bar watching the others enjoy themselves, that I stop feeling almost as out of place as I used to. I down my second, shake off my concern, tell myself I'm smokin', and walk over to the girls.

Tammy glances at me as I approach the table, then goes back to listening to Sophia tell a story. A moment passes as I step closer, then she whips her head my way. "Jennifer?"

"Hey gals," I say, giving my best smile. "How is everyone? It's been forever!"

All of them stop and stare, then the rounds of 'Wow' and 'You look great' and 'How did you do it?' begin.

"One at a time, one at a time," I say, setting my third drink of the night on the table.

"So, that's why you've been hiding away," says Yolanda. "You look like a different person."

"I feel like a different person," I say, sliding onto a stool.

"Well, you look it," says Samra. "Good for you."

As the questions continue at a slower pace, I answer them casually, like it's not that big of a deal, though I do admit I've worked really hard, found a killer-hot trainer who really knew how to push me, and that he's been a big motivation. I wink as I say this.

Tammy's kept quiet the whole time, though now she questions. "Isn't your trainer Autumn's boyfriend? Isn't that what you said?"

"Yeah," I say, annoyed by her question. "But there's no harm in noticing his looks. It would be impossible not to. Anyway, I didn't know he was going to be my trainer when I signed up." I shrug and toss a hand to the side, as if sweeping away her words. "It was fate I guess."

"I guess." Tammy purses her lips.

"Maybe I should get myself one of these super-hot trainers," says Samra, laughing. "Think I could look like you?"

"Sure," I say, "all of you could." I sense a shift in the mood as my words come out and add, "not that you need to, of course, it's just something I wanted to do, for me." I put my head down for a moment and use the card; "I mean, after my mom…" I let the words trail off.

Yolanda puts her hand on my arm. "We know," she says, "we can't imagine how that must have been for you, to—"

"Anyway," I say, letting my face brighten. I don't even want to think of Mom. Not now. "Tonight is about having a good time, right?"

"Yeah!" says Chrissy, the shyest girl in the group. "Having a trainer, that's all it took?"

"Well," I smile, "he was a full-service trainer. He assessed my goals, came up with a plan for me, including an eating plan," I let out a puff of air, "which was not the easiest thing in the world. But I was motivated and determined and when I started seeing the results, started feeling so much better, it just made it that much easier to stick to the plan and not indulge. It wasn't worth it to sabotage all that torture I was going through at the gym."

"Wow," says Chrissy, "I don't know that I could have that much discipline."

"You could," I say, "if you really wanted to."

"I don't know that I'd want to," says Tammy. "Give up chocolate? Give up French fries? Turn into a sweaty mess multiple times a week? No, thank you!" The other girls laugh and the conversation transitions to talking about Yolanda's new job at some marketing firm. Tammy casts me a look. I can't read it, but I sense it isn't good.

In some ways I'm having a better time with these girls than I usually do, but I still feel like an outcast. I don't belong. I glance at other tables, other groupings, and realize they're my people now, or at least closer to it than this group. I feel bad for thinking this, judging and assessing people based on their weight—the way so many have judged me. I've had similar thoughts before, obviously, but when I was including myself in the fat group, it seemed different.

Once we've all had another drink or two, some of the

girls head to the dance floor and for the first time I join them. Except for a couple of the dance inspired classes I've taken at the gym, it's the only time I've danced in public. Even at the one high school dance I went to I stood against the wall the whole time then left two hours early. But this is fun. One advantage to being the skinny girl in this group, I know I stand out. I know I look good, even if my moves are technically not as good as some of theirs. The way Yolanda and Sophia move their hips absolutely blows me away. They look beautiful. Sexy. Confident. We laugh and I let loose as they try to guide me, helping me follow their motions. I haven't felt this relaxed or happy since the day of the hike. Being tipsy probably contributes to the feeling, but what does that matter? For the first time in a long time I don't even care what I look like. I'm just having fun. On our way back to the table, sweaty and giggling, I'm intercepted by a brown-eyed wonder. I can tell, even through his dress shirt, that he works out.

"I couldn't help but notice you out there," he says, a practised drawl to his voice. "These ladies were teaching you to move, huh?"

"I guess so." I glance back to Yolanda and Sophia, who look thoroughly impressed. "Though I don't know how well I was catching on."

"Oh, you were doing all right." He grins. "Maybe I can offer you a drink then teach you some more moves." He scans me, head to foot. "What do you say?"

"Well," I glance again at the girls, who smile and nod, "sure, why not?" I follow him over to the bar and take the screwdriver he offers me.

"So," he says, "do you recognize me?"

"Recognize you?" My brow furrows. "Should I?"

"Aww, I'm hurt." He flashes a row of perfectly straight white teeth and leans in closer. "I've been noticing you, but you haven't noticed me."

"I guess not." I'm not sure if I should be curious or

nervous.

"Don't worry," he says. "I'm not a psycho or anything. I've just seen you at the gym. You go to Fit4Life, right?"

"Oh." Fear flashes through me that he knows what I was, "Yeah."

"Matt's your trainer," he says. "I've seen you work—you're intense."

"Thanks."

"I just started going there about a month ago, and you're one of the first things I liked about that gym."

Only a month. Relief floods me, followed by shock that he noticed me. Me. "Really," I say, trying to figure out what it is to flirt. "Then why'd you never talk to me before?"

"Well," he says, looking shy, "it's a little weird isn't it? A little invasive to go up to a woman while she's trying to get her workout on. I didn't want to seem too forward. You're always so focused."

"And it's less invasive here?" I tease.

"Well," he says, "that's what nightclubs," he raises his glass, "and alcohol is for, isn't it? Liquid courage."

"You need courage to talk to me?" I say, genuinely astonished that this guy could be insecure. He's so cute.

"Seems so." He flashes that smile again. "But I don't feel too shy right now." He sets down his drink and leans back. "You look good," he says, "really good. You are wearing that dress."

"Thanks." I try to ignore the cheesiness of his line, if you can even call it that.

"What's your name?"

"Jennifer."

"Jennifer," he says, then repeats it two times, like it's a new sound in his mouth. "I like that."

"And you are?" I give my most coy smile as I say this, leaning against the bar, matching my body language to his.

"I'm Marshall." He finishes his drink then motions to the bartender. "Two shots of tequila for me and the lady."

I'm pretty sure that screwdriver put me beyond tipsy, but I don't want to look inexperienced, so I take the drink when it's offered and do my shot—salt, lime, and all.

"Time to dance." He grabs my wrist and pulls me to the floor.

I'm nervous at first, uncertain, but as the liquor works its way into me, as Marshall's arms guide me, I relax and let the music move me. The room spins but I don't mind. All I'm thinking of is how good Marshall's hands feel on me. I find myself imagining they're Matt's hands and am transported to a state of ecstasy that turns into a torrent of guilt. I'm done with Matt. Done. Yet within moments, Marshall and Matt meld again in my mind until Marshall bends and joins his lips to mine, sending Matt out of my head completely.

It's not like I've never been kissed before. There was that game of spin the bottle in grade eight and one night in college when I'd gotten really loaded and made out with this chubby guy with braces from my Chemistry class—braces, in college, the poor guy—but I've never been kissed like this. It's a little intense, a little wet, but it's also good, so very good. Just as I pull my arms up to wrap them around his neck, a hand drags me away. "What," I snap, as Tammy's flushed face comes into view, "do you think you're doing?"

"I think I'm taking you home."

"You are not." I transition from a scowl to a smile. "I'm dancing here. With Mattall, Matshall." I laugh.

"Marshall, honey," he says, taking a step closer to us. "Marshall."

"No, you're not," says Tammy. "Whatever it is you're doing is not dancing."

"Seems like dancing to me," says Marshall.

"Right," says Tammy, turning from him. She focuses her gaze on me. "You're too drunk to do anything but go to bed."

"Maybe that's the plan," I say, joking, but then I wonder if my words could be true.

"It's not." She pulls me toward the edge of the dance-floor.

"Just a minute." I turn back to Marshall. "Just give me one minute." He shrugs his shoulders and goes to lean against a nearby bar. "Tammy," I say, turning on her. "I'm fine, okay?" I focus on my words, making sure they don't slur. "He's a nice guy. He's from my gym."

"You know him?" Her determination seems to waver.

"Well, no," I say, "but he said he goes to my gym. He said he's noticed me."

"Well, that's creepy."

"Tammy," I can't hide the annoyance in my voice, "what's your problem? I'm just having a little fun. I thought you always wanted me to have more fun."

"Not fun you'll regret tomorrow morning."

"What's to regret?" I whisper. "Maybe I'll finally get laid." I've never said anything like this before. There's never been anything to say. I giggle. "By something that isn't silicon," I whisper even lower.

"Jenn," she says, holding me close, "you've had way too much."

"I've only had…" I try to count but am a little uncertain. "Five? Or six maybe? No." I hold up my fingers, attempting to count on them. "Five, five for sure…if not seven. I don't know," I say, "but that's not that much."

"That wasn't that much maybe," she says, "when you were seventy pounds heavier, but now—"

"Seventy-nine," I say.

"What?"

"Seventy-nine pounds."

"Well, good for you," she says. "Good for you."

"You could do it too." My hand rests on her shoulder. "You could. If you didn't eat so much." I lean forward. "You don't have to be fat," I whisper. "You can be like me."

"I don't want to be like you." She shrugs away from my

hand. "I'm happy just the way I am."

"You're not happy." I return my grasp, using her shoulder as a support. "Fat people can't be happy. Fat people are losers." I draw out the final word like there's a string attached to it. "But me? I'm almost there. I'm so close to happy tonight I feel it."

She pushes me off of her, and I've never seen this look on her face. "Really, Jenn. You're happy? Or, sorry, close to it? You've been holding in your gut all night, checking yourself out in every mirror or glass surface you've passed. You're about to go home with some strange man who could be a serial rapist for all you know. That's happy?" The room's really spinning now, and Tammy leads me over to a stool by our table. She grasps my arm so firm she leaves red marks on it.

"Take this." She hands me her water.

I take a few swigs then put it down. "You're just jealous," I sneer.

"What?"

"You're just jealous that now I'm getting all the attention. That the hot sexy guy wants me, and you," I laugh, "you're stuck with Colin."

Tammy takes a step back, as if I've hit her. "You know," she says, "I was trying to be understanding when you kept blowing me off. I was trying to think of it from your perspective. You had this goal and it would have been hard for you to keep to your plan and see me eat what I wanted. I couldn't figure out why we couldn't do other things though. The movies?"

"Popcorn," I interject.

"I could have skipped the popcorn, if you'd asked," she says, and I think she may be crying, but my own eyes are too blurred to tell. "I would have. Because I thought this was about health, about your mom. But it's just about you hating yourself, and hating me too, hating everyone who doesn't fit your ideal. You think I'm jealous of you, do you? Well, you've got it all wrong, Miss. Hot Stuff. I pity you."

I stare at her and blink away my disbelief. "You pity me?"

"Yeah," she says, "I do. Go off if you want. The two of you probably deserve each other."

"We do," I say, only understanding her meaning later. I down the rest of the water and hop off the stool.

"Jenn," she says, and I turn. "Just don't be too stupid, okay? Use protection."

"Whatever," I say, no longer looking at her.

CHAPTER EIGHTEEN

I wobble my way across the club back to Marshall. The shoes I'm wearing are entirely too tall.

"You're back." He gives a slow grin.

"I'm back." What is meant to be an enticing smile slinks onto my lips.

"What do you say we get out of here?"

"Sure."

He keeps a hand on my elbow and the support is welcome, especially as we make our way down the steep flight of stairs. He hails a cab then opens the door for me when it pulls up to the curb. "What's the address?" he asks and I'm shocked that he expects we're going to my place. I hesitate and mumble something about not knowing if I want to tell him. "I've got a roommate." He rubs a hand along the back of my neck. "Can't we go to your place?"

"No problem." I want to sound casual, like I take basic strangers back to my place all the time, like my stomach isn't rolling at the thought. Marshall lowers his hand to my thigh and rubs it gently. Part of me screams, 'No!' while the other is all yes. He leans over and kisses me, his hand cupping the side of my face, and I don't resist. When the driver pulls in front of my building, Marshall looks at me with what looks to be false embarrassment on his face.

"I was using credit at the bar. You wouldn't mind covering it, would you?"

I shake my head and pay the driver. I would have been

paying if I'd come home alone, anyway. We make our way up to my apartment and the first thing I do is yank off my shoes then breathe a sigh of relief. I glance around, glad I tidied up just a couple of days ago. The place is presentable.

Marshall walks into the living room then turns to me. "Cute place."

"Yeah," I smile, amazed a man like him is standing in my apartment, staring at me like he wants me—though this is not quite the way I pictured it would be. I imagined being wined and dined. I imagined at least a handful of dates before I welcomed a guy into my apartment. In recent months, it'd been Matt I imagined would stand here, where Marshall is. We would have spent months growing close first, connecting on a deeper level while I helped him heal his broken heart. Then eventually, one day, when Autumn seemed like a distant memory, this day would come. But I'm not getting Matt, and Marshall is as good looking, maybe even better looking, and he is here, and he wants me.

He steps toward me, a shy but intense smile on his face. "You're not as tall as you seemed." He slides his hands along my waist. I shake my head. "A good height though." He steps even closer, his body pressing against mine. I tilt my head up, look into his chocolate brown eyes, and, amazingly, he pulls me even closer. He kisses me with a ferocity that almost frightens me then pushes my back against the wall. My blood races and my mind whirls until suddenly everything stills, and nothing but excitement fills my being. He lifts me, my legs wrap around his waist, and instinctively he finds the bedroom. He throws me against the bed, and I land with my legs spread wide. He grins at this and crawls onto the bed as he undoes his shirt. I marvel at his contours. Sitting up, I rub my hands down his pecs and lean forward to kiss them. As I do this, he works at his belt then peels off his pants. He kisses me again and his hands push my dress up then strip my panties off. I have a brief moment of wishing I didn't wear these huge tummy tuckers, but he doesn't seem to notice. He pushes my dress up higher. One hand gropes my breast as the other reaches below. He draws his hand away and seems to fumble with something. Then it happens. He's inside me and it's an unexpected frenzied mix of pain and pleasure that ends all too soon. He shakes, groans, pants for a few moments, then draws away from me. I lie there, propped up on my elbows, staring as he searches for his boxers, pulls them on, and gets dressed. As he does this, I pull the strap back up on my dress and pull the skirt of it down. I scoot my way over to the edge of the bed and realize what's happening. I never thought my first time would be like this.

"You don't have to rush off," I almost plead.

"Oh," he glances at me, "work tomorrow."

"You could sleep here if you want. You'd get to bed sooner." I try not to let my voice sound desperate.

"No." He pauses in buttoning his shirt then smiles at me. "Thanks, though."

"Yeah." I stand. "Okay."

He grabs his belt and grins. "That was great though. Really good."

"Yeah," I say. "Mm-hmm"

"Was it good for you?" he asks, securing his belt buckle.

"Sure."

"Great." He leans forward and kisses my forehead. "Maybe we'll do it again sometime."

"Maybe." I swallow. "You want my number?" I regret the words as soon as they're out of my mouth. Marshall will not want my number.

"Oh," he says, "I'm sure I'll see you at the gym. Besides, I know where you live," he winks.

"Yeah," I nod, "of course." I follow him to the living room and stand there, stupidly, as he puts on his shoes. "Hey," I say, and he looks up. "You, uh…did you use protection?"

He laughs, and my stomach tightens. "Check your trash

can."

I nod, then close the door behind him. I rest my back against the wall, reliving the past hour. It wasn't all awful. The kissing was nice. It was what I should have expected, what Tammy expected. Tammy, I think with a groan, remembering my hateful words. I wasn't even saying them to her, not really. But say them I did.

I sink to the floor and want to wind back the clock. I can't do that though. I think again of my mother, the person Tammy thought this weight loss was for, or because of. Whether Mom would be proud of my success, my discipline, or not, I don't know. I know though, she wouldn't be proud of the person I've become. I stand, walk through the living room, and see my reflection in the window as I pass. The rouches in the dress don't seem to be doing such a good job of hiding my remaining bulges anymore. But it's worse than that. I step closer and stare into the eyes that look back at me. They haven't changed, and the person they reflect isn't kind, isn't compassionate, isn't happy. She's bitter. She's judgemental. She's gross. Worst of all, she's alone.

Tears threaten to come but I don't want to cry over this, over him, he's not worth it. I can cry for Tammy though, and as I think of this, I quickly wipe the moisture away. I continue to the bedroom, feeling sticky and cheap in my dress and not even a little sexy. I stand over the trash can and look for the evidence of our love—what I always thought that act would represent anyway. It's there. That's something. I grab a Kleenex and wrap the condom up. I don't want to see it again. I don't want to see him again. I've already considered getting a new trainer. Maybe I'll get a whole new gym.

❦

WHEN I WAKE THE NEXT morning, my head feels like it's been hammered, and I realize where that term comes from. I slowly try to stand. Once I manage that task, I make my way to the bathroom. The room sways and rocks and I have to brace myself against the wall, feeling repulsive. I stand in front of the sink and splash water on my face. The mirror lets me know I didn't remember to remove my makeup before falling into bed. A woman with a bad case of raccoon eyes stares back at me. As I continue to splash my face, hoping the fresh water will clear my head, the night plays through my mind. The time with Marshall is clear enough and thinking of it makes me sick and sad. But it was what it was. It just wasn't what I really wanted, or the way I wanted it.

I stare at my reflection with resolve—I gave the experience enough tears last night. If I'm honest, not all my crying was for Tammy. It wasn't for Marshall either. It was for me. But Tammy is who I think of now. I can't remember the exact words I said to her, but I know it was bad. As I struggle to remember everything I said, shame creeps over me. She was trying to help me, to watch out for me—she knows me better than I know myself apparently—and the things I said…I shake my head and let it hang as the water droplets drip into the sink. Despicable.

A quick splashing isn't enough, so I turn on the water in the shower and head for my phone. "Matt, hi."

"Hey there, she said yes!"

"I know." I can't help but smile at the joy in his voice, despite how it cuts me. "I'm so happy for you two."

"I have to admit," he says, "I was a little nervous. Especially after our talk. I mean you had some points. I was kind of taking her by surprise."

"Yeah," I lean my head against the wall, still feeling

dizzy, "well, I'm glad it's all working out." I want to mean the words. I do on some level. "I'm just calling to let you know I won't be able to make our session today. It's such short notice, just charge it like normal, I don't want you to get gypped."

"That's no problem, but what's up—You okay?"

"Yeah," my voice wavers, "I'm fine. Just not feeling too hot today."

"You sick?"

"In a manner of speaking. I went out with some friends last night, had a little too much fun."

"Ah," I can almost see his sweet smile, "that kind of sick. Well, feel better, okay? Have lots of liquids and a banana."

"Sure." The shower must be more than hot by now. I shouldn't waste more water. "I have to go—"

"See you Wednesday?" he asks.

I take a breath, eager for the pounding in my head to go away. "I'll let you know." I end the call and peel off my clothing as I walk back to the bathroom. While the water pours over me, I realize how different it feels, how much more room I have to maneuver in my stand-up shower, how the water flows easily, rather than pooling in my copious amounts of flesh. I wonder if I'm exaggerating the different sensation. I wonder if I've exaggerated my whole life. All the girls last night seemed pretty interested in my weight loss, perhaps a little envious, but once the initial shock wore off, they treated me like they always had. The only difference was the way I responded. They'd always asked me about my life. They'd always invited me onto the dance floor—I'd just never said yes before. And the biggest realization—they all seemed pretty happy with their lives, happy with themselves, despite the extra weight. They were all decently successful too, more successful than I've ever been. So, is it likely I'm the only one who always had prejudiced interviewers, or was it something else? Something about me, specifically?

As I work the shampoo through my hair, the words I

said to Tammy replay in my mind. They were ridiculous. Cruel. So untrue. Colin is a good guy, a stable guy, a guy who I'm sure would never go home with a girl then walk out the moment he'd been satisfied. He wasn't with Tammy for the thrill or because he didn't think he could do any better—at least it didn't seem like it. He loves her. And who am I to say anything about them, anyway? I'm no authority on any type of relationship. I didn't even do so great with the one person I knew would love me no matter what. I cringe to think of the way I treated Mom on my darker days.

If she had been different, if she had been stronger, if she hadn't let food do this to her, to us, everything would be better. My moments of hatred didn't come from nowhere. If Mom had made better choices Dad never would have left, Billy and I may have actually been friends, and she'd still be here.

I bang my hands against the glass wall. She'd still be here. The anger bubbles up again and for the first time I don't try to ignore it. I don't push it down. I yell. I yell at her, saying all the things I never said.

It's not until I'm done that I hear how empty the words are, how there's no weight to them, then laugh at the unintended pun. Mom did what she did. I've done what I've done. We can't change the past.

I see again the look in Tammy's eyes and step out of the shower. Before I've even dried off, I pick up the phone and dial her number. It rings, once, twice, three times, then cuts to the answering machine. I've phoned enough to know her machine is set to five rings. "Tammy," I take a deep breath, "it's Jenn. I'm really sorry. Last night…I'm just really sorry. Call back, K? Please?" I hold the phone in front of me and wait about four minutes before setting it down to get dressed.

As I do, I find myself getting a little annoyed at Tammy. Yes, I messed up. Yes, I said some things I shouldn't have, but she's supposed to be my best friend, and just because I got a little nasty while drunk, just because I said some things she knows I never would have said in my right mind, she decides to write me off? She let me go off with that guy. Like she said, he could have been a rapist, he could have given me AIDS. I was too drunk to even make sure he was using a condom. I was lucky he wasn't so drunk. She was lucky he wasn't. Friends are supposed to watch out for each other, yet she doesn't pick up this morning. What if I'd been calling from the hospital? What if I'd been in a ditch somewhere? She could have at least figured that out before deciding to dismiss me.

Part of me knows I'm reaching here, but being angry feels a hell of a lot better than letting the guilt and shame take over. I let the anger simmer, and it flows again toward my mother. As much as she was wonderful, a lot of my problems really were her fault. Whenever I tried to make healthy changes, she would always be my downfall. In high school she'd make big delicious dinners. After I moved out, she'd visit with fresh-baked cupcakes or cookies and, when I'd say I was trying to lose weight, she'd tell me to just live, to just enjoy life. She didn't want me to be thin. She wanted me to stay fat, just like her. Just enjoy life—What irony. Her 'enjoyment' had robbed her of the very thing she was trying to enjoy. Robbed me of her. Her obsession with cakes and burgers and poutine was why I had to crouch over her, trying to make her heart start, enduring the stench of her failed bladder. Her selfish obsession was why I'd never be able to see her again, talk with her again, why she'd never meet my husband, never hold her grandchildren. "Fuck her," I say to the room. And the forcefulness of my voice shocks me. But I like it. "Fuck her!" I yell, the horror she put me through racing through my mind. I'm shaking with the words but scream them once more.

And those girls last night. They were good actors, nothing more. I know what it is to look in the mirror and hate what you see. I know they can't like their bodies. I know they can't be happy with their obesity—not that they were all obese, but still. I've experienced the difference in the way people look at me now from how they looked at me then. Tammy's friends might not be miserable all the time, but there is no way they don't dream about letting go of the weight. There is no way they didn't see me last night and wish they were me.

But they're not me. I'm the only one who had the discipline to transform my life, the self-control. They think I didn't crave cookies and chips and Taquitos? They think it was easy? They think every time I pass a bakery window I don't yearn to sink my teeth into the wondrous delicacies? Well, I do. But I don't! Because I'm better than that, not like them. Not like my own mother. I'm better.

I get off my knees, where I've fallen in my yelling, and pull off the bra and t-shirt I had put on. Instead, I put on a sports bra and long-sleeved technical shirt. I pull on a pair of gym pants. Matt was right. He didn't do this. I did this. And I can continue to do it without him, without anybody. I have a goal and I'm going to achieve it. I have a dream and it's going to be realized.

I start my run at an easy jog but quickly pick up the pace. I turn down to the harbour, my feet slamming into the wood of the boardwalk. I make my way up toward the Commons, the incline not even phasing me, and then away from downtown. I run faster and harder than I've ever run. My lungs burn, my legs ache, but I keep going. I have to keep going. I'm running for my life. When I feel as if my heart is about to burst, I slow ever so slightly and focus all my thoughts and all my energy into my body. My mind is attuned to every footfall, every breath, every sweep of my arm.

When I can't push myself anymore, I'm probably about ten kilometres from home with no money and no bus fare. My head is dizzy, my pulse is racing, and my throat is dry. I close my eyes and realize how stupid I've been. I take a few deep breaths of the cool winter air. Spring is a couple of months away and now that I'm standing still, I wish I had brought a jacket. I should have known I wouldn't last forever. I should have run in a loop. Thankfully, there's a bus terminal nearby and I slip in and drink greedily from the fountain. I head to the bathroom and pat off what sweat I can with a paper towel. Then I start my walk. It's a long one, but I'll do it—all on my own.

CHAPTER NINETEEN

The next morning, I call Fit4Life and say I'd like to cancel my membership. Mayhem tries to dissuade me, but when I tell her I've had a wonderful experience, that it's transformed me and given me the skills to maintain my fitness on my own, she seems happy with that. Before I hang up, she says I need to come in and sign some papers. I grudgingly agree and hope Matt isn't there when I do. I know it's cowardly, to just step away like that. I know it'll come back to bite me since our paths will cross again sooner or later—most likely sooner—but I'm just not ready to see him, to see him and know he'll never be mine, to face the embarrassment of thinking he could be. I also dread seeing Marshall. I don't know the protocol. Do I say 'Hi,' like we're casual friends? Am I expected to ignore him, keep it the anonymous, casual encounter he obviously wanted it to be? I don't want to find out.

Before sitting down at my computer, I contemplate calling Tammy again. My anger has faded. I don't want to lose her, but still feel miffed she hasn't shown more concern for me. As I'm debating whether to phone her again, a call comes in from Autumn and I let it ring. Her joy is not something I want to bask in at the moment. I flip open my laptop and start on my latest assignment, and this is what I do for the next week. I write, I eat healthy—following Matt's guidelines—I workout, and I keep away from everyone I know. Tammy hasn't called yet, but Autumn called three times and Dad once. I texted Autumn back so she wouldn't show up at my doorstep—*I've been really swamped with some big work projects. I'll get in touch soon to help with all the wedding planning! :) :) :)* It's held her off so far—she respects work ethic—but I know it won't last much longer; the day will come when I actually have to start helping her.

There are a lot of things I'll actually have to do pretty soon. And so, on a sunny, cloudless day I decide it's time to knock one of them off my list. It's silly to pay for a membership I'm not using, and the only reason I'm still paying is I'm scared to see Matt, but I'll have to see him at some point anyway. His schedule changes all the time, so if I'm lucky I won't run into him. After my workout at home I shower, carefully do my hair and my makeup, put on some casual but flattering clothes, and make my way to the gym. While I'm signing the final document and passing it to Mayhem, a familiar set of shoulders comes into view.

"Jenn!" Matt says something to the client he's with, a middle-aged man who could pass for a pregnant woman in silhouette, and trots over to me. "Hey."

"Hey." I smile back.

"I've been worried about you," his face holds genuine concern, "so has Autumn. She says you've been swamped with work. So swamped you cancel our appointments? Your membership? You're not giving up, are you?"

"No, no." I smile casually. "Not at all. I'm just doing my workouts from home now and around the neighbourhood." I hand the document back to Mayhem and turn toward Matt. "You gave me the skills I need, so I'm making use of them, like you said."

He nods, but it doesn't look confident. "That's great. That's good." He rocks back on his heels. "It would have been nice, you know, though, if you'd called me, or texted, or anything…"

"Yeah," I say, with a shake of my head. "I'm sorry about that. I've just been so overwhelmed." I'm silent for a moment and so is he. "Once I get things under control it'll be better. We should all go out—maybe a day hike or even for lunch or something."

"So, you're eating enough again?"

"Yep," I say. "Following your guidelines."

"And you know you'll want to up that again once you get to your goal—or are you there already?" He gives me a once over. "You're looking fit."

"I haven't checked in a few days," I lie. "But I think I still have a few more to go." I smile. "They'll go when they go though, no rush, no worry." It's surprising how believable I sound.

"That's good, Jenn. That's a good way to be." There's that silence again. "So, you're sure everything's okay though? With you? With us?"

"Just peachy." I mentally slap myself. "Things are good. As I said, I've been really busy. And I know it would have been nice to call—I mean I called the club. They said they'd tell you. They did, right?"

"Yeah," his words come out slowly, "they did."

"Good. I mean I wouldn't have wanted you to think I was just ditching you after all the hard work we put in. I never could have…well, I mean I could have but you really helped me out. I'll always be thankful for that."

"That's my job." He rocks back on his heels again.

"That's your job," I parrot. "Anyway, I'll be in touch with Autumn when things slow down. I'm sure I'll see you soon."

"Okay."

I nod goodbye and can feel him watching me, but, strangely, thankfully, feel almost nothing of what I've felt for him these past months. I'm happy for him, I am. I'm happy for him and Autumn, for the life they'll have, but still, I feel miserable for me, for stupid, pathetic, dreamer me. Lust is one thing. I can lust any number of guys, but it was more with Matt. Though my feelings for him have faded, the loss is still there. I try not to feel it, but it's hard. He made me believe he cared about me, not in a sexual way, but in a way that made me feel worthwhile; an incredible feat. How could I not care about him? I guess though, that doesn't have to change—him caring about me, us being friends. He'll be my cousin. He'll still be in my life. And I'll find 'my' Matt. I'll get to where I want to be and then I'll find him. I have to. A good guy. A sexy guy. A guy who would never cheat on me with his secretary if I put a few pounds back on—not that I will—but if I did, he wouldn't.

I exit the club and head down the street. That could have gone worse. At least I didn't have to face Marshall. I try to take my mind somewhere else. Although there'll be fewer options this time of year, I remember the Seaport Farmer's Market is open today. I'm running low on my fruits and veggies. A detour is exactly what I need.

THE SUN IS WARM AGAINST my back and despite a cool breeze, it seems like the type of day wonderful things are bound to happen. I enter the market and browse the vegetable stands, deciding between spaghetti squash or cauliflower for supper, then hear my name called in a high-pitched, overly zealous voice that resembles nails on a chalkboard. I turn and am hit with more than I imagined. Not only is it the tart, as Mom always liked to call her, but it's one of the little tartlets and my father as well. I push out a smile, trying to make it look as genuine as possible. My dad's new family all smile in return as we endure what seems to be an unending moment of silence.

"You look fabulous," gushes Evita, and I'm not sure if there's a hint of poison in her tone or if I'm the one who puts it there.

"Yeah," says Dad, "you look great, Jenny. I'm so proud

of you."

I don't know what to say to that. I don't want to be a bitch, but don't see why Dad has any right to feel pride, so I just nod. I glance at Melinda who is looking away, looking bored. I know she's not actually bored. It's a cultivated look, one she always wears when I'm around—a way to let me know I'm not worth her attention. Evita shuffles by the vegetable stand and makes her way to my side. She gives me a gentle hug, as if I'm a bubble that may burst if she squeezes too firmly. I can't blame her. I've erupted in her presence more than once. Good for her for still making an effort at some form of affection. I return her embrace with a barely noticeable pat on the shoulder.

My father makes his way around the stand as well but doesn't attempt a hug. His lips turn up in this weird smile and he stares at me as if he's looking through me rather than at me. He does this as Evita rambles on about all the wonderful produce and the beauty of the day. Finally, he speaks, interrupting Evita mid-sentence. "You look so much like her." His voice is soft, full of wonder and admiration. "When she was about your age." He clears his throat. "Your mother, she would be proud of you too."

His words hit me like a blow to the chest. I don't recall ever hearing such tenderness in his voice when speaking of Mom, when speaking to me. It makes me love him and hate him all at once. I can't think what to say, but Evita makes it so I don't have to.

"We just came back from visiting your brother," she says, "Billy," as if I need to be reminded of his name. I nod and she waits a moment for me to speak. When I don't, she continues. "He's doing very well, isn't he, dear?"

"Yes," says Dad, still looking at me in that odd way, as if he's lost in the past.

"The doctors say he'll probably be released in the next two to three weeks." Evita looks from Dad to me. "We suppose he'll come stay with us at first, until he's really on his feet again. Your aunt offered to help but I think it's better if he's with our family. In his old room. Don't you?"

I'm not sure whether she's talking to me or my father, but I answer this time. "Yeah, that'd be good."

"He's talking well again too. He asked about you, Jennifer." Evita's voice rises an octave. "He asked why you never came to see him."

"Jenny will see him when she's ready," says Dad, and it's the most shocking thing I've ever heard come out of his mouth. Just the other week he was chastising me over the phone for my lack of interest in Billy, but I guess the bond of blood is strong. He won't let her chastise me. It almost makes me want to hug him.

"Well," this time I'm sure venom seeps through Evita's cherry tone, "I just thought it'd be nice if she paid him a visit. She is his sister after all. His other sisters have visited him plenty."

"Well, that's very nice of them." I keep the words I'm really thinking to myself.

"I guess with all the time and energy you've obviously put into completely transforming yourself, it would be hard to find time." She gives me a close-lipped smile. "We all have our priorities."

"Can we go?" says Melinda, "I'm going to be late for class."

"Melinda's got her one-on-one dance training," says Evita. "After she won the last regional competition, we decided it'd be best to get more focused training, so she's not missing any opportunities."

"That's excellent." I offer an overly wide smile. "Well, you'd better get going then."

Dad puts his hand on my shoulder. "I'll call you later this week. Maybe we can go for lunch?" He asks it so hesitantly I feel like an even bigger bitch than Evita—he's scared to ask his own daughter to lunch. But I remember the reason I've made him scared. I remember the way he abandoned me, the way I've never felt good enough for him, the way he went out and got this new family that now stands in front of me. A family that lives up to the standards Mom and I never could. Maybe it's only now that I've lost the weight, he sees me as worthy. Well, I don't need him to think I'm worthy. His approval is the last thing I need.

"Maybe," I say. "If I can find time." Dad nods. He turns away and I watch them weave down the aisle of the market. I watch and wonder if I'll ever consider any of them family, if I'll ever want to. When it comes down to it, Autumn, Aunt Lucille, and Daniel are the only people I really think of as family, and I've even been ostracizing myself from them. I've been ostracizing myself from everyone. Tammy comes to mind and shame rises within me—I wish my emotions would just make up their mind. Next, I think of the night with Marshall. How different could my first time have been if I hadn't blown off Rajeev? He's nice, so nice, if not what I think I want, what I think I deserve, but I know he wouldn't have walked out never to be heard from again. I know it would have been an entirely different experience. A better experience. If I'm honest with myself, I Rajeev is more than I deserve, not less.

I walk away from the market, squash in hand, and determine to be happy, to be proud of how far I've come, despite what I may have lost in the process. I'll continue to work toward my goal. I'll achieve it, not just the weight, but becoming a better person, the person I've always wanted to be. That's what matters most.

People pass me—friends laughing and chatting, couples hand in hand, parents with children—and I'm not sure I've ever felt so alone.

CHAPTER TWENTY

Several weeks later I've just finished my workout when there's a knock at my door. Despite the five or six messages I've left, Tammy still hasn't returned my calls. I'm beyond pissed. Who does she think she is—to throw away twelve years of friendship over one measly fight? I rush to the door anyway, hoping it's her, ready to make up, ready to settle down on the couch and throw on a Rom Com.

I wrench the door open without looking in the peephole and take a step back. My hand drops from the doorknob. I take two more steps back. It's Billy, but it's not. He's so thin he looks more like a prisoner of war than the brother I remember. He wears his hair shorn close to his head, shorter than it's been since he was a toddler. His eyes are hollow. His shoulders hunch forward. A cane is in his right hand and he leans on it for support. The biggest change of all is how timid he looks. All the bravado I'm used to seeing has drained away. He looks as shocked to see me as I am to see him. His eyes question at first, then brighten with the surety of recognition. Still, his voice has a lilt to it. "Jennifer?"

I nod.

He steps toward the door, using his cane for leverage, then takes a step back. "May I?" I nod and he crosses my threshold. "Wow," he says. "Wow. You look great. Really great. If Dad hadn't told me, I may not have known it was you." I'm not sure whether to take this as a compliment or an insult—my reaction is to take it as the latter but the look in his eyes and tone of his voice tell me it's not intended as one. I take a few steps further into the apartment then turn toward the living room. He follows me. "This is a nice place you have here," He smiles, fidgeting with the toque in his left hand. He's not one for hats but with his newly short hair and slender frame it makes sense.

We sit across from each other and as I take him in, realize what he must have gone through to look the way he looks, realize that I, his blood sister, didn't help him through any of it, I feel sick with guilt. "I'm sorry," I blurt, and he waves my words away. "I should have—" but he waves again.

"That's not why I'm here, Jenn." He looks at the toque, at his hands as he wrings it. "I'm not here to hear your apologies." I hold my breath, anticipating the verbal lashing, the shaming I'm due. "I came to apologize to you."

I blink and release my breath, uncertain I've heard correctly. He looks up at me, offers the slightest of smiles, then looks back down again. "I understand why you didn't come visit me." He swallows, his Adam's apple protruding from his thin neck. "I understand why it would have been hard for you," he takes a breath, "to pretend everything was okay, to pretend you loved me when…" His voice trails off and I finally speak.

"I love you." I lean forward. "You're my brother. Of course, I—"

"Yeah, well, if you do that's a sign of your character, not mine. I've had a lot of time to think," his brow furrows, "laid up the way I was, for a time unable to even speak. I could still think though. At first, when you and Mom never came to see me, when I never remembered hearing your voices in my hospital room before I fully came to, I was angry. Obviously, Mom had a good reason…" He stops here and I don't know what to say; apparently neither does he, but at last he continues.

"I kept thinking I couldn't believe it: Mom was dead, and I'd never see her again. It made me mad that she was gone for such a stupid, avoidable reason, but it also made me ashamed. I was not the son I should have been." He takes a deep breath. "Though, when it comes to stupid, avoidable reasons, who was I to talk?" He lets out a short hard laugh then presses his lips together. "She was excused, but not you. I was so mad at you. You're my big sister and you never came to see me, not once." He turns his head to the window. "I knew I hadn't been the greatest brother to you, but still. You always made an effort to be in my life when I didn't even care, didn't want you there, when I was embarrassed by you...and then when I wanted you, you chose not to be there. You abandoned me."

I purse my lips, wanting to defend myself, but respect the fact that he's clearly not done, that it must be hard for him to be this vulnerable. "People made excuses for you—Aunt Lucille, Autumn, Dad even. They said you were going through a rough time yourself, that you were the one who found Mom, that it hit you hard—not being able to save her. They said you were trying to transform your life, focus on that. They said it was consuming you." I want to defend this as well, but I know it's true. "That still wasn't enough though. It just made me angrier. I told myself if you did come, I would ignore you. I'd have nothing to do with you. So I teased you from time to time, so I was embarrassed by you and let it be known. So what? I was a kid, and you were fat. I told myself you should have just expected that from me. I told myself it was your choice, being fat. But then I started thinking more and more. I thought about Dad and his new family—how much I wanted to be a part of that family, how much I wanted distance from ours. And they accepted me, Evita, the girls. They never accepted you, not that you made it easy for them, but still." He stops, takes a breath. "You may have abandoned me, but I abandoned you first."

Tears run down my face. Silently, so as not to interrupt his words.

"I brought it up to one of my buddies when he helped me move my stuff out of storage and into Dad's, said how my bitch of a sister never came to visit me once. He said that was harsh but not surprising, seeing the way I treated you." He brings his gaze back to his hands. "I questioned him. It surprised me he even knew who you were. I didn't remember anything from the day of the accident, so he told me. He told me what I'd said the last time you saw me, how I acted." He looks at me. "I'm sorry, Jenny. I was a bastard. You didn't deserve that. You never deserved any of it." He's crying now too. I haven't seen Billy cry since he was a little boy and it almost breaks me. "So, I understand why you didn't want to see me. I understand how you must hate me and that's okay. I understand. But I still had to come and say I'm sorry. I don't expect your forgiveness, but I—"

I cut him off by launching myself from the couch and wrapping my arms around him. We cry together, clutching each other. I'm crying for so much, I can't tell one emotion from the next. I'm crying for the pain he's caused me over the years, the pain of that night. I'm crying for our lost mother and the anger I still have at the way he treated her— the way he treated me. I'm crying because he can never apologize to her and how that must haunt him. I'm crying for how petty and small I've been, letting my hate and anger make him feel abandoned. I'm crying because he's not the man he once was and may never be again—the fit, strong man he worked so hard to become. I'm crying because I'm afraid he wouldn't have said these words if I were still the me I used to be, that if I were sitting in front of him, his lardo sister, he would have only been able to see me as that, and not worthy of this apology, this love. Perhaps most of all, I'm crying because I don't know if I can ever fully forgive him or if I'm even willing to try.

He pulls away and wipes his sleeved arm across his nose, just like he used to as a boy. But I can't see the little boy in him anymore. Not even in his eyes. They're not the same eyes of the man I spent the last year hating either. He smiles at me, a genuine smile. A smile of relief, of hope. "I should get going. I still get tired pretty early." He shrugs. "I'll get it back," and I see a flash of the bravado I remember. "I'm staying at Dad's for now. It'd be nice if you'd come by and visit. Maybe come to dinner—" He must see the look in my eyes. "Or we could go out to dinner, or coffee, or a walk."

I nod and I smile, but I can't confirm with my words. He stands and I do too. We walk to the door. "Thanks for coming by," I say. "I'm sorry, I—" He cuts me off again by giving me another hug. It's more hugging than we've done in twenty years.

"I haven't gone to see her grave yet," he says, looking at the floor, or his shoes—I can't be sure. "I'd really like it if you came with me. Maybe next week."

"I haven't been back either," I say. "Not since the funeral." I feel weak as I say it, selfish, but I say it anyway. "I don't know that I'm ready yet."

He nods and steps into the hall. "Well, I'll let you know when I'm going. I'll give you a call. If you want to join me, that'd be good. If you don't, that's cool too."

I close the door behind my brother and lean against the faux wood. After taking a few deep breaths I head back to my room and pull out a technical shirt and jogging pants. I remember a jacket this time, a toque, and fingerless gloves. It's approaching eight o'clock and I've already done my workout for today, but I need to run. The old me would have eaten through my pain and confusion and anger—my interactions with Billy have always had that affect on me. The new me needs this other method.

I step out into the cold air and run hard, barely noticing the icy breeze. I know I'm running from the past year, but I'm also running toward my future. The problem is, I don't know what future I'm running toward. That elusive, perfect me—the happy, beautiful, skinny me—seems somehow not as important as I always thought she was. I've almost found her, at least as far as the scale is concerned, but at this moment I don't feel any better, any different. Sure, it's great to not turn in disgust from my own reflection and to exercise without fear of a heart attack, but beyond that not much of significance has changed, not much that's real.

I pick up my pace and see Billy, sitting before me, apologizing. He went to hell and back this past year—A coma, learning how to form words again, learning how to walk, and he apologizes to me. He forgives me who cared too much about my own pain, my own anger, to visit him even once. And still, despite seeing his frail and wasted self, I felt bitter and angry. This is not the me I dreamed of. I receive a once over and nod of appreciation from a man jogging by. He's cute and fit—the type of guy I should be thrilled would notice me, but I find his roving eyes distasteful. All he sees is a body—almost skinny. He has no idea who I really am, who I've always been. Selfish. Unforgiving. Mean.

As I continue to run, pushing myself, I think of Tammy again, how beautiful she is, how happy and self-assured and sweet. She has lots of friends. She has a man who loves her. She likes herself—and people like her. Her weight hasn't held her back from life or from success. Her company was downsized a few years back, but she made it past the new interview process and now has an even better job. Tammy's had hard times too, she has people she could be mad at, but she doesn't carry that anger around with her like I do. Despite all my disparaging talk of chubby chasers over the years, I know she's never had a guy walk away from her the way Marshall walked away from me.

I think of my Mom. She lost Dad, yes, but she had lots of friends, way more than me. And most of the time she was happy. Most of the time she seemed to feel good about herself. I turn from the noisy street and onto a paved trail surrounded by trees. It's one I usually avoid. I slow to a walk, and take a deep breath, the only other sound the wind through the barren branches and my feet hitting the frost-covered lawn.

What did Mom have that I don't? What does Tammy have? No one could call me fat now, not even overweight, and yet I'm more alone than I ever was. I can't even be around Autumn without feeling jealous—I mean I'm happy for her but so sad for me. To add to that, I've probably ruined my friendship with Tammy. And my reaction to seeing my father with Evita…half of my life is consumed with anger for the people I should be loving.

I don't even know what I'm thinking or where my thoughts are going. They're all jumbled up within me. The other girls too, the ones who are really more Tammy's friends than mine, they always seemed happier than me. They still do. They have their complaints—their work problems, their boy problems, their family problems—but they have something else too, something that carries them through all the crap. Something I've never had.

A pain shoots through my right hip. I know I've pushed too far, and I'll suffer tomorrow for it, but I continue on. It's taken a long time to get here, but here I am, at last. The sun is about to set, and I'm chilled as the sweat continues to push its way through my pores. But it doesn't matter. I can't turn back now. As I approach my mother's gravesite, I make one foot go in front of the other. The days following Mom's death are a bit of a haze, and it takes me a moment to remember exactly where she's buried. All I remember clearly is the muted pain. At last I find the plot. It's been a little over a year since I stood here. I look at the words and it doesn't seem real. Her name shouldn't be here.

Cynthia Mary Carpenter
June 7, 1966 - January 17, 2013

It always bothered me that she never went back to her maiden name. I saw it as not being able to let go of Dad. She said she wanted to have the same name as her children, and what's in a name, anyway. A statement of contradiction. I gaze at the rest of the text.

Beloved Mother, Sister, Aunt, and Friend.
Life is a blessing. Celebrate being alive.

I'm shocked that I didn't know these are the words she chose. But how would I know? Aunt Lucille handled all the details. The headstone wouldn't have gone up until after she was interred. I'm sure though, that it must have been Mom's request to have those words engraved. It's surprising she thought of the words she wanted on her tombstone. She was so young. It angers me all over again—she must have known her death was a near possibility, maybe the doctor told her she had a heart condition, maybe she didn't think I was worth telling. Almost as quickly as the thought enters my mind, I push it out. Whether she knew or not, it had nothing to do with her belief in my worth.

I read the words again—*Life is a blessing. Celebrate being alive.* They were taken from a song she liked to play. It was on a mixed CD of hers and she'd smile as she hummed or sang along. Sometimes she'd sing the words under her breath as she cooked or cleaned, almost like a chant, like a mantra, like a reminder. At times, it made me angry to hear it, how happy she sounded while humming those words. What in her life was so blessed? What was there to celebrate? I called her out on it once—only once. She'd just looked at me. 'Jennifer,' she said, disappointment and dismay flooding her face, followed by this pitying look of love. 'Just open your eyes, baby. Just open your eyes.' I stared at her ample frame, her lovely face marred by the extra pounds, and felt sorry for her, sorry that she thought it made sense to feel sorry for me. At least I was in touch with reality, I had thought. At least I didn't pretend that designer clothes and salon hairdos and carefully applied makeup could actually make a difference to the way the world looked at me. But now I think back to her smile, her joy, and am pretty sure I was wrong.

When I'd watched her coffin lowered into the ground, at least fifty people stood around me. Even more people had been at the funeral home. Many of the faces I'd looked into had been tear streaked. Afterward, at Aunt Lucille's, people talked fondly about moments they'd shared with my mom— how she'd made them laugh, how she knew just the right time to show up with a lovingly made casserole or tin of cookies, how she'd always known how to diffuse the tension at work or family gatherings. Yet all I'd focused on that night was the words Uncle Leo spouted in a drunken moment of idiocy. The good things everyone else had to say seemed nothing more than words, but they were what really mattered. Life is a blessing. Celebrate being alive.

Despite my fight toward a healthier life, a happier life, I've rarely celebrated life. The closest I'd come in years was probably on that hike, or those few minutes on the dance floor with Tammy's friends, just a few weeks ago. I smile. In those moments I forgot about my insecurities, my anger, and let myself become enthralled with the beauty and fun around me.

Rajeev's words, as we gazed at the stars, come back to me. He was more right than I wanted to admit. I kneel on the cold, hard ground before my mother's tombstone. I have been letting my past, the pain in it, rule me. Even worse, I've been letting it blind me. "Mom," I say, then check to make sure no one is around to hear my words. "I don't think you'd be very proud of me if you were here right now." It's weird talking to a stone, but I don't stop. "I think I've had the wrong idea about a lot of my life. I think I've had things skewed." My mind travels back to what started this whole journey—standing in the street holding my hand over my split pants, mortified. But it was more than that. It was all the moments leading up to that moment. All the moments that made me feel like nothing. For so much of my life I felt hated and judged when, ironically, it was probably because I spent so much of my time hating and judging others.

I place my hand flat against the cool headstone. "I'm sorry for all the things I thought about you over the years. I know you know I loved you. I always loved you. But there were times when I was ashamed of you too, when I was embarrassed." I notice a piece of mud to the side of her name and brush it off. "I always hated Billy so much for being embarrassed, for wanting Evita to be his mother, but sometimes I wanted her too…I just knew she'd never want me. But most of all I wanted you. The you I'd seen in the pictures when Dad fell in love with you.

"I hated you sometimes for not being that woman anymore, for letting me be as I was. I was judging your worth based on how much you weighed…I was judging my own by that same scale." I stop and debate whether to continue. I feel kinda stupid. But talking to her, it also feels kinda good. "You probably wouldn't recognize me if you were to see me right now. I'm eighty-six pounds lighter than I was—at least I think I am. I haven't checked in a few days, actually." I let my words fade into the silence. "I'm eighty-six pounds lighter but I'm not really any happier. In some ways I may be less…" I think again of Tammy. I think of Billy. I think of Marshall. I think of Dad. I think of Autumn. I think of Matt. I think of Rajeev. I want to say more but I don't know what to say, so instead I kiss my fingers and gently place them against the engraved stone of her name. I'm shaking with the cold and know I have at least an hour walk ahead of me. I consider turning back but pull out my phone instead and do something I never in a million years thought I would. I call my Dad for help.

CHAPTER TWENTY-ONE

Dad pulls his car up to the entrance of the cemetery in less than six minutes. When I open the passenger door, he reaches into the back then passes me a flannel hoodie. He doesn't ask what I'm doing in the cemetery at nine-thirty at night. He just smiles and waits as I pull off my jacket, put the hoodie on, then buckle my seatbelt. He pulls back onto the road. "Home?"

I nod.

"Mine or yours?" He's hesitant as he asks this, his hands firmly on 10 and 2. "Just if you didn't want to be alone. We have leftover casserole we could heat up in a minute, and an extra bed."

"That's okay," I say and feel the urge to cry. "But thank you." I've never meant those words so much.

"Okay." He smiles back. Does he know Billy came to see me today? Most likely. He probably has questions, but we drive in silence. When he pulls up in front of my apartment, he keeps his eyes ahead but reaches over and takes my hand, gives it a quick squeeze, then releases it. He glances over then looks away quickly. "Thank you for calling me." My mouth drops open. He's the one who has just left whatever he was doing on a moment's notice to come and get me. "I appreciate it," he says.

Again, the tears fight to surface. "Uh, I...Yeah." I open the door, feeling awkward about saying thank you now. But I am thankful, not just because he came to get me, no questions asked, but for what he's said, the care he's shown. This is still the same man who left me and started a new family, the same man who's always made me feel like I wasn't enough for him, who clearly cared about his new perfect family more than Mom and me…but it's also the man who continues to call me—albeit sporadically—despite my blatant disinterest in him. And thought I never believed it as genuine, he did invite me to come live with him and Evita—not just that first time, but multiple times throughout my life—for summers, at the start of high school, when I had finished University and was looking for a place to live closer to the city. I'd always assumed they were just words. I'd always said no. For the first time, I think—*maybe it's me who abandoned him.*

He sits smiling at me, tentative, like Billy was, as I step out and hold my hand on the door. "Hey, Dad," I say. He waits for me to continue. "If you all aren't busy, maybe I could come over this week—for Sunday dinner."

"That'd be great," he says, nodding his approval. "I'll let Evita know to make extra." My gut reaction is to take this as a jab—gotta make sure there's enough for the fat girl—but as I look into his eyes, I know that's not what he meant. How many other times was it not what other people meant either? I waver at the door then speak again. "How's Courtney doing?"

"Oh," he says, seemingly taken aback, "she's doing a lot better. Got rid of that boyfriend. She still doesn't want to go back to University, but she's working at a drugstore, thinking of going to school to become a hairstylist."

I nod. "Well, that's something."

"It's not what we had planned for her," he pauses, "but things don't always go according to plan."

"No," I offer a soft smile, "they don't." We stare at each other a moment. "Thanks for the drive, Dad. Goodnight."

"Goodnight, Jenny. Oh," he shakes his head give an embarrased smile, "Jenn."

"Jenny's okay." I smile back. "It's just a name, right?"

He nods.

I close the door, walk up my apartment steps, and realize I still have the hoodie. It's okay though, I'll give it back on Sunday. A simple interaction from all outward appearances: A father picks up his daughter, drops her off, they exchange a few words. Nothing monumental. But outward appearances never tell the whole story. I step into the shower and let the hot water stream over my body. I feel changed. I'm awash with shame, I'm awash with regret, but more than that I'm awash with hope. I've got a lot of mending to do, a lot of apologizing, a lot of restructuring the way I do life.

WHEN I GET OUT OF THE shower, I look at the clock— 10:49—and make a decision. I can't undo the choices in my life, I can't relive the wasted years, but I can celebrate the ones I have left. It's late, but I imagine Autumn will still be awake. In some ways this will be one of the easiest fixes I have ahead of me. But in some ways, it may be one of the hardest.

"Autumn, hey," I say into the phone. "No, no, everything is okay." I respond to her query. "I just wanted to see if there was anything I could help you out with this weekend—for the wedding planning. I know I've been…unavailable, but I'm available now. I want to help with anything I can." Autumn's quiet for a moment then starts in with enthusiasm, filling me in on everything that's already been done and the mountain of tasks still to be tackled. I agree to meet her at eleven the next morning for a third round of dress shopping.

"Third time's a charm," she says. "I feel it in my bones. Tomorrow's the day I'm going to find my dress."

I can't help but smile at her excitement. I push away the old dream of Matt watching me walk down the aisle that threatens to surface. Then I realize—he will watch me walk down the aisle. I just won't be wearing the colour dress I imagined. I picture the words on Mom's gravestone. It's Autumn's life I need to celebrate right now. And who knows, maybe I'll find my person at the wedding, the memory of Rajeev and the way he looked in the starlight pops into my mind, and I can't help but smile.

Fixing things with Tammy is the next fix on my list but it's too late to call, not that calling has done much good. Instead, I'll stop in at her apartment after dress shopping. She'll be less likely to slam the door in my face than to ignore another call.

∽

WHEN AUTUMN AND AUNT Lucille pull up to my apartment, Autumn is a ball of nervous excitement.

"I went with Tracey and Eloise last week," she says. "I found a couple of nice ones, but nothing that really popped, you know?"

"Yeah?"

"I think today's going to be the day."

"It'll be your 'Say Yes to the Dress' moment." Aunt Lucille grins. It's impossible not to smile at the way she says this, with such energy.

"Mom's been watching bridal shows obsessively." Autumn laughs, glances back at me, and gives a joking eye roll. "Obsessively."

"Oh, come on," says Aunt Lucille. "You've been watching too."

"I've watched a few." Autumn laughs again. "Like maybe two or three? Didn't you watch a marathon last weekend?"

"It wasn't all weekend," says Aunt Lucille. "It didn't start till Saturday morning." We all laugh, and it feels good being with them. Neither Autumn nor Aunt Lucille seem even slightly annoyed with me, despite the fact that I've basically ignored all their attempts at contact the past few weeks. I breathe a sigh of relief, and thankfulness.

When we get to the first shop, the saleslady is all business. She walks around Autumn like she's a prize filly. She lifts her arm, takes a chunk of Autumn's hair, holds it in her hand, then lets it fall. What the texture of Autumn's hair has to do with a dress choice I can't fathom.

"And when is the wedding?" The lady asks, her chin propped in her hand, her elbow propped on her opposite hand.

"In about five months."

"Five months!" The lady gasps, her hand clasping below her throat. "Why didn't you come sooner? That's barely time to put an order in, to get the sizing right." The woman is legitimately stressed. I couldn't imagine her being more appalled if Autumn had told her she likes to eat babies for lunch.

"I was actually planning to get something off the rack if I can," says Autumn. "Hopefully it wouldn't need more than a few alterations."

"Oh." Immediately the woman's enthusiasm wanes.

"We have more important things to spend thousands of dollars on," says Autumn.

"I see. Well, come over here. Jane can help you." The lady points us toward Jane then walks away. I share a look with Autumn and Aunt Lucille, and we stifle a laugh.

Jane is much more pleasant. She seems down to earth. "So, do you have any idea what you're looking for?" she asks.

"I have some ideas," says Autumn. "It's a beach wedding, so I don't want anything too out there. It needs to be something I can move around in. But I also want to feel like I'm wearing a wedding dress. Not just a white summer dress…You know?"

"Absolutely." Jane smiles. "Let's get you started."

Fourteen dresses in, and we all feel a little worn. Every dress looks good on Autumn; anything would look good on Autumn. But none of them pop. As a much-needed break, Autumn suggests we look for some bridesmaids' dresses. I hesitate. My first thought is—nothing in here will fit me, and then I remember it will. We riffle through the assortment of dresses. Autumn knows she wants something light and airy looking for the bridesmaids. The first dress I try is delicate, three-quarter length, and a soft lilac hue. It reminds me of a cloud at sunset. When I slip it on and step out of the change-room, I barely believe the woman looking back at me. I'm lovely. I. Am. Lovely. Autumn leans over my shoulder and I know she sees it too but, unlike me, her expression isn't shocked. I glance at Aunt Lucille, standing off to the side. She's smiling at my reflection.

"Your mom would have loved to see this," she says, "loved to be here." Her eyes glisten. "When your day comes…"

"You'll be here," I say, and she takes my hand. "That'll make her happy."

"You bet I will." Both Aunt Lucille and Autumn wrap their arms around me.

I wipe my palm across my cheeks, smoothing away the wetness. Autumn swipes her thumb under my left eye. "You missed a spot."

"Thanks."

"Do we even need to try any others?" she asks.

"I don't know." I shrug. "It's what you think."

"I think this is the one. Are you happy in it?"

"Definitely."

"Well, that was easy." She laughs. "So, I guess back to me?" She rolls her eyes and I can't believe I almost didn't share this with her, I can't believe I've been so selfish and self-absorbed.

"This will be the one," says Jane, coming toward us with a dress that doesn't look like much on the hanger. It's of a light and frilly material, similar to my dress, but with more substance underneath. Autumn takes it from Jane and shrugs.

She calls from the change room. "The shoulders, are they supposed to be kind of falling off? Like just on the edge?"

"Yes," says Jane.

"Okay, then."

When Autumn steps out, Aunt Lucille makes this little noise like she's in pain. Autumn looks at her Mom, a slight smile on her face. "Is that good?" Aunt Lucille motions for Autumn to turn to the mirror and step on the little podium. She does and her face softens. She holds her arms to the side and lightly grasps the skirt of the dress, pulling it out then letting it fall. "This is it," she speaks quietly, as if in awe. "This is the one."

The neckline stretches from shoulder to shoulder, dipping slightly in the centre, but only enough to give the faintest suggestion of cleavage. The dress hugs her torso, down to her waist, and then flares at just the right spot, falling gently.

"Jenn?" She turns to me.

"It's perfect." I smile at Autumn then grin at the way Aunt Lucille just stands there, trying and failing to hold back her tears, her hands clasped in front of her chest. "Matt will be blown away. You're beautiful." Autumn looks shy, uncertain. An expression I'm not used to seeing on her.

"I want him to love it," she says.

"He will."

She steps off the podium and bites her lower lip.

Jane grins. "Are you saying, 'Yes to the Dress?'"

Autumn nods.

"Well, say it."

"Yes." She laughs. "At last!"

The seamstress takes measurements for alterations; we finalize the order, then slip in line for brunch at a restaurant down the street. Aunt Lucille goes to the restroom and I step aside to look at the menu on the wall when I hear a voice that makes my muscles tense. I turn to see Marshall standing beside a woman Autumn chats with excitedly. The woman's curly blond hair, bright blue eyes, and smile all create the picture of a person it'd be hard to dislike. Her arm loops casually through Marshall's.

"This is my cousin, Jenn. Jenn, Tanya," says Autumn. I shake the hand that's outstretched to me, my smile firm. "We met at a fitness conference last month. And now she works at our studio. Tanya is a yoga queen."

Tanya laughs.

"And this is Mar—"

"We've met," I say, and his eyes dart over to mine. "We go to the same gym."

"Yeah," says Marshall, back to being cool as ever. "I think I've seen you around. Jenn, you said it was?"

"Yes," I say, "Jenn." I try to keep my breathing even. I try to keep my face calm. He must have been drunk—I am nothing compared to Tanya.

"Oh right," says Tanya, squeezing his arm affectionately. "He just loves that gym. I can't convince him to come over and join ours."

Autumn laughs. "One day we'll convert him."

"Well," says Tanya, "at least I convinced him to move in with me a few months ago. Finally got this old hound dog on a leash."

So, this is the roommate. I can't help thinking she needs a stronger leash. Not only did I lose my virginity to a one-night stand, a guy who couldn't leave fast enough—

"Anyway, we have an appointment," says Marshall, cutting off my thoughts. "It was nice seeing you again, Autumn, Jenn." He looks at me the same way he does Autumn, casually, like I'm nothing more than an acquaintance he's run into on the street, because that's all I am—to him.

"Yeah, great to see you two." Autumn lifts her hand in a small wave. "I'm definitely hitting up your class next Monday, Tanya. It's been too long."

"Awesome." Tanya's smile is electric. She and Marshall walk off, arm in arm, just as Aunt Lucille returns and we're ushered to our seats.

"You all right?" asks Autumn while we weave through the tables.

"Yeah," I push out a soft breath of air, "just hungry is all." I sit down and try to push the images out of my head—the way he drew away from me, pulling up his pants like he couldn't get away fast enough. The way he chuckled as he told me to check the trash can.

Aunt Lucille and Autumn drop me off a couple of hours later and I glance at my watch. It's too late to head over to Tammy's. She and Colin have a standing dinner date Saturday evenings. I don't want to ruin her night if things with us don't go well. This feels a bit like a cop-out but—one step at a time. I try to keep Mom's final message in my head. I use it to push out the memories of Marshall that fight to take over my mind. I use it when I'm tempted to cancel the dinner at Dad's tomorrow. Life is worth celebrating, even Evita's, even Courtney's and Melinda's. Billy's too.

∽

THE NEW SHIRT AND skirt Autumn helped me pick out yesterday helps me feel a shred of confidence at the prospect of an evening at Dad and Evita's. Albeit with effort, I'm smiling when Evita opens the door.

"Don't you look lovely." She ushers me in. "Arnold,

Jennifer is here."

"Hi." I keep my smile on. I'm going to be positive. I'm going to be non-judgemental. My father gives me a light hug. I glance around the room. "Where's Billy?"

"He'll be here soon. He went for a walk."

Someone plays a piano in another room. I can't even picture which one. That's how few times I've been here; I don't know which room holds a piano. In the living room, where I stand, pictures line the walls—of the girls, of Billy, of Dad and Evita. There's even a picture of me. I turn away from it—the image is not one I want to be reminded of. But it's there. That's something.

"And how is the writing going?" asks Evita as she sits down on the plush couch across from me. "Your father tells me you've been doing very well at it."

I glance over at him then back to her. "It's good."

"I'm so glad." Her knees are tight together, her hands are on her knees, her back is straight. I see her as if for the first time. She's not prim. She's not a cold bitch. She's scared—of me.

"What about you?" I ask. I try to remember what it is she does. "How is work?"

"Oh, just the same as always," she says, and slaps my father's knee. "Though I wouldn't mind a better boss." She still works for my father, I realize. I guess I just assumed she wouldn't anymore.

Courtney enters the room and sits on the opposite end of the couch from me. "Hey," she says.

"Hey." She looks at her phone, barely acknowledges me, but then she doesn't acknowledge her parents at all.

Billy walks in. Again, his gauntness, the way he leans on the cane, shocks me. He smiles his half smile. This I recognize. He sits down.

"Still throws me off," he says. I know what he's referring to, but instead of getting pissed I accept the fact that it's a legitimate comment. He throws me off too. We've both changed.

"Well, I guess we might as well get eating," says Evita. I smile at her and she glances away then back, her smile hesitant. As the evening progresses, she relaxes. I wouldn't go so far as to say I like her, but I can admit that she is a likable person. I can see what Dad sees in her. She's pleasant. I watch her with my father. She's attentive, and so is he. I still feel wary around my father, but I also feel sorry for how hard I've made things for him over the years. He's a man who fell in love with another woman. It happens. It doesn't mean he's a man who fell out of love with me.

With Billy, it's harder. Every glance at his wasted body is a reminder of how I've deserted him, but it's also a reminder of the reason for my desertion. Billy was awful—no way to reason around that one. I was not making up his mockery. I was not inserting my own anger or distaste into his words and expressions the way I think I may have been with Evita and the girls. I still don't know that Billy wouldn't be mocking me right now if I weighed what I used to. I'll never know.

"So, how's rehab?" I ask him as we're eating dessert. I declined the ice cream and am just eating the berries meant as a topping.

"It sucks," he says. "It's really painful." He shrugs. "But it's a challenge, right? I'm lucky to be alive..." He hesitates. "I'll be back on the bike in no time."

"You're going to ride again?"

"Sure." He rubs his hand across his head in the way he used to push the long strands of hair out of his face. "Of course."

"Not too soon though," says Evita. "And not at night in the rain?"

"Nah." He smiles at her in a way I never saw him smile at Mom. "Not then."

When I'm at the door, ready to leave, Evita pats my shoulder almost like I'm a puppy. My father hugs me and so does Billy. I make an effort not to tense. He's trying. I have to believe he never fully understood the damage he was doing. I have to believe he was just a stupid little boy and then an insecure young man who didn't want to be ostracized by his peers the way his sister was by hers. It probably became a habit. It probably stemmed from some lingering fear that my fate could become his. I lift my arms and hug him back.

It'll take time, full forgiveness, but Billy and I are the last living bit of Mom. That has to count for something.

CHAPTER TWENTY-TWO

When Monday evening rolls around I grab my bag, lock the apartment door, and walk the ten blocks to Tammy's house. I need this time to think, to hope. I need peace. No chance of that on a noisy bus. When I knock on the door, I hear the rustling noises of Tammy rising from the couch then making her way down the hall. The sound stops and I imagine she's looking at me through the pinhole, deciding. I almost call out to her but stop myself, respecting her freedom to make a choice without my influence. She deserves that. I take a deep breath and turn to leave just as the deadbolt turns. I turn back. The door slowly opens to reveal Tammy standing there, a hard but hurt look on her face.

Neither one of us speaks and so I say the first stupid thing that comes to mind. "You get my messages?"

"You mean all two dozen of them?"

"Was it really two dozen?" I ask.

"Seemed like it." She steps away from the door, indicating I can step in. She crosses both arms in front of her chest, making it clear all has not been forgiven. "It was at least seven." I can't be sure, but think I see the slightest hint of a grin.

"You got new curtains." I gesture to the peach lace that now covers her living room windows. She nods. "I like them."

"Why are you here, Jenn?"

213

"To apologize," I say, "again."

"Words, words." Tammy walks further into the room, turning away from me. "You wouldn't have said what you did unless you thought it, felt it, at least on some level. That's what really hurts. That's why I don't know that an apology means anything—that it can mean anything."

"I know," I say. "I was drunk. And that was a big part of it. But you're right, on some level I thought those words." I take a step toward her and she turns to look at me again. "But that's only a reflection of me, not of you. That just shows how misguided and messed up I was in my thinking, in everything. That just shows I was sad and jealous and pathetic."

Something I've said has piqued her interest. Her body visually relaxes, her defences settling down. "What do you mean?"

"I mean you were right," I say. "I was unhappy—miserable, really. I thought being thin was the only way I could get past that. I despised being fat—what that meant—and I guess I despised everyone else who was fat too, especially if they'd found some way to be happy. It was unreachable for me. And so it made me jealous, angry, bitter."

"And now," she says, looking curious but distrustful.

"And now I realize how awful I was and how I blamed all my problems and unhappiness on my weight when really, when it comes down to it, it was all just on me." I motion to the couch, asking with my gesture if I can sit down, and she nods. "You were right. I was just unhappy, and I hated that other people weren't. I hated that you were happy, and I couldn't figure out how that was possible. I wasn't even any happier once the weight came off. Not really." I can tell Tammy's listening, but she doesn't say anything. She does sit down across from me, apparently waiting for me to go on.

"I wish I could take it back. I'm really sorry for what I said," I bite my lip, "when you were just trying to watch out for me. But more than that, I'm sorry for even thinking it. You deserve a better friend than me. I know that. But I think I can be that better friend." Tammy remains silent and my first reaction is to get frustrated, to feel indignant that she's making this so hard, but I push those feelings away. This is not about me. It's about her, and how I hurt her. It's not even about whether or not she forgives me. It's about me admitting that I did something that requires forgiveness, me acknowledging I was in the wrong. "It's okay if you don't want to be my friend anymore, or if you can't. I'd get that. Either way though, I want you to know I truly am sorry, I respect you, I appreciate the way you've been my friend over the years, and I admire you." I take a breath. "I see you as somewhat of a role model now. The way you find the joy in things. The way you're giving and kind and full of life." I smile. "You're like my mom in that way. I had you both in my life as examples for years, there to show me a better way to live, and I didn't see it. I do now." A small smile twitches at the corner of her mouth. "I went to see my mom's grave."

"You did?" She leans forward.

"Yeah," I press my lips together and nod, "I finally did. The words she chose...they changed something in me."

Tammy nods back, her smile growing bigger. "Your mom was a cool lady."

"And I saw Billy—well, he came to see me. But we talked. He's staying with Dad now. And I went over for dinner. I asked to go over for dinner."

"Wow." She leans back in her seat. "How was it?"

"It was good, actually." I rub a hand across my chin. "I had a nice time. Evita's not so bad."

Tammy laughs. The big boisterous laugh I've missed. "You really are changing."

I laugh too. It feels good. Natural.

"So," she leans forward again, "how did things go with that guy? Marshall, was it?"

"Wham, bam, thank you, ma'am." I roll my eyes and shake my head. "You were so right."

"I'm sorry." Tammy puts a hand on my knee, there isn't a hint of I-told-you-so in her voice.

"Yeah," I swipe a hand through the air, as if erasing the memory, "lesson learned. I'm more sorry for his lovely girlfriend."

"He has a girlfriend?" she says, confusion and disgust flooding her face. "And he told you? Or you…?"

"I ran into them the other day," I say, "she's friends with Autumn. Apparently, he and this girlfriend have been living together for a couple months. Explains why he insisted on going to my apartment."

"Oh, Jenn," she sighs, "I'm really sorry."

"It is what it is." I shrug. "I made a mistake and now I won't make that same mistake again."

"Right." She gives a short nod.

"And how's Colin?" I ask.

Almost two hours later, I rise from the couch and Tammy rises too. She wraps her arms around me and I squeeze back, relief flooding through me—this friendship is not lost. We make plans for next weekend and I walk into the cool night air feeling refreshed.

∽

BACK AT HOME, I LOG into Facebook and see a new event invite. 'Autumn and Matt. Together at last. Together forever.' If I've been walking around with a bit of a dagger in my chest, it's just been turned. Matt was a crush. An idea. But I'm still worried it will be awkward seeing him, seeing how in love they are, and how ridiculous I was to think it'd be me and him one day. I haven't seen Matt since that day at the club. But even that wasn't so bad. The party is the same night I'm supposed to hang out with Tammy. I scan through the guest list and find her name. I pick up my cell.

"Did you just see the invite?" she asks into the phone before I have a chance to say hello.

"Yeah, that's why I'm calling."

"That's so exciting!" says Tammy. "I've been wanting to meet this guy. Why didn't you tell me? You knew, right?"

"Yeah, I knew. I don't know. I just…"

"You were talking about how hot he was that night…you don't have a crush on him or something, do you?"

"I…"

"Jenn."

"I may have, a bit. It was just a passing thing though, no big deal."

"Okay. So, we're going, right? We'll watch that movie another night?"

"Yeah. I think so."

"You think so?"

"Yeah, we're going."

I hang up the phone a few minutes later, after Tammy has gone on about all the things she likes about weddings. I look around my apartment. I've been doing better at keeping things tidy so cleaning can't distract me. I already did my workout today—no more multiples. TV doesn't seem appealing. I notice the Toews book on the coffee table and pick it up. Rajeev will probably be at the party too. It wouldn't be the worst thing to have something extra to talk about.

MATT AND AUTUMN'S ENGAGEMENT party is at Aunt Lucille and Uncle Leo's and I decide to walk there—all six and a half kilometres of the way, in my knitted navy-blue dress and tights. The dress is nice, but not showy, not something anyone would do a double look at, and neither am I. I'm just a young woman walking on a cool spring evening. I'm not a spectacle, but I probably never was—not really.

Cars line the street in front of the house and my gut twists when I see Uncle Leo directing people where to park. "Jennifer." His eyes widen as I walk toward him.

"Hi, Uncle Leo." I hug him. It's something I used to do. Years ago.

"You look—"

"I know," I say. "I lost a lot of weight."

"I was going to say," says Uncle Leo, "you look just like your mother…when she was your age."

My chest clenches. I didn't expect these words from him. "My dad said that too."

"He was right."

I smile in reply, my lips pressed tight together, my cheekbones making my eyes squint. He pats my shoulder with his large hand and I feel tiny underneath it. I walk up the driveway as he directs the next car, slip in the front door, and am amazed at the number of people they've squeezed in. The air is warm and moist. Chatting and laughter travels through the back door and I make my way to the porch. While slipping through the crowd, I don't bounce a single person. I step back into the night air and notice Matt by the barbecue with some of his friends from the gym. He's sweating over the grill—in a t-shirt despite the cool weather. His muscles glisten. I look away. "Billy?"

"Hey." Billy leans against the railing, a beer in his hand, eyeing me.

"I didn't know you'd be here."

"You kidding me? I wouldn't miss it."

"It's just that—"

"Things change, right? Autumn and Aunt Lucille, in the hospital…" He doesn't have to say more. We both know they were there for him. I wasn't. "You look nice." He gives his half-grin. "I like your hair like that. Better than the red."

"Thanks." I dyed it back to its natural hue a few days ago. I step toward him and we stand there beside each other, watching people walk in and out of the house. He raises his arm then rests it on the railing behind my back. His fingers graze my shoulder.

"My cousins!" Autumn traipses across the balcony. "Hello!" She hugs us both and kisses Billy's cheeks. I grin. I have never seen Autumn tipsy. It looks good on her. She skips down the steps and wraps an arm around Matt's middle.

"Careful, babe," he says. "I'm dealing with fire here."

"She's pretty happy," says Billy, watching them.

"Yeah."

"It's good." His smile softens. "She deserves a good guy."

"You've met Matt before?"

"Oh yeah, he came with Autumn a few times." I turn my gaze to the deck. Even Matt went to visit Billy.

"Nature calls." My brother pulls his arm away and picks up his cane. I watch as he limps away from me. His walk is getting better. It's not his old, practised gait, but this new one has a certain swag to it too. I head into the house and make my way to the dining room. A lot of the faces are familiar, but they don't seem to recognize me...or maybe they're used to me not acknowledging them. A plethora of dishes line the table and I pile my plate with carrots, tomatoes, cucumber, and one cupcake. Nothing wrong with a little indulgence; it's all a part of celebrating life.

"You and your veggies."

Rajeev's voice makes me turn. I take a bite into a carrot. "They're good."

He nudges me. "I see you've got a cupcake too—that's better."

"Maybe." He puts food on his plate, no longer looking at me. "I read the book," I say.

He looks up. "Yeah?"

"Yeah."

"What did you think?"

"At first I thought it was somewhat self-indulgent—forced," I pause, "but then it was beautiful. It made me ache."

His eyes have a look I can't read, but I think it's good. "I wouldn't argue that."

"Thank you for getting it for me."

He nods and gestures to a vacant corner. I follow him. "You excited for the wedding? I hear you're Maid of Honour."

"Yeah. It will be beautiful, I'm sure." I pause. "I'm just happy for them." It's not a lie, not at all, not anymore. "I think they're really good for each other. I think they're the type that will last, you know?"

"I know."

He smiles then, and I remember looking into his almond eyes by that boulder, how close our bodies were—how close they are now. His shoulder almost touches mine. We're silent as we chew. Side by side, we watch the guests mingle around throughout the room. "Have you had any difficult cases lately?" I ask.

He expels a breath of air and looks over at me. "There's this one young mother..." He tells me a story that makes my heart break and makes me see him for the amazing man he really is.

The party goes late into the night. There's Karaoke. Tammy does an amazing rendition of 'All By Myself' and no one laughs. They just hoot and holler in appreciation. And why wouldn't they? At the end of the night Rajeev offers to take me home and Billy comes along. Based on where we live, I'm dropped off first and am left wondering exactly what Rajeev and my brother will talk about in the last few minutes of the drive. Billy knows things I wouldn't want Rajeev to, but as I put the key in the door to my apartment and flip on the light, I feel certain it will be okay.

❧

SEVERAL WEEKS LATER I wake up and realize I've missed my goal day. I haven't even been looking at the scale. Just living my life. I saw Rajeev again at the birthday party Tammy organized for me. We chatted, and it was friendly, fun, but he said nothing to indicate he still wants to ask me out. I couldn't help thinking how he said I wasn't ready, but I think I'm closer now. Not quite there, maybe, but closer. Old habits die hard, and day by day I have to work on learning how to celebrate this life I've got, not letting the fear of a pound here or there destroy me. But I decide to step on the scale—just to see. I'm still working out. I still eat healthy the majority of the time, but I'm not letting it rule me.

When I step off the scale, I'm a little disappointed, but only a little. I'm nine pounds away from where I wanted to be, from the goal I'd worked so hard for, but it doesn't matter so much now. Maybe Matt was right. Maybe the number was arbitrary.

The reflection in the mirror doesn't look a lot like the woman I envisioned all those months ago—with large perky breasts and a firm, high booty. I see now that nine pounds wouldn't have made me look like her, anyway. That's just not me. The person I see has some bulges, some loose skin—that should tighten up in time. The stretch marks may never disappear, and that's okay. I like the way I look. I've worked hard to look like this. This body lets me do so much more. We have another hiking trip planned—girls only—a few weeks before Matt and Autumn's wedding, and I'm taking salsa lessons at this little joint in the North End with Tammy's friend Sophia. My joints don't ache like they used to, and my grumpy old doctor has given me a clean bill of health.

Nine pounds won't make me happy. Nor will that 'skinny me' I've wasted so much time dreaming about. I don't need her. I have better things to focus on.

The woman looking back at me is no Victoria Secret's model, not even close, but she's smiling. She's happy. I'm happy. It's a happiness that's far more stable than a number on the scale will ever be. It's enough.

WONDERING WHAT'S NEXT?

Sign up for my reader's group to get a free online or ebook bonus chapter for *When Comes the Joy*.
https://www.charlenecarr.com/WhenComesBonusSignU
p
See what happens when romance blooms between Jennifer and Rajeev AND get a first-row seat to Matt and Autumn's wedding!

Just so you know, this bonus chapter was written six months after publishing When Comes The Joy. *Don't worry, it's not the final chapter, you just read that! However, my readers wanted to know more, so I obliged. :)*

Go to charlenecarr.com/whencomesbonussignup to get your bonus chapter PLUS get an extended ebook excerpt of *Where There Is Life*, the next book in the *A New Start* series for free.

Dear Reader,

Thank you for taking the time to read *When Comes The Joy*, the first book in my *A New Start* series! If you've made it this far, hopefully you enjoyed Jennifer's story. It would mean so much if you took a moment to leave a quick, honest review on Goodreads and/or your favourite online retailer. Reviews are incredibly important. They're the reason readers decide to give a book a chance and your review could be the one that helps a fellow book lover find a new story to enjoy!

If you decide not to sign up for the bonus chapter, I still think you'll love the rest of the series. Each of these books digs deep to look at the heart of a woman struggling with all life's thrown at her. These novels are real and raw, thought-provoking, and written from the heart.

They're also all stand-alones. You can read book 3 without reading book 2, but they are chronological, so if you plan to read them all, you'll enjoy them most if you read them in order.

If you'd like to know the next time I release a new book or have a great promotion, please follow me on BookBub. And if you've read *When Comes The Joy* as part of a book club, keep turning pages for a Book Club Discussion Guide.

Turn the page to learn about the rest of the books in the *A New Start Series.*

Read on, my friend,

Charlene Carr

OTHER BOOKS IN THE A NEW START SERIES

Where There Is Life
Book 2

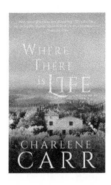

What would you do if you woke up in a hospital bed, only to realize all your dreams were shattered?

Autumn's blissful newlywed life abruptly ends when she wakes after a life-threatening accident, unable to remember what happened or why her husband isn't by her side.
As the haze clears and Autumn's memory returns, will she be able to confront the truth?
Evocative and complex.
Honest and emotional.
The second book in the *A New Start* Stand-alone Series, *Where There Is Life* is a riveting story about love, loss, and finding your way.

By What We Love
Book 3

Sometimes getting exactly what you want is the worst thing ever.

Dream job? Check. Man to make every woman you know stop and turn? Check. But when having one means giving up the other, what's a girl ...excuse me, *woman* to do?

Eloise Grant, a successful and driven Public Relations Consultant, has worked her whole life to make sure she never has to depend on anyone but herself.

But when she's offered a promotion she feels she can't refuse, depending on herself means leaving her friends, her family, and the man she loves behind.

Whatever choice she makes, it seems like Eloise's life is about to unravel.

Smart and engaging.

Heart wrenching and unpredictable.

By What We Love, book 3 in the *A New Start* stand-alone series, is the story of a woman desperate to have it all, while battling with memories of a past she'd rather forget.

Forever In My Heart
Book 4

**Tracey Sampson has finally met the man she's ready
to start her life with. He's perfect.
But is she?**

Struggling with the unknown and desperate for answers,
Tracey embarks on a journey to reveal the secrets of a past
she vowed she'd never explore.
Heartfelt and honest.
Courageous and compelling.
Forever In My Heart, book 4 in the *A New Start* stand-
alone series, is a deep and passionate read about coming to
terms with your imperfections and insecurities in order to let
love in.

Whispers of Hope
Book 5

The act every woman is supposed to be capable of, she's failing at, over and over again.

A year ago, Tracey Sampson met and married the man who helped her finally believe she is worthy of love, just as she is.

But she's yet to fulfill her greatest dream—to hold her own child in her arms.

As month by month that dream drifts further and further away, Tracey is forced to acknowledge that not everyone gets their happily every after.

Engrossing and inspiring.

Heart-wrenching and passionate.

As real as it gets.

Whisper of Hope, book 5 in the *A New Start* stand-alone series bares the heart and soul of a woman heartfelt and emotional story of a woman pursuing her life's dream despite heartache and disappointment. Witness the power of hope to transform a life.

ACKNOWLEDGMENTS

I would like to thank my husband, Peter, who was my first reader and is a constant support. I would also like to thank my mother, who is always there to listen and offer her opinion on my work. Finally, I would like to thank my wonderful beta readers who gave generously of their time and provided invaluable feedback.

This book would not be what it is without you all!

BOOK CLUB DISCUSSION QUESTIONS

1. What did you think of Jennifer's motivation to lose the weight? Did it seem believable to you that her mother's death was a strong motivating factor, or do you think her general frustration with her life played a bigger role?

2. *"This will be a life change. This will be different. I will wake up exactly one year from today and I will be the person I've always wanted to be. The person I was born to be."*

How misguided was Jennifer's belief that becoming the 'person she was [born] to be" had something to do with reaching a certain number on a scale. Do you feel society pushes that belief on women – that they're only worthy and lovable if they fit into a certain mold?

3. Jennifer is quite unlikable at times. Were you able to look past this, to feel empathy and/or understanding for her character, or did she continually frustrate you?

4. Do you think many people judge themselves on their physical appearance and whether they do or do not meet some outward expectation of beauty? How do you think this affects self-esteem and self-worth? Did anything in Jennifer's experience speak to you?

5. What were your thoughts regarding Jennifer's relationships with her father and Billy? If in Jennifer's shoes, would you have forgiven them for the way they treated her, or do you think Jennifer was exaggerating their negative behaviour toward her?

6. Were you glad Jennifer didn't reach her goal weight, just a healthy one? Why?

7. *"We look into a past that no longer exists, looking as if it's real. We hold onto things in our life that there's no reason to hold onto anymore because, unlike the stars, they don't bring us beauty, they bring us pain."*

In the scene on Mount Carleton, looking up at the stars, Rajeev talks to Jennifer about living in the past and how when we hold onto the past, letting it determine our future, it can cripples our chance at happiness. What do you think of this?

ABOUT THE AUTHOR

 I'm a lover of words. Pursuing this life-long obsession, I studied literature in university, attaining both a BA and MA in English. Still craving more, I attained a degree in Journalism. After travelling the globe for several years and working as a freelance writer, editor, facilitator, and starting my own Communications business, I decided the time had come to focus exclusively on my true love - novel writing.

My goal is to write books that are almost impossible to put down, not because of some great mystery, or high-speed chase, or sexy scene, but because they're full of characters who enrage and delight you; Imperfect people in circumstances that could hit any one of us.

Characters full of human frailties who make awful, sometimes stupid choices ...

But who don't give up when they're knocked down. Who struggle and fight and come out on the other side stronger, braver, ready to live a life of their own making.

Read more at www.charlenecarr.com/books

Lightning Source UK Ltd.
Milton Keynes UK
UKHW011034041022
409908UK00005B/914